The Lady in the Car

The Lady in the Car

William Le Queux

MINT EDITIONS

The Lady in the Car was first published in 1908.

This edition published by Mint Editions 2021.

ISBN 9781513280998 | E-ISBN 9781513286013

Published by Mint Editions®

 MINT
EDITIONS

minteditionbooks.com

Publishing Director: Jennifer Newens
Design & Production: Rachel Lopez Metzger
Project Manager: Micaela Clark
Typesetting: Westchester Publishing Services

Contents

Preface

An Apology

I hereby tender an apology to the reader for being compelled, in these curious chronicles of an adventurous motorist and his actions towards certain of his female acquaintances, to omit real names, and to substitute assumed ones. With the law of libel looming darkly, the reason is obvious.

Since the days when, as lads, we played cricket together at Cheltenham "the Prince," always a sportsman and always generous to the poor, has ever been my friend. In the course of my own wandering life of the past dozen years or so, I have come across him in all sorts of unexpected places up and down Europe, and more especially in those countries beyond the Danube which we term the Balkans.

For certain of his actions, and for the ingenuity of his somewhat questionable friends, I make no apology. While the game of "mug-hunting" remains so easy and so profitable, there will be always both hunters and hunted. As my friend's escapades were related to me, so have I set them down in the following pages, in the belief that my readers may perhaps care to make more intimate acquaintance with the clever, fearless, and altogether remarkable man whose exploits have already, from time to time, been referred to in guarded and mysterious terms by the daily press.

William Le Queux

I

HIS HIGHNESS'S LOVE AFFAIR

The Prince broke open a big box of choice "Petroffs," selected one, lit it slowly, and walked pensively to the window.

He was in a good mood that morning, for he had just got rid of a troublesome visitor.

The big *salon* was elegantly furnished with long mirrors, gilt chairs covered with sky-blue silk upholstery, a piano, and a pretty writing-table set close to the long window, which led out to a balcony shaded by a red-and-white sun-blind—the *salon* of the best suite in the Majestic, that huge hotel facing the sea in King's Road, Brighton.

He was a tall, well-set-up man of about thirty-three; dark-haired, good-looking, easy-going, and refined, who, for the exception of the slightest trace of foreign accent in his speech, might easily have been mistaken for an Englishman. In his well-cut dark brown flannels and brown shoes he went to the balcony, and, leaning over, gazed down upon the sun-lit promenade, full of life and movement below.

His arrival a few days before had caused quite a flutter in the big hotel. He had not noticed it, of course, being too used to it. He travelled a great deal—indeed, he was always travelling nowadays—and had learned to treat the constant endeavours of unknown persons to scrape acquaintance with him with the utter disregard they deserved.

Not often did the Majestic, so freely patronised by the stockbroker and the newly-rich, hold as guest any person equalling the Prince in social distinction, yet at the same time so modest and retiring. The blatant persons overcrowding the hotel that August Sunday, those pompous, red-faced men in summer clothes and white boots, and those over-dressed women in cream silk blouses and golden chatelaines, mostly denizens of Kensington or Regent's Park, had been surprised when an hour ago he had walked along the hall and gone outside to speak with his chauffeur. He was so very good-looking, such a sportsman, and so very English they whispered. And half of those City men's wives were instantly dying for an opportunity of speaking with him, so that they could return to their suburban friends and tell of their acquaintance with the cousin of his Imperial Majesty the Kaiser.

But Prince Albert of Hesse-Holstein was thinking of other things. He had no use for that over-fed Sunday crowd, with their slang chatter, their motor-cars and their gossip of "bithneth," through which he had just passed. He drew half a dozen times at his yellow Russian cigarette, tossed it away, and lit another.

He was thinking of his visitor who had just left, and—well, there remained a nasty taste in his mouth. The man had told him something— something that was not exactly pleasant. Anyhow, he had got rid of him. So Prince Albert Ernst Karl Wilhelm, head of the great house of Hesse-Holstein, grand-cross of the Orders of the Black Eagle, Saint Sava and the Elephant, and Commander of St. Hubert and of the Crown of Italy, returned again to the balcony, smoked on, and watched.

In the meantime, in the big hall below, sat a well-dressed elderly lady with her daughter, a pretty, fair-haired, blue-eyed girl of twenty, a dainty figure in white, who wore a jade bangle upon her left wrist. They were Americans on a tour with "poppa" through Europe. Mr. Robert K. Jesup, of Goldfields, Nevada, had gone to pay a pilgrimage to Stratford-on-Avon, while his wife and daughter were awaiting him in Brighton.

With the inquisitiveness of the American girl Mary Jesup had obtained the "Almanach de Gotha" from the reading-room, and both mother and daughter were, with difficulty, translating into English the following notice of the Prince's family which they found within the little red-covered book:

"Evangeliques—Souche: Widukind III, comte de Schwalenberg (principaute de Holstein), 1116–1137; bailli a Arolsen et acquisition du chateau de Hesse vers, 1150; Comte du Saint Empire de Hesse, 1349, dignite confirme, 22 juin, 1548; bailli de Wildungen, 1475; acquisition d'Eisenberg (chateau fort, aujourd'hui en ruines, situe sur la montagne du meme nom) vers, 1485; acquisition par heritage du comte de Pyrmont, 1631; coll. du titre de 'Hoch et Wohlgeboren,' Vienne, 25 fevr., 1627; pretention a l'heritage du comte de Rappolstein (Ribeaupierre Haute-Alsace) et des seigneuries de Hohenack et de Geroldseck (ibidem) par suite du mariage (2 juill, 1658) du cte Chretien-Louis, ne 29 juill, 1635, + 12 dec. 1706, avec Elisabeth de Rappolstein, nee 7 Mars, 1644, + 6 dec. 1676, apres la mort de son oncle Jean-Jacques dernier comte de Rappolstein, 28 juill, 1673; les lignes ci-dessus descendent de deux fils (freres consaiguins) du susdit Chretien-Louis comte de Hesse-Eisenberg, de Pyrmont et Rappolstein, etc.—V. L'edition de 1832 (Page 84)."

"There, mother!" exclaimed the pretty girl. "Why, they were an ancient family even before America was discovered! Isn't he real nice? Say! I only wish we knew him."

"Ah, my dear," replied the elder woman with a sigh. "Those kind of people never know us. He's a royalty."

"But he looks such a nice man. What a lovely car he's got—real fine! I've been out to see it. How I wish he'd take us for a ride."

"You'd better ask him, my dear," laughed her mother.

"Guess I shouldn't be backward. I believe he would in a moment, if I asked him very nicely," she exclaimed, laughing in chorus. Truth to tell, she had admired him when she had first encountered him two days ago. She had been seated in one of those wicker chairs outside the door in King's Road, when he had come out and taken the chair next to hers, awaiting his car—a big sixty "Mercedes" painted cream, with the princely arms and crown upon its panels.

He was talking in English to his man, who had carried out his motor-coat. He was a prince—one of the wealthiest of all the German princes, a keen automobilist, a sportsman who had hunted big game in German East Africa, a landlord who owned a principality with half a dozen mediaeval castles and some of the finest estates in the German Empire, and one of the Kaiser's most intimate relatives. And yet he was travelling with only his man and his motor-car.

Though Mary Jesup was heiress to the two millions sterling which her father had made during the past three years—as half the people in the hotel knew—yet she was aware that even her father's wealth could not purchase for her the title of Princess of Hesse-Holstein. She was a very charming girl, bright, athletic and go-ahead—a typical American girl of to-day—and as she strolled out along the pier with her mother, her thoughts constantly reverted to the young man in brown who had given her more than one glance when he had passed.

Meanwhile, there had entered to the Prince his faithful valet Charles, a tall, thin, clean-shaven Englishman, some four years his senior.

"Well?" asked his Highness sharply casting himself into an easy-chair, and taking another "Petroff."

"Got rid of him—eh?"

"Yes—but it was difficult. I gave him a couple of sovereigns, and made an appointment to meet him in the bar of the Cecil, in London, next Thursday at four."

"Good. That gives us time," remarked the Prince with a sigh of relief. "And about the girl? What have you found out?"

"She and her mother dined in the *table-d'hote* room last night, and took coffee afterwards in the Palm Court. The father is the man who owns the gold-mines in Nevada—worth ten million dollars. Last year he gave half a million dollars to charity, and bought the Bourbon pearls for his wife. Gave eighty thousand pounds for them. She's got them here, a long string twice round her neck and reaches to her waist. She's wearing them to-day, and everybody, of course, thinks they're false."

"How foolish these American women are! Fancy wearing pearls of that price in the open street! Why, she might easily be robbed," his master remarked.

"But who'd believe they're genuine? They're too big to take a thiefs fancy," replied the faithful Charles. "The Jesups seem fond of jewellery. Miss Mary has a lovely diamond necklet—"

"And wore it last night, I suppose?"

"Of course. They are newly-rich people, and crowd it all on. Yet, what does it matter? Men like Jesup can easily buy more if they lose it. Why, to have her jewels stolen is only a big advertisement for the American woman. Haven't you seen cases in the paper—mostly at Newport they seem to occur."

"The girl is pretty—distinctly pretty, Charles," remarked the Prince slowly, with a philosophic air.

"Yes, your Highness. And she'd esteem it a great honour if you spoke to her, I'm sure."

Prince Albert pursed his lips.

"I think not. These American girls have a good deal of spirit. She'd most probably snub me."

"I think not. I passed through the hall five minutes ago, and she was looking you up in the 'Almanach de Gotha.'"

His Highness started.

"Was she?" he cried with quick interest. "Then she evidently knows all about me by this time! I wonder—" and he paused without concluding his sentence.

Charles saw that his master was thinking deeply, so he busied himself by putting some papers in order.

"She's uncommonly pretty," his Highness declared presently. "But dare I speak to her, Charles? You know what these Americans are."

"By all means speak to her. The mother and daughter would be company for you for a few days. You could invite them to go motoring, and they'd no doubt accept," the man suggested.

WILLIAM LE QUEUX

"I don't want the same experience that we had in Vichy, you know."

"Oh, never fear. These people are quite possible. Their wealth hasn't spoilt them—as far as I can hear."

"Very well, Charles." The Prince laughed, tossing his cigarette-end into the grate, and rising. "I'll make some excuse to speak with them."

And Charles, on his part, entertained shrewd suspicions that his master, confirmed bachelor that he was, had, at last, been attracted by a girl's fresh, fair beauty, and that girl an American.

Time hung heavily upon the Prince's hands. That afternoon he ran over in his car to Worthing, where he dined at Warne's, and the evening he spent in lonely state in a box at the Brighton Alhambra. Truth to tell, he found himself thinking always of the sweet-faced, rather saucy American girl, whose waist was so neat, whose tiny shoes were so pointed, and whose fair hair was always drawn straight back from her intelligent brow.

Yes. He felt he must know her. The morrow came, and with it an opportunity occurred to speak with her mother.

They were sitting, as it is usual to sit, at the door of the hotel, when a mishap to a dog-cart driven by a well-known actress gave him the desired opportunity, and ten minutes later he had the satisfaction of bowing before Mary Jesup herself.

He strolled with them on to the Pier, chatting so very affably that both mother and daughter could hardly believe that he was the cousin of an Emperor. Then, at his request to be allowed to join them at their table at luncheon, they had their midday meal together.

The girl in white was altogether charming, and so unlike the milk-and-water misses of Germany, or the shy, dark-eyed minxes of France or Italy, so many of whom had designed to become Princess of Hesse-Holstein. Her frank open manner, her slight American twang, and her Americanisms he found all delightful. Mrs. Jesup, too, was a sensible woman, although this being the first occasion that either mother or daughter had even met a prince, they used "Your Highness" a trifle too frequently.

Nevertheless, he found this companionship of both women most charming.

"What a splendid motor-car you have!" Mary remarked when, after luncheon, they were taking their coffee in the Palm Court at the back of the hotel.

"I'm very fond of motoring, Miss Jesup. Are you?" was his Highness's reply.

"I love it. Poppa's got a car. We brought it over with us and ran around France in it. We left it in Paris till we get back to the Continent in the fall. Then we do Italy," she said.

"Perhaps you would like to have a run with me and your mother to-morrow," the Prince suggested. "It's quite pretty about the neighbourhood."

"I'm sure you're very kind, Prince," responded the elder woman. "We should be charmed. And further, I guess my husband'll be most delighted to meet you when he gets down here. He's been in Germany a lot."

"I shall be very pleased to meet Mr. Jesup," the young patrician responded. "Till he comes, there's no reason why we should not have a few runs—that is, if you're agreeable."

"Oh! it'll be real lovely!" declared Mary, her pretty face brightening in anticipation of the pleasure of motoring with the man she so admired.

"Then what about running over to Eastbourne to tea to-day?" he suggested.

Mother and daughter exchanged glances. "Well," replied Mrs. Jesup, "we don't wish to put you out in the least, Prince. I'm sure—"

"Good! You'll both come. I'll order the car for three o'clock."

The Prince ascended the stairs much gratified. He had made a very creditable commencement. The hundred or so of other girls of various nations who had been presented to him with matrimonial intent could not compare with her, either for beauty, for charm, or for intelligence.

It was a pity, he reflected, that she was not of royal, or even noble birth.

Charles helped him on with a light motor-coat, and, as he did so, asked:

"If the Parson calls, what am I to say?"

"Say what you like, only send him back to London. Tell him he is better off in Bayswater than in Brighton. He'll understand."

"He may want some money. He wrote to you yesterday, remember."

"Then give him fifty pounds, and tell him that when I want to see him I'll wire. I want to be alone just now, Charles," he added a trifle impatiently. "You've got the key of my despatch-box, eh?"

"Yes, your Highness."

Below, he found the big cream-coloured car in waiting. Some of the guests were admiring it, for it had an extra long wheelbase and a big touring body and hood—a car that was the last word in all that was comfort in automobilism.

The English chauffeur, Garrett, in drab livery faced with scarlet, and with the princely cipher and crown upon his buttons, raised his hat on the appearance of his master. And again when a moment later the two ladies, in smart motor-coats, white caps, and champagne-coloured veils, emerged and entered the car, being covered carefully by the fine otter-skin rug.

The bystanders at the door of the hotel regarded mother and daughter with envy, especially when the Prince got in at the girl's side, and, with a light laugh, gave the order to start.

A few moments later they were gliding along the King's Road eastward, in the direction of Lewes and Eastbourne.

"You motor a great deal, I suppose?" she asked him, as they turned the corner by the Aquarium.

"A good deal. It helps to pass the time away, you know," he laughed. "When I have no guests I usually drive myself. Quite recently I've been making a tour up in Scotland."

"We're going up there this autumn. To the Trossachs. They say they're fine! And we're going to see Scott's country, and Edinburgh. I'm dying to see Melrose Abbey. It must be lovely from the pictures."

"You ought to get your father to have his car over," the Prince suggested. "It's a magnificent run up north from London."

The millionaire's wife was carefully examining the Prince with covert glances. His Highness was unaware that the maternal gaze was so searching, otherwise he would probably have acted somewhat differently.

A splendid run brought them to Lewes, the old-world Sussex capital. There, with a long blast of the electric siren, they shot down the hill and out again upon the Eastbourne Road, never pulling up until they were in the small garden before the Queen's.

Mary Jesup stepped out, full of girlish enthusiasm. Her only regret was that the people idling in the hall of the hotel could not be told that their companion was a real live Prince.

They took tea under an awning overlooking the sea, and his Highness was particularly gracious towards Mrs. Jesup, until both mother and daughter were filled with delight at his pleasant companionship. He treated both women as equals; his manner, as they afterwards put it, being devoid of any side, and yet he was every inch a prince.

That run was the first of many they had together.

Robert K. Jesup had been suddenly summoned by cable to Paris on business connected with his mining interests, therefore his wife and daughter remained in Brighton. And on account of their presence the Prince lingered there through another fortnight. Mostly he spent his days walking or motoring with Mrs. Jesup and her daughter, and sometimes—on very rare occasions—he contrived to walk with Mary alone.

One morning, when he had been with her along the pier listening to the band, he returned to luncheon to find in his own room a rather tall, clean-shaven, middle-aged clergyman, whose round face and ruddy complexion gave him rather the air of a *bon vivant*.

Sight of his unexpected visitor caused the Prince to hold his breath for a second. It was the Parson.

"Sorry I was out," his Highness exclaimed. "Charles told you where I was, I suppose?"

"Yes, Prince," replied the cleric. "I helped myself to a whisky and soda. Hope you won't mind. It was a nice morning in town, so I thought I'd run down to see you."

"You want another fifty, I suppose—eh?" asked his Highness sharply. "Some other work of charity—eh?"

"My dear Prince, you've guessed it at once. You are, indeed, very good."

His Highness rang the bell, and when the valet appeared, gave him orders to go and get fifty pounds, which he handed to the clergyman.

Then the pair had luncheon brought up to the room, and as they sat together their conversation was mostly about mutual friends. For a cleric the Reverend Thomas Clayton was an extremely easy-going man, a thorough sportsman of a type now alas! dying out in England.

It was plain to see that they were old friends, and plainer still when, on parting a couple of hours later, the Prince said:

"When I leave here, old fellow, you'll join me for a little, won't you? Don't worry me any more at present for your Confounded—er charities—will you? Fresh air for the children, and whisky for yourself— eh? By Jove, if I hadn't been a Prince, I'd have liked to have been a parson! Good-bye, old fellow." And the rubicund cleric shook his friend's hand heartily and went down the broad staircase.

The instant his visitor had gone he called Charles and asked excitedly:

"Did any one know the Parson came to see me?"

"No, your Highness. I fortunately met him in King's Road, and brought him up here. He never inquired at the office."

"He's a fool! He could easily have written," cried the Prince eagerly.

WILLIAM LE QUEUX

"Where are those women, I wonder?" he asked, indicating Mrs. Jesup and her daughter.

"I told them you would be engaged all the afternoon."

"Good. I shan't go out again to-day, Charles. I want to think. Go to them with my compliments, and say that if they would like to use the car for a run this afternoon they are very welcome. You know what to say. And—and see that a bouquet of roses is sent up to the young lady's room before she goes to dress. Put one of my cards on it."

"Yes, your Highness," replied the valet, and turning, left his master to himself.

The visit of the Reverend Thomas Clayton had, in some way, perturbed and annoyed him. And yet their meeting had been fraught by a marked cordiality.

Presently he flung himself into a big armchair, and lighting one of his choice "Petroffs" which he specially imported, sat ruminating.

"Ah! If I were not a Prince!" he exclaimed aloud to himself. "I could do it—do it quite easily. But it's my confounded social position that prevents so much. And yet—yet I must tell her. It's imperative. I must contrive somehow or other to evade that steely maternal eye. I wonder if the mother has any suspicion—whether—?"

But he replaced his cigarette between his lips without completing the expression of his doubts.

As the sunlight began to mellow, he still sat alone, thinking deeply. Then he moved to go and dress, having resolved to dine in the public restaurant with his American friends. Just then Charles opened the door, ushering in a rather pale-faced, clean-shaven man in dark grey tweeds. He entered with a jaunty air and was somewhat arrogant of manner, as he strode across the room.

The Prince's greeting was greatly the reverse of cordial.

"What brings you here, Max?" he inquired sharply. "Didn't I telegraph to you only this morning?"

"Yes. But I wanted a breath of sea-air, so came down. I want to know if you're going to keep the appointment next Monday—or not."

"I can't tell yet."

"Hylda is anxious to know. You promised her, remember."

"I know. But apologise, and say that—well, I have some private business here. You know what to say, Max. And I may want you down here in a hurry. Come at once if I wire."

The man looked him straight in the face for a few moments.

"Oh!" he exclaimed, and then without being invited, crossed and took a cigarette.

"Charles," said the visitor to the valet who had remained in the room, "give me a drink. Let me wish success to matrimony." And with a knowing laugh he tossed off the whisky and soda handed to him. For half an hour he remained chatting confidentially with the Prince, then he left, saying that he should dine alone at the Old Ship, and return to London at ten.

When Max Mason had gone, Prince Albert heaved a long sigh, and passed into the adjoining room to dress.

That night proved a momentous one in his Highness's life, for after dinner Mrs. Jesup complained of a bad headache, and retiring at once to her room, left the young people together. What more natural, therefore, than that his Highness should invite Mary to put on her wrap and go for a stroll along the promenade in the moonlight. She accepted the invitation eagerly, and went up to her mother's room.

"I'm going for a walk with him, mother," she cried excitedly as she burst into the room where Mrs. Jesup, with all traces of headache gone, was lazily reading a novel.

"That's real good. Put on something thick, child, for its chilly," was the maternal reply. "And, remember, you don't go flirting with Princes very often."

"No, mother, but just leave him to me. I've been thinking over what you say, and I mean to be Princess of Hesse-Holstein before the year's out. Or else—"

"Or else there'll be trouble—eh?" laughed her mother.

But the girl had disappeared to join the man who loved her, and who was waiting below.

In the bright August moonlight they strolled together as far as Hove, where they sat upon a seat outside the Lawns. The evening was perfect, and there were many passers-by, mostly couples more or less amatory.

Never had a girl so attracted him as had Mary that calm and glorious night. Never had he looked into a woman's eyes and seen there love reflected as in hers. They rose and strolled back again, back to the pier which they traversed to its head. There they found a seat unoccupied, and rested upon it.

And there, taking her little hand tenderly in his, he blurted forth, in the blundering words of a blundering man, the story of his affection.

She heard him in silence to the end.

"I—I think, Prince, you have not fully considered what all this means. What—"

"It means, Mary, that I love you—love you deeply and devotedly as no other man has ever loved a woman! I am not given to ecstasies over affection, for I long ago thought every spark of it was dead within my heart. I repeat, however, that I love you." And ere she could prevent him, he had raised her hand and pressed it to his lips.

She tried to withdraw it, but he held it firmly. The moon shone full upon her sweet face, and he noticed how pale and beautiful she looked. She gave him one glance, and in that instant he saw the light of unshed tears. But she was silent, and her silence puzzled him.

"Ah!" he sighed despondently. "Am I correct, then, in suspecting that you already have a lover?"

"A lover? Whom do you mean?"

"That tall, fair-haired, mysterious man who, during the past week, has been so interested in your movements. Have you not noticed him? He's staying at the hotel. I've seen him twenty times at least, and it is only too apparent that he admires you."

"I've never even seen him," she exclaimed in surprise. "You must point him out to me. I don't like mysterious men."

"I'm not mysterious, am I?" asked the Prince, laughing, and again raising her hand to his lips tenderly. "Will you not answer my question? Do you think you can love me sufficiently—sufficiently to become my wife?"

"But—but all this is so sudden, Prince. I—I—"

"Can you love me?" he interrupted.

For answer she bent her head. Next moment his lips met hers in a hot passionate caress. And thus did their hearts beat in unison.

Before they rose from the seat Mary Jesup had promised to become Princess of Hesse-Holstein.

Next morning, the happy girl told her mother the gratifying news, and when Mrs. Jesup entered the Prince's private *salon* his Highness asked her, at least for the present, to keep their engagement secret.

That day the Prince was occupied by a quantity of correspondence, but the future Princess, after a tender kiss upon her white brow, went out in the car with her mother as far as Bognor. Two hours later the Prince sent a telegram to the Rev. Thomas Clayton, despatched Charles post-haste to London by the Pullman express, and then went out for a stroll along King's Road.

He was one of the happiest men in all the world.

Not until dinner did he again meet Mrs. Jesup and her daughter. After describing what an excellent run they had had, the millionaire's wife said:

"Oh, Mary has been telling me something about a mysterious fair-haired man whom you say has been watching her."

"Yes," replied his Highness. "He's been hanging about for some days. I fancy he's no good—one of those fellows who live in hotels on the look-out for pigeons."

"What we call in America a crook—eh?"

"Exactly. At least that's my opinion," he declared in confidence.

Mrs. Jesup and her daughter appeared both very uneasy, a circumstance which the Prince did not fail to notice. They went up to his *salon* where they had coffee, and then retired early.

Half an hour later, while his Highness was lazily enjoying one of his brown "Petroffs," the millionaire's wife, with blanched face, burst into the room crying:

"Prince! Oh, Prince! The whole of my jewels and Mary's have been stolen! Both cases have been broken open and the contents gone! My pearls too! What shall we do?" His Highness started to his feet astounded. "Do? Why find that fair-haired man!" he replied. "I'll go at once to the manager." He sped downstairs, and all was quickly in confusion. The manager recollected the man, who had given the name of Mason, and who had left suddenly on the previous morning. The police were telephoned for, and over the wires to London news of the great jewel robbery was flashed to New Scotland Yard.

There was little sleep for either of the trio that night. Examination showed that whoever the thief was, he had either been in possession of the keys of the ladies' trunks, wherein were the jewel-cases, or had obtained impressions of them, for after the jewels had been abstracted the trunks had been relocked.

The Prince was very active, while the two ladies and their maid were in utter despair. Their only consolation was that, though Mary had lost her diamonds, she had gained a husband.

About noon on the following day, while his Highness was reading the paper as he lolled lazily in the depths of the big armchair, a tap came at the door and a waiter ushered in a thin, spare, grey-faced, grey-bearded man.

The Prince sprang to his feet as though he had received an electric shock.

The two men faced each other, both utterly dumbfounded.

"Wal!" exclaimed the visitor at last, when he found tongue. "If this don't beat hog-stickin'! Say, young Tentoes, do you know I'm Robert K. Jesup?"

"You—Jesup! My dear Uncle Jim!" gasped the other. "What does this mean?"

"Yes. Things in New York over that little poker job are a bit hot just now, so Lil and the old Lady are working the matrimonial trick this side—a spoony jay, secret engagement, and blackmail. Worked it in Paris two years ago. Great success! Done neatly, it's real good. I thought they'd got hold of a real live prince this time—and rushed right here to find it's only you! They ought really to be more careful!"

"And I tell you, uncle, I too have been completely deceived. I thought I'd got a soft thing—those Bourbon pearls, you know? They left their keys about, I got casts, and when they were out bagged the boodle."

"Wal, my boy, you'd better cough 'em up right away," urged the old American criminal, whose name was Ford, and who was known to his associates as "Uncle Jim."

"I suppose the Parson's in it, as usual—eh? Say! the whole lot of sparklers aren't worth fifty dollars, but the old woman and the girl look well in 'em. My! ain't we all been taken in finely! Order me a cocktail to take the taste away. Guess Lil'll want to twist your rubber-neck when she sees you, so you'd better get into that famous car of yours and make yourself scarce, young man!"

THE SUSSEX DAILY NEWS NEXT morning contained the following announcement:

"His Royal Highness Prince Albert of Hesse-Holstein has left Brighton for the Continent."

II

The Prince and the Parson

H is Royal Highness descended from the big cream-coloured "Mercedes" in the Place Royale, drew off his gloves, and entered the quiet, eminently aristocratic Hotel de l'Europe.

All Brussels knew that Prince Albert of Hesse-Holstein was staying there. Hence, as the car pulled up, and the young man in long dust-coat and motor-goggles rose from the wheel and gave the car over to the smart chauffeur Garrett in the grey uniform with crimson facings, a small crowd of gaping idlers assembled to watch his entrance to the hotel. In the hall a few British tourists in tweeds or walking-skirts stared at him, as though a real live prince was of different clay, while on ascending the main staircase to his private suite, two waiters bowed themselves almost in two.

In his sitting-room his middle-aged English man-servant was arranging his newspapers, and closing the door sharply behind him he said: "Charles! That girl is quite a sweet little thing. I've seen her again!"

"And your Highness has fallen in love with her?" sniffed the man.

"Well, I might, Charles. One never knows." And he took a "Petroff" from the big silver box, and lit it with care. "I am very lonely, you know."

Charles's lips relaxed into a smile, but he made no remark. He was well aware how confirmed was his master's bachelordom. He often admired pretty girls, just as much as they adored him—because he was a prince—but his admiration was tinged with the acidity of sarcasm.

When Charles had gone, his Highness flung off his motor-coat and threw himself into a big chair to think. With a smart rat-a-plan, an infantry regiment of *les braves Belges* was crossing the Place to relieve the guard at the Palace. He rose and gazed across the square:

"Ah!" he laughed to himself, "my dear uncle, the Red Rubber King, is closely guarded, it seems! I suppose I ought to call upon him. He's at home, judging from the royal standard. Whew! What a bore it is to have been born a prince! If I'd been a policeman or a pork-butcher I daresay I'd have had a much better time. The world never guesses how badly we fellows are handicapped. Men like myself cannot cross the road without some scoundrelly journalist working up a 'royal scandal' or a political complication."

Then his thoughts ran off into another direction—the direction in which they had constantly flowed during the past week—towards a certain very charming, sweet-faced girl, scarcely out of her teens, who was staying with her father and mother at the Grand Hotel, down on the boulevard.

The Northovers were English—decidedly English. They were of that insular type who, in a Continental hotel, demand bacon and eggs for breakfast, denounce every dish as a "foreign mess," and sigh for the roast beef and Yorkshire pudding of middle-class suburbia. James Northover, Charles had discovered to be a very estimable and trusted person, manager of the Stamford branch of the London and North Western Bank, who was now tasting the delights of Continental travel by three weeks' vacation in Belgium. His wife was somewhat obese and rather strong-minded, while little Nellie was decidedly pretty, her light brown hair dressed low and secured by a big black velvet bow, a pair of grey, rather mischievous eyes, sweetly dimpled cheeks, and a perfect complexion. Not yet nineteen, she had only left the High School a year before, and was now being afforded an opportunity of inflicting her school-girl French upon all and sundry with whom she came into contact.

And it was French—French with those pronounced "ong" and "onny" endings for which the tourist-agents are so terribly responsible.

But with all her linguistical shortcomings little Nelly Northover, the slim-waisted school-miss with the tiny wisp of unruly hair straying across her brow, and the rather smart and intelligent chatter, had attracted him. Indeed, he could not get the thought of her out of his head.

They had met at a little inn at the village of Anseremme, on the Meuse, close to Dinant—that paradise of the cheap "hotel-included" tourist. Something had gone wrong with the clutch of his car, and he had been held up there for two days while an engineer had come out from Brussels to repair the damage. Being the only other guest in the place beside the eminently respectable bank manager and his wife and daughter, he lost no time in ingratiating himself with them, and more especially with the last-named.

Though he spoke English perfectly and with but the very slightest accent, he had given his name at the inn as Herr Birkenfeld, for was not that one of his names? He was Count of Birkenfeld, and seigneur of a dozen other places, in addition to being Prince of the royal house of Hesse-Holstein. The bank manager and his wife, of course, believed him to be a young German gentleman of means until, on the morning of the day of his departure, Charles, in greatest confidence, revealed to them who his master really was.

The English trio were utterly staggered. To Nellie, there was an element of romance at meeting a real prince in those rural solitudes of river and forest. As she declared to her mother, he was so nice and so unassuming. Just, indeed, like any ordinary man.

And in her young mind she compared Albert Prince of Hesse-Holstein with the provincial young gentlemen whom she had met last season at the popular county function, the Stamford Ball.

As constantly Nellie Northover's thoughts reverted to the affable prince, so did his Highness, on his part, sit hour upon hour smoking his pet Russian cigarettes in quick succession, pondering and wondering.

His position was one of terrible weariness. Ah! how often he wished that he had not been born a prince. As an ordinary mortal he might have dared to aspire to the hand of the sweet young English miss. But as Prince Albert of Hesse-Holstein, such a marriage would be denounced by press and public as a *misalliance*.

He liked James Northover. There was something of the John Bull about him which he admired. A keen, hard-headed business man, tall and bald, who spoke with a Nottingham brogue, and who had been over thirty years in the service of the bank, he was a highly trusted servant of his directors. In allowing overdrafts he seldom made mistakes, while his courtesy had brought the bank a considerably increased business.

The Prince knew all that. A couple of days after meeting Nellie in Anseremme he had written to a certain Reverend Thomas Clayton, who lived in Bayswater, and had only that morning received a long letter bearing the Stamford postmark.

It was on account of this letter that he went out after luncheon in the car along the Rue Royale, and down the Boulevard Botanique, to the Grand Hotel on the Boulevard d'Anspach.

He found Nellie alone in the big *salon*, reading an English paper. On seeing him the girl flushed slightly and jumped to her feet, surprised that he should call unexpectedly.

"Miss Northover!" he exclaimed, raising his motor-cap, "I've called to take you all for a little run this afternoon—if you can come. I have the car outside."

WILLIAM LE QUEUX

"I'm sure it's awfully kind of you, Prince," the girl replied with some confusion. "I—well, I don't know what to say. Father and mother are out."

"Ah!" he laughed; "and of course you cannot come with me alone. It is against your English ideas of *les convenances*—eh?"

She laughed in chorus, afterwards saying:

"I expect them back in half an hour."

"Oh, then, I'll wait," he exclaimed, and taking off his motor-coat, he seated himself in a chair and began to chat with her, asking what sights of Brussels she had seen, at the same time being filled with admiration at her fresh sweetness and *chic*. They were alone in the room, and he found an indescribable charm in her almost childlike face and girlish chatter. She was so unlike the artificial women of cosmopolitan society who were his friends.

Yes. He was deeply in love with her, and by her manner towards him he could not fail to notice that his affection was reciprocated.

Presently her parents appeared. They had noticed the big cream-coloured car with the chauffeur standing outside, and at once a flutter had run through both their hearts, knowing that the august visitor had arrived to call upon them.

Northover was full of apologies, but the Prince cut them short, and within a quarter of an hour they were all in the car and on the road to that goal of every British tourist, the battlefield of Waterloo. The autumn afternoon was perfect. The leaves had scarcely begun to turn, and the sun so hot that it might still have been August.

Nellie's father was just as proud of the Prince's acquaintance as she was herself, while Mrs. Northover was filled with pleasurable anticipations of going back to quiet, old-world Stamford—a place where nothing ever happens—and referring, in the hearing of her own tea-drinking circle, to "my friend Prince Albert."

A week passed. Mr. and Mrs. Northover could not fail to notice how constantly the Prince was in Nellie's society.

Only once, however, did her father mention it to his wife, and then in confidence.

"Nellie seems much struck by the Prince, don't you think? And I'm sure he admires her. He's such a good fellow. I like him. I suppose it's a mere harmless flirtation—and it amuses them both."

"Fancy, if she became Princess of Hesse-Holstein, James!"

But James Northover only grunted dubiously. He was ignorant of the truth; ignorant of the fact that on the previous night, while they had been taking a stroll along the boulevard after dinner, the Prince, who had been walking with Nellie, had actually whispered to her a declaration of love.

It had all been done so secretly. The pair had been following a little distance behind her worthy parents, and in the star-lit night he had pressed her hand. He had told her hurriedly, whispering low, how fondly he had loved her from the very first moment they had met. How devoted he was to her, and declaring that no woman had ever touched the chord of love in his heart as she had done.

"To-morrow, dearest, we shall part," he whispered; "but before we do so will you not give me one word of hope—hope that you may some day be mine! Tell me, can you ever reciprocate my love?" he whispered in deep earnestness, as he bent to her, still holding her little hand in his strong grip as they walked.

For a few moments she was silent; her dimpled chin sank upon her breast. He felt her quivering with emotion, and as the light of a gas-lamp fell across her beautiful face he saw tears in her eyes.

She turned to him and lifted her gaze to his. Then he knew the truth without her spoken word. She was his—his own!

"We will keep our secret, dearest," he said presently. "No one must know. For family reasons it must not yet leak out. Think how lonely I shall be at this hour to-morrow—when you have left!"

"And I also," she sobbed. "You know—you must have seen—that I love you!"

At that moment her mother turned to look back, and consequently they both instantly assumed an attitude of utter unconcern. And next afternoon when he saw the three off from the Gare du Nord by the Harwich service, neither the estimable Northover, nor his rather obese spouse, had the slightest idea of the true secret of the two young hearts.

Nellie grasped her lover's hand in adieu. Their eyes met for a single instant, and it was all-sufficient. Each trusted the other implicitly. It was surely a charming love-idyll between prince and school-girl.

His Highness remained in Brussels for about three weeks, then crossed to London. He stayed at the Carlton, where, on the night of his arrival, he was visited by the rather ruddy-faced jovial-looking clergyman, the Reverend Thomas Clayton.

It was Charles who announced him, saying in an abrupt manner:

"The Parson's called, your Highness."

"Show him in," was the Prince's reply. "I was expecting him."

The greeting between Prince Albert and his old clerical friend was hearty, and the two men spent a couple of hours over whisky and sodas and cigarettes, chatting confidentially.

"You're in love with her, Prince!" laughed his reverend friend.

"Yes, I really and honestly believe I am," the other admitted, "and especially so, after your report."

"My inquiries were perfectly satisfactory," the clergyman said.

"I want to have an excuse for going up to Stamford, but don't see well how it can be managed," remarked the Prince pensively, between whiffs of his cigarette.

"With my assistance it might, my dear boy," replied the Reverend Thomas. "It wants a little thinking over. You're a prince, remember."

"Yes," sighed the other wearily. "That's just the confounded difficulty. I wonder what the world would say if they knew my secret?"

"Say?" and the clergyman pulled a wry face. "Why bother about what the world thinks? I never do."

"Yes. But you're a parson, and a parson can do practically just what he likes."

"As long as he's popular with his parishioners."

And it was not till near midnight, after a dainty snack of supper, served in the Prince's sitting-room, that the pair parted.

A fortnight later Mr. James Northover was agreeably impressed to receive a letter from the Prince stating that a great friend of his, the Rev. Thomas Clayton, of St. Ethelburga's, Bayswater, was staying in Stamford, convalescent after an illness, and that he was coming to visit him.

The Northover household was thrown into instant confusion. Its head was for inviting the Prince to stay with them, but Mrs. Northover and Nellie both declared that he would be far more comfortable at the Stamford Hotel, or at the "George." Besides, he was a prince, and Alice, the cook, could not possibly do things as was his Highness's habit to have them done. So a telegram was sent to the Carlton saying that the Northovers were most delighted at the prospect of seeing the Prince again.

Next day his Highness arrived in the big cream-coloured car at the Stamford Hotel, causing great excitement in the town. Charles had come down by the morning train and engaged rooms for his master, and within half an hour of the Prince's arrival the worthy mayor called and left his card.

The Prince's first visit, however, was to his old friend, the Rev. Thos. Clayton, whom he found in rather shabby apartments in Rock Terrace seated in an armchair, looking very pale, and quite unlike his usual self.

"I'm sure it's awfully good of you to become an invalid on my account?" exclaimed the Prince the moment they were alone. "However do you pass your days in this sleepy hollow?"

"By study, my dear boy! Study's a grand thing! See!" And he exhibited a big dry-as-dust volume on "The Extinct Civilisations of Africa."

He remained an hour, and then, remounting into the car, drove out along the Tinwell Road, where, half a mile from the town, Mr. Northover's comfortable, red-brick villa was situated. He found the whole family assembled to welcome him—as they had, indeed, been assembled in eager expectation for the past four hours.

Nellie he found looking particularly dainty, with the usual big black velvet bow in her hair, and wearing a neat blouse of cream washing-silk and a short black skirt. She was essentially the type of healthy hockey-playing English girl.

As he grasped her hand and greeted her with formality, he felt it tremble within his grasp. She had kept his secret; of that there was no doubt.

The home life of the Northovers he found quite pleasant. It was so unlike anything he had even been used to. He remained to tea, and he returned there to dine and spend a pleasant evening listening to Nellie's performances on the piano.

Afterwards, when the ladies had retired as they did discreetly at half-past ten, he sat smoking his "Petroffs" and chatting with Mr. Northover.

"I hope you found your friend, the clergyman, better, Prince. Where is he living?"

"Oh, yes; he's much better, thanks. But he has rather wretched quarters, in a house in Rock Terrace. I've urged him to move into an hotel. He says, however, that he hates hotels. He's such a good fellow—gives nearly all he has to the poor."

"I suppose he's down here for fresh air?"

"Yes. He's very fond of this neighbourhood. Often came here when a boy, I believe."

"When you go again I'd like to call upon him. We must not allow him to be lonely."

"I shall call to-morrow. Perhaps you could go with me, after the bank has closed?"

WILLIAM LE QUEUX

"Yes. At four-thirty. Will you call at the bank for me?"

And so it was arranged.

Punctually at the hour named the Prince stepped from his car before the bank—which was situated in a side street between two shops—and was at once admitted and ushered through to the manager's room.

Then the pair went on to Rock Terrace to pay the visit. The invalid was much better, and Northover found him a man entirely after his own heart. He was a man of the world, as well as a clergyman.

In the week that followed, Nellie's father made several visits, and once, on a particularly bright day, the Prince brought the Rev. Thomas round in the car to return the visit at Tinwell Road.

Within ten days the vicar of St. Ethelburga's, Bayswater, had become quite an intimate friend of the Northovers; so much so, indeed, that they compelled him to give up his rooms in Rock Terrace, and come and stay as their guest. Perhaps it was more for the Prince's sake they did this—perhaps because they admired Clayton as "a splendid fellow for a parson."

Anyhow, all this gave the Prince plenty of opportunities for meeting Nellie clandestinely. Instead of going to her music-lesson, or to her hockey-club, or visiting an old schoolfellow, she went daily to a certain secluded spot on the Worthope Road, where she was joined by the man she loved.

Her romance was complete. She adored Albert, utterly and devotedly; while he, on his part, was her slave. On the third day after his arrival in Stamford she had promised to become Princess of Hesse-Holstein, and now they were closely preserving their secret.

The advent of his Highness had raised Mrs. Northover to the very pinnacle of the social scale in Stamford. Times without number she tried to obtain from Nellie the true state of affairs, but the girl was sly enough to preserve her lover's secret.

If the truth were yet known to the family of Hesse-Holstein, all sorts of complications would assuredly ensue. Besides, it would, he felt certain, bring upon him the displeasure of the Emperor. He must go to Potsdam, and announce to the Kaiser his engagement with his own lips.

And so little Nellie Northover, the chosen Princess of Hesse-Holstein, the girl destined to become husband of the ruler of a principality half the size of England, and the wealthiest of the German princes, often wandered the country roads alone, and tried to peer into her brilliant future. What would the girls of Stamford say when they found that Nellie Northover was actually a princess! Why, even the Marchioness who lived at the great ancestral mansion, mentioned in Tennyson's well-known poem, would then receive her!

And all through the mere failing of a motor-car clutch at that tiny obscure Belgian village.

The Reverend Thomas gradually grew stronger while guest of Mr. Northover, and both he and the Prince, together with the Northovers, Mr. Henry Ashdown, the assistant manager of the bank who lived on the premises, and others of the Northovers' friends went for frequent runs in the nobleman's car.

The Prince never hedged himself in by etiquette. Every friend of Northover at once became his friend; hence, within a fortnight, his Highness was the most popular figure in that quaint old market town.

One afternoon while the Prince and the clergyman were walking together up the High Street, they passed a thin, pale-faced man in dark grey flannels.

Glances of recognition were exchanged, but no word was uttered.

"Max is at the 'George,' isn't he?" asked the Prince.

"Yes," replied his companion. "Arrived the night before last, and having a particularly dull time, I should think."

"So should I," laughed the Prince.

That evening, the two ladies being away at the Milton Hound Show, they took Northover and his assistant, Ashdown, after their business, over to Peterborough to bring them back. Ashdown was some ten years younger than his chief, and rather fond of his whisky and soda. At the Great Northern Hotel in Peterborough they found the ladies; and on their return to Stamford the whole party dined together at the Prince's hotel, an old-fashioned hostelry with old-fashioned English fare.

And so another fortnight went past. The autumn winds grew more chilly, and the leaves fell with the advance of October.

Nellie constantly met the Prince, in secret, the only person knowing the truth besides themselves being the Parson, who had now become one of the girl's particular friends.

While the Prince was dressing for dinner one evening, Charles being engaged in putting the links in his shirt-cuffs, he suddenly asked:

"Max is still in Stamford, I suppose?"

"I believe so, your Highness."

"Well, I want you to take this up to London to-night, Charles." And he drew from a locked drawer a small sealed packet about four inches square, looking like jewellery. "You'll see the address on it. Take it there, then go to the Suffolk Hotel, in Suffolk Street, Strand, and wait till I send you instructions to return."

"Very well, your Highness," answered the man who always carried out his master's instructions with blind obedience.

Next day, in conversation with Mr. Northover, the Prince expressed regret that he had been compelled to discharge his man Charles at a moment's notice.

"The man is a thief," he said briefly. "I lost a valuable scarf-pin the other day—one given me by the Emperor. But I never suspected him until a few days ago when I received an anonymous letter telling me that my trusted man, Charles, had, before I took him into my service, been convicted of theft, and was, indeed, one of a gang of clever swindlers! I made inquiries, and discovered this to be the actual truth."

"By Jove!" remarked the Reverend Thomas. "Think what an escape the Prince has had! All his jewellery might have suddenly disappeared!"

"How very fortunate you were warned!" declared Mr. Northover. "Your correspondent was anonymous, you say?"

"Yes. Some one must have recognised him in London, I think, and, therefore, given me warning. A most disagreeable affair—I assure you."

"Then you've lost the Emperor's present?" asked Nellie.

"Yes," sighed the Prince; "It's gone for ever. I've given notice to the police. They're sending a detective from London to see me, I believe, but I feel certain I shall never see it again."

This conversation was repeated by Mrs. Northover to her husband, when he returned from business that evening.

About the same hour, however, while the Prince was smoking with his clerical friend in his private room at the hotel, the waiter entered, saying that a Mr. Mason had called upon his Highness.

"That's the man from Scotland Yard!" exclaimed the Prince aloud. "Show him up."

A few moments later a rather pale-faced, fair-haired man in shabby brown tweeds was ushered in, and the waiter, who knew the story of Charles's sudden discharge, retired.

"Good evening, Prince," exclaimed the new-comer. "I got your wire and came at once." At the same time he produced from his pocket a small cartridge envelope containing something slightly bulky, but carefully sealed.

"Right! Go over there, Max, and help yourself to a drink. You're at the 'George,' I suppose?"

"No. I've got a room here—so as to be near you—in case of necessity, you know," he added meaningly.

The two men exchanged glances.

It was evident at once that Mr. Mason was no stranger, for he helped himself to a cigarette uninvited, and, mixing a small drink, drained it off at a single gulp.

Then, after chatting for a quarter of an hour or so, he went out "just to get a wash," as he put it.

The Prince, when he had gone, turned over the small packet in his hand without opening it.

Then he rose, walked to the window, and in silence looked out upon the old church opposite, deep in thought.

The Parson, watching him without a word, knit his brows, and pursed his lips.

Next morning the Prince sent Garrett with the car to London, as he wanted some alteration to the hood, and that afternoon, as he crossed the marketplace, he again met Max. Neither spoke. A glance of recognition was all that passed between them. Meanwhile, the detective from London had been making a good many inquiries in Stamford, concerning the associates and friends of the discharged valet Charles.

The latter was, the detective declared, an old hand, and his Highness had been very fortunate in getting rid of him when he did.

That evening Mr. and Mrs. Ashdown invited the Prince and the clergyman to dinner, at which they were joined by the sweet-faced Nellie and her father and mother. With true provincial habit, the party broke up at ten-thirty, and while the Parson walked home with the Northovers, his Highness lit a cigar and strolled back to the hotel alone.

Until nearly two o'clock he sat smoking, reading, and thinking— thinking always of pretty Nellie—and now and then glancing at the clock. After the church-bell had struck two he had a final "peg," and then turned in.

Next morning, when the waiter brought his coffee, the man blurted forth breathlessly:

"There's been a great robbery, your Highness, last night. The London and North Western Bank has been entered, and they say that four thousand pounds in gold has been stolen."

"What!" gasped the Prince, springing up. "Mr. Northover's bank?"

"Yes, sir. The whole town is in an uproar! I've told Mr. Mason, and he's gone down to see. They say that a week ago a youngish man from London took the empty shop next door to the bank, and it's believed the thieves were secreted in there. There doesn't seem any evidence of any of the locks being tampered with, for the front door was opened with a key, and they had keys of both the doors of the strong-room. The police are utterly mystified, for Mr. Northover has one key, and Mr. Ashdown the other, and the doors can't be opened unless they are both there together. Both gentlemen say their keys have never left them, and none of the burglar-alarms rang."

"Then it's an absolute mystery—eh," remarked the Prince, utterly astonished. "Perhaps that scoundrel Charles has had something to do with it! He went to the bank for me on several occasions!"

"That's what Mr. Mason and the other police officers think, sir," the waiter said. "And it seems that the men must have got out the coin, brought it into the empty shop, carried it through the back of the premises and packed it into a dark-green motor-car. A policeman out on the Worthorpe Road, saw the car pass just before two o'clock this morning. There were two men in it, besides the driver."

The Prince dressed hastily, and was about to rush down to the bank to condole with Northover when the latter burst into his room in a great state of mind.

"It's an absolute mystery, and so daring!" he declared. "The thieves must have had duplicate keys of the whole bank! They left all the notes, but cleared out every bit of gold coin. We had some unusually heavy deposits lately, and they've taken three thousand four hundred and thirty-two pounds!"

"What about that man who took the shop next door?"

"He's perfectly respectable, the police assure me. He knows nothing about it. He's hardly finished stocking the place with groceries, and opens the day after to-morrow. His name is Newman."

"Then how did they get their booty away?"

"That's the mystery. Unless through the back of the shop next door. No motor-car came along the street in the night, for Ashdown's child was ill, and Mrs. Ashdown was up all night and heard nothing. The means by which they got such a heavy lot of coin away so neatly is as mysterious as how they obtained the keys."

"Depend upon it that my scoundrelly valet has had a finger in this!" the Prince declared. "I'll assist you to try and find him. I happen to know some of his friends in London."

Northover was delighted, and at the police-station the superintendent thanked his Highness for his kind promise of assistance. Mr. Mason was ubiquitous, and the parson full of astonishment at the daring coup of the unknown thieves. Two bank directors came down from town in the afternoon, and after a discussion, a full report was telegraphed to New Scotland Yard.

That same evening the Prince went up to London, accompanied by the keen-eyed Mr. Mason, leaving the Parson still the guest of Mr. Northover.

The latter, however, would scarcely have continued to entertain him, had he known that, on arrival at King's Cross, his Highness and Mr. Mason took a cab to a certain house in Hereford Road, Bayswater, where Charles and Garrett were eagerly awaiting him. In the room were two other men whom the Prince shook by the hand and warmly congratulated.

Charles opened the door of the adjoining room, a poorly furnished bedroom, where stood a chest of drawers. One drawer after the other he opened.

They were full of bags of golden sovereigns!

"Those impressions you sent us, Prince, gave us a lot of trouble," declared the elder of the two men, with a pronounced American accent. "The keys were very difficult to make, and when you sent us word that the parson had tried them and they wouldn't act, we began to fear that it was no go. But we did the trick all right, after all, didn't we? Guess we spent a pretty miserable week in Stamford, but you seemed to be having quite a good time. Where's the Sky-pilot?"

"He's remaining—convalescent, you know. And as for Bob Newman, he'll be compelled to carry on that confounded grocery business next door for at least a couple of months—before he fails, and shuts up."

"Well," exclaimed the man Mason, whom everybody in Stamford—even the police themselves—believed to be a detective. "It was a close shave! You know, Prince, when you came out of the bank after dinner and I slipped in past you, I only just got into the shadow before that slip of a girl of Northover's ran down the stairs after you. I saw you give her a kiss in the darkness."

"She deserved a kiss, the little dear," replied his Highness, "for without her we could never have brought off so complete a thing."

"Ah! you always come in for the good things," Charles remarked.

"Because I'm a prince," was his Highness's reply.

The police are still looking for the Prince's valet, and his Highness has, of course, assisted them. Charles, however, got away to Copenhagen to a place of complete safety, and he being the only person suspected, it is very unlikely that the bank will ever see their money again—neither is Nellie Northover ever likely to see her prince.

III

The Mysterious Sixty

When the smart chauffeur, Garrett, entered the cosy chambers of his Highness Prince Albert of Hesse-Holstein, alias Charles Fotheringham, alias Henry Tremlett, in Dover Street, Piccadilly, he found him stretched lazily on the couch before the fire. He had exchanged his dinner jacket for an easy coat of brown velvet; between his lips was a Russian cigarette of his pet brand, and at his elbow a brandy and soda.

"Ah! Garrett," he exclaimed as the chauffeur entered. "Come here, and sit down. Shut the door first. I want to talk to you."

As chauffeur to the Prince and his ingenious companions, Garrett had met with many queer adventures and been in many a tight corner. To this day he wonders he was not "pinched" by the police a dozen times, and certainly would have been if it were not that the gay, good-looking, devil-may-care Prince Albert never left anything to chance. When a *coup* was to be made he thought out every minute detail, and took precaution against every risk of detection. To his marvellous ingenuity and wonderful foresight Garrett, with his friends, owed his liberty.

During the three years through which he had thrown in his lot with that select little circle of "crooks," he had really had a very interesting time, and had driven them thousands of miles, mostly on the Continent, in the big "Mercedes" or the "sixty" six-cylinder "Minerva."

His Highness's share in the plunder had been very considerable. At his bankers he possessed quite a respectable balance, and he lived in easy affluence the life of a prince. In the drawing-rooms of London and Paris he was known as essentially a ladies' man; while in Italy he was usually Henry Tremlett, of London, and in France he was Charles Fotheringham, an Anglo-Frenchman and Chevalier of the Legion d'Honneur.

"Look here, Garrett," he said, raising himself on his elbow and looking the man in the face as he tossed his cigarette in the grate. "To-day, let's see, is December 16. You must start in the car to-morrow for San Remo. We shall spend a week or two there."

"To-morrow!" the chauffeur echoed. "The roads from Paris down to the Riviera are pretty bad just now. I saw in the paper yesterday that there's heavy snow around Valence."

"Snow, or no snow, we must go," the Prince said decisively. "We have a little matter in hand down there—you understand?" he remarked, his dark eyes still fixed upon the chauffeur.

The man wondered what was the nature of the *coup* intended.

"And now," he went on, "let me explain something else. There may be some funny proceedings down at San Remo. But just disregard everything you see, and don't trouble your head about the why, or wherefore. You're paid to be chauffeur, Garrett—and paid well, too, by your share of the profits—so nothing else concerns you. It isn't, sparklers we're after this time—it's something else."

The Prince who, speaking English so well, turned his birth and standing to such good account, never told the chauffeur of his plans. His confederates, indeed, were generally kept completely in the dark until the very last moment. Therefore, they were all very frequently puzzled by what seemed to be extraordinary and motiveless actions by the leader of the party of adventurers.

The last *coup* made was in the previous month, at Aix-les-Bains, the proceeds being sold to the old Jew in Amsterdam for four thousand pounds sterling, this sum being divided up between the Prince, the Parson, a neat-ankled little Parisienne named Valentine Dejardin, and Garrett. And they were now going to spend a week or two in that rather dull and much over-rated little Italian seaside town, where the sharper and crook flourish to such a great extent in spring—San Remo.

They were evidently about to change their tactics, for it was not diamonds they were after, but something else. Garrett wondered as the Count told him to help himself to a whisky and soda what that "something else" would turn out to be.

"I daresay you'll be a bit puzzled," he said, lazily lighting a fresh cigarette, "but don't trouble your head about the why or wherefore. Leave that to me. Stay at the Hotel Regina at San Remo—that big place up on the hill—you know it. You'll find the Parson there. Let's see, when we were there a year ago I was Tremlett, wasn't I?—so I must be that again, I suppose."

He rose from his couch, stretched himself, and pulling a bookcase from the high old-fashioned wainscoting slid back one of the white enamelled panels disclosing a secret cavity wherein, Garrett knew, reposed a quantity of stolen jewels that he had failed to get rid of to the Jew diamond dealer in Amsterdam, who acted in most cases as receiver.

The chauffeur saw within that small cavity, of about a foot square, a number of little parcels each wrapped in tissue paper—jewels for which the police of Europe for a year or so had been hunting high and low. Putting his hand into the back the Prince produced a bundle of banknotes, from which he counted one "fifty" and ten fivers, and handed them to his man.

"They're all right. You'll want money, for I think that, after all, you'd better go to San Remo as a gentleman and owner of the car. Both the Parson and I will be perfect strangers to you—you understand?"

"Perfectly," was Garrett's reply, as he watched him replace the notes, push back the panel into its place, and move the bookcase into its original position.

"Then get away to-morrow night by Newhaven and Dieppe," he said. "If I were you I'd go by Valence and Die, instead of by Grenoble. There's sure to be less snow there. Wire me when you get down to Cannes." And he pushed across his big silver box of cigarettes, one of which the chauffeur took, and seating himself, listened to his further instructions. They, however, gave no insight into the adventure which was about to be undertaken.

At half-past seven on the following night, with his smartly-cut clothes packed in two suit-cases, his chauffeur's dress discarded for a big leather-lined coat of dark-green frieze and motor-cap and goggles, and a false number-plate concealed beneath the cushion, Garrett drew the car out of the garage in Oxford Street, and sped along the Embankment and over Westminster Bridge on the first stage of his long and lonely journey.

The night was dark, with threatening rain, but out in the country the big searchlight shone brilliantly, and he tore along the Brighton road while the rhythmic splutter of his open exhaust awakened the echoes of the country-side. With a loud shriek of the siren he passed village after village until at Brighton he turned to the left along that very dangerous switchback road that leads to Newhaven.

How he shipped the car, or how for four weary days—such was the hopeless state of the roads—he journeyed due south, has no bearing upon this narrative of an adventurer's adventure. Fortunately the car ran magnificently, the engines beating in perfect time against rain and blizzard, and tyre-troubles were few. The road—known well to him, for

WILLIAM LE QUEUX

he had traversed it with the Prince at least a dozen times to and from Monte Carlo—was snow-covered right from Lyons down to Aix in Provence, making progress difficult, and causing him constant fear lest he should run into some deep drift.

At last, however, in the bright Riviera sunshine, so different to the London weather he had left behind five days ago, and with the turquoise Mediterranean lying calm and picturesque on his right, he found himself passing along the Lower Corniche from Nice through Beaulieu, Monaco, and Mentone to Ventimiglia, the Italian frontier. Arrived there, he paid the Customs deposit at the little roadside bureau of the Italian dogana, got a leaden seal impressed upon the front of the chassis, and drew away up the hill again for a few short miles through Bordighera and Ospedaletti to the picturesque little town of San Remo, which so bravely but vainly endeavours to place itself forward as the Nice of the Italian Riviera.

The Hotel Regina, the best and most fashionable, stands high above the sea-road, embowered in palms, oranges, and flowers, and as Garrett turned with a swing into the gateway and ran up the steep incline on his "second," his arrival, dirty and travel-worn as he was, caused some stir among the smartly dressed visitors taking their tea *al fresco*.

With an air of nonchalance the gentleman chauffeur sprang out, gave over the mud-covered car to a man from the hotel garage, and entering the place, booked a pretty but expensive sitting-room and bedroom overlooking the sea.

Having tubbed and exchanged his rough tweeds for grey flannels and a straw hat, he descended to see if he could find the Parson, who, by the list in the hall, he saw was among the guests. He strolled about the town, and looked in at a couple of *cafes*, but saw nothing of the Prince's clever confederate.

Not until he went in to dinner did he discover him.

Wearing a faultless clerical collar and perfect-fitting clerical coat, and on his nose gold pince-nez, he was sitting a few tables away, dining with two well-dressed ladies—mother and daughter he took them to be, though afterwards he found they were aunt and niece. The elder woman, handsome and well-preserved, evidently a foreigner from her very dark hair and fine eyes, was dressed handsomely in black, with a bunch of scarlet roses in her corsage. As far as Garrett could see, she wore no jewellery.

The younger of the pair was certainly not more than nineteen, fair-haired, with a sweet girlish face, blue eyes almost childlike in their softness, and a pretty dimpled cheek, and a perfectly formed mouth that invited kisses. She was in pale carnation—a colour that suited her admirably, and in her bodice, cut slightly low, was a bunch of those sweet-smelling flowers which grow in such profusion along the Italian coast as to supply the European markets in winter.

Both women were looking at Garrett, noticing that he was a fresh arrival.

In a Riviera hotel, where nearly every guest makes a long stay, a fresh arrival early in the season is always an event, and he or she is discussed and criticised, approved or condemned. Garrett could see that the two ladies were discussing him with the Reverend Thomas, who glared at him for a moment through his glasses as though he had never before seen him in his life, and then with some words to his companions, he went on eating his fish.

He knew quite well of Garrett's advent, but part of the mysterious game was that they did not recognise each other.

When dinner was over, and everyone went into the hall to lounge and take coffee, Garrett inquired of the hall-porter the names of the two ladies in question.

"The elder one, m'sieur," he replied, in French, in a confidential tone, "is Roumanian, the Princess Charles of Krajova, and the young lady is her niece, Mademoiselle Dalrymple."

"Dalrymple!" he echoed. "Then mademoiselle must be English!"

"Certainly, m'sieur."

And Garrett turned away, wondering with what ulterior object our friend "the Parson" was ingratiating himself with La Princesse.

Next day, the gay devil-may-care Prince, giving his name as Mr. Henry Tremlett, of London, arrived, bringing the faithful Charles, to whose keen observation more than one successful *coup* had owed its genesis. There were now four of them staying in the hotel, but with what object Garrett could not discern.

The Prince gave no sign of recognition to the Parson or the chauffeur. He dined at a little table alone, and was apparently as interested in the two women as Garrett was himself.

Garrett's main object was to create interest, so acting upon the instructions the Prince had given him in London, he posed as the owner of the fine car, swaggered in the hall in his big coat and cap, and took runs up and down the white winding coast-road, envied by many of the guests, who, he knew, dearly wanted to explore the beauties of the neighbourhood.

It was not, therefore, surprising that more than one of the guests of both sexes got into casual conversation with Garrett, and among them, on the second day after his arrival, the Princess Charles of Krajova.

She was, he found, an enthusiastic motorist, and as they stood that sunny afternoon by the car, which was before the hotel, she made many inquiries regarding the long stretch from Dieppe to the Italian frontier. While they were chatting, the Parson, with Mademoiselle approached. The Rev. Thomas started a conversation, in which the young lady joined. The latter Garrett decided was very charming. Her speech was that of an educated English girl only lately from her school, yet she had evidently been well trained for her position in society, and though so young, carried herself extremely well.

As yet, nobody had spoken to Tremlett. He seemed to keep himself very much to himself. Why, the chauffeur wondered?

That evening he spent in the hall, chatting with the Parson and the ladies. He had invited them all to go for a run on the morrow by the seashore as far as Savona, then inland to Ceva, and back by Ormeo and Oneglia, and they had accepted enthusiastically. Then, when aunt and niece rose to retire, he invited the Rev. Thomas up to his sitting-room for a final whisky and soda.

When they were alone with the door shut, Clayton said:

"Look here, Garrett! This is a big game we're playing. The Prince lies low, while we work it. To-morrow you must attract the girl, while I make myself agreeable to the aunt—a very decent old body, after all. Recollect, you must not fall in love with the girl. She admires you, I know."

"Not very difficult to fall in love with her," laughed the other. "She's uncommonly good-looking."

"Yes, but be careful that you don't make a fool of yourself, and really allow yourself to be smitten," he urged.

"But what is the nature of this fresh game?" Garrett inquired, eager to ascertain what was intended.

"Don't worry about that, my dear fellow," was his reply. "Only make love to the girl. Leave the rest to his Highness and myself."

And so it came about that next day, with the pretty Winnie—for that was her name—seated at his side, Garrett drove the car along to Savona, chatting merrily with her, and discovering her to be most *chic* and charming. Her parents lived in London, she informed him, in Queen's Gate. Her father was in Parliament, sitting for one of the Welsh boroughs.

The run was delightful, and was the commencement of a very pleasant friendship. He saw that his little friend was in no way averse to a violent flirtation, and indeed, he spent nearly the whole of the next morning with her in the garden.

The chauffeur had already disregarded the Parson's advice, and had fallen desperately in love with her.

As they sat in the garden she told him that her mother was a Roumanian lady, of Bucharest, whose sister had married the enormously wealthy landowner, Prince Charles of Krajova. For the past two years she had lived in Paris, Vienna and Bucharest, with her aunt, and they were now at San Remo to spend the whole winter.

"But," she added, with a wistful look, "I far prefer England. I was at school at Folkestone, and had a most jolly time there. I was so sorry to leave to come out here."

"Then you know but little of London?"

"Very little," she declared. "I know Folkestone better. We used to walk on the Leas every day, or play hockey and tennis. I miss my games so very much," she added, raising her fine big eyes to his.

At his invitation she walked down to the town and back before luncheon, but not without some hesitation, as perhaps she thought her aunt might not like it. On the Promenade they met his Highness, but he gave them no sign of recognition.

"That gentleman is staying at our hotel," she remarked after he had passed. "I saw on the list that he is a Mr. Tremlett, from London."

"Yes—I also saw that," remarked the chauffeur. "Looks a decent kind of fellow."

"Rather a fop, I think," she declared. "My aunt, however, is anxious to know him, so if you make his acquaintance, will you please introduce him to us?"

"I'll be most delighted, of course, Miss Dalrymple," he said, inwardly congratulating himself upon his good fortune.

And an hour later he wrote a note to the Prince and posted it, telling him of what the girl had said.

While the Parson monopolised the Princess, Garrett spent most of the time in the company of Winifred Dalrymple. That afternoon he took the Parson and the ladies for a run on the car, and that evening, it being Christmas Eve, there was a dance, during which he was on several occasions her partner.

She waltzed splendidly, and Garrett found himself each hour more deeply in love with her. During the dance, he managed to feign to scrape acquaintance with the Prince, and presented him to his dainty little friend, as well as her aunt, whereat the latter at once went out of her way to be most gracious and affable. Already the handsome Tremlett knew most of the ladies in the hotel, as his coming and going always caused a flutter within the hearts of the gentler sex, for he was essentially a ladies' man. Indeed, to his easy courtly manner towards them was due the great success of his many ingenious schemes.

He would kiss a woman one moment and rifle her jewel-case the next, so utterly unscrupulous was he. He was assuredly a perfect type of the well-bred, audacious young adventurer.

While the dance was proceeding Garrett was standing with Winifred in the hall, when they heard the sound of an arriving motor-car coming up the incline from the road, and going to the door he saw that it was a very fine sixty horse-power "Fiat" limousine. There were no passengers, but the driver was a queer grey-haired, hunchbacked old man. His face was splashed, his grey goat's-skin coat was muddy, like the car, for it was evident that he had come a long distance.

As he entered the big brilliantly-lit hall, his small black eyes cast a searching look around. Winifred, whom Garrett was at that moment leading back to the ballroom, started quickly. Had she, he wondered, recognised him? If so, why had she started. That she was acquainted with the stranger, and that she did not wish to meet him he quickly saw, for a few moments later she whispered something to the Princess, whose face instantly changed, and the pair pleading fatigue a few minutes later, ascended in the lift to their own apartments.

So curious was the incident, that Garrett determined to ascertain something regarding the queer, wizened-faced old hunchback who acted as chauffeur, but to his surprise when he returned to the hall, he found the car had already left. The little old man in the fur motor-coat had merely called to make inquiry whether a certain German baron was staying in the hotel, and had then left immediately.

He was much puzzled at the marked uneasiness of both the Princess and Winifred at the appearance of the mysterious "sixty." Indeed, he saw her Highness's maid descend the stairs half an hour later, evidently in order to gather some facts concerning the movements of the hunchback. Prince and Parson were both playing bridge, therefore Garrett was unable to relate to them what he had seen, so he retired to bed wondering what the truth might really be.

Morning dawned. The Prince and his friend were both down unusually early, walking in the garden, and discussing something very seriously. But its nature they kept from their chauffeur.

The morning he spent with Winifred, who looked very sweet and charming in her white serge gown, white shoes and big black hat. They idled in the garden among the orange groves for an hour, and then walked down to the town and back.

At luncheon a surprise awaited them, for quite close to Garrett sat the little old man, clean and well-dressed, eating his meal and apparently taking no notice of anybody. Yet he saw what effect the man's presence had produced upon the Princess and her niece, who having taken their seats could not well escape.

Where was the big "sixty"? It was certainly not in the garage at the hotel! And why had the old man returned?

Reviewing all the circumstances, together with what the Prince had explained to him in Dover Street, he found himself utterly puzzled. The whole affair was an enigma. What were the intentions of his ingenious and unscrupulous friends? The Prince had, he recollected, distinctly told him that diamonds were not in the present instance the object of their manoeuvres.

About three o'clock that afternoon he invited the Princess and her pretty niece to go out for a run in the car to Taggia, the road to which first runs along by the sea, and afterwards turns inland up a beautiful fertile valley. They accepted, but both Prince and Parson pleaded other engagements, therefore he took the two ladies alone.

The afternoon was bright and warm, with that blue sky and deep blue sea which is so characteristic of the Riviera, and the run to Taggia was delightful. They had coffee at a clean little osteria—coffee that was not altogether good, but quite passable—and then with Winifred up beside him, Garrett started to run home in the sundown.

They had not gone more than a couple of miles when, of a sudden, almost before he could realise it, Garrett was seized by a contraction of the throat so violent that he could not breathe. He felt choking. The sensation was most unusual, for he broke out into a cold perspiration, and his head beginning to reel, he slowed down and put on the brake, for they were travelling at a brisk pace, but beyond that he remembered absolutely nothing. All he knew was that an excruciating pain shot through his heart, and then in an instant all was blank!

Of only one other thing he had a hazy recollection, and it was this.

Just at the moment when he lost consciousness the girl at his side, leant towards him, and took the steering-wheel, saying:

"Let go, you fool!—let go, will you!" her words being followed by a weird peal of laughter.

THE DARKNESS WAS IMPENETRABLE. FOR many hours Garrett had remained oblivious to everything. Yet as he slowly struggled back to consciousness he became aware that his legs were benumbed, and that water was lapping about him. He was lying in a cramped position, so cramped that to move was impossible. He was chilled to the bone. For a full hour he lay half-conscious, and wondering. The pains in his head were awful. He raised his hand, and discovered a nasty wound upon his left temple. Then he at last realised the astounding truth. He was lying upon rocks on the seashore, and it was night! How long he had been there, or how he had come there he had no idea.

That woman's laughter rang in his ears. It was a laugh of triumph, and caused him to suspect strongly that he had been the victim of feminine treachery. But with what motive?

Was it possible that at Taggia, while he had been outside looking around the car, something had been placed in his coffee! He recollected that it tasted rather bitter. But where was the car? Where were the Princess and her pretty niece?

It was a long time before his cramped limbs were sufficiently supple to enable him to walk, and then in the faint grey dawn he managed to crawl along a white unfamiliar high road that ran beside the rocky shore. For nearly two hours he walked in his wet clothes until he came to a tiny town which he discovered, was called Voltri, and was quite a short distance from Genoa.

The fascinating Winifred had evidently driven the car with his unconscious form covered up in the tonneau for some time before the pair had deposited him in the water, their intention being that the sea should itself dispose of his body.

For an hour he remained in the little inn drying his clothes and having his wound attended to, and then when able to travel, he took train back to San Remo, arriving late in the afternoon. He found to his astonishment he had remained unconscious at the edge of the tideless sea for about thirty hours.

His bandaged head was put down by the guests as due to an accident in the car, for he made no explanation. Presently, however, the hotel proprietor came to his room, and asked the whereabouts of the Princess and her niece, as they had not been seen since they left with him. In addition, the maid had suddenly disappeared, while the party owed a little bill of nearly one hundred pounds sterling.

"And Mr. Tremlett?" Garrett asked. "He is still here, of course?"

"No, signore," was the courtly Italian's reply. "He left in a motor-car with Mr. Clayton and his valet late the same night."

Their destination was unknown. The little old hunchback had also left, Garrett was informed.

A WEEK LATER, AS GARRETT entered the cosy sitting-room in Dover Street the Prince sprang from his chair, exclaiming:

"By Jove, Garrett! I'm glad to see you back. We began to fear that you'd met with foul play. What happened to you? Sit down, and tell me. Where's the car?"

The chauffeur was compelled to admit his ignorance of its whereabouts, and then related his exciting and perilous adventure.

"Yes," replied the handsome young adventurer, gaily. "It was a crooked bit of business, but we needn't trouble further about the car, Garrett, for the fact is we've exchanged our 'forty' for that old hunchback's mysterious 'sixty.' It's at Meunier's garage in Paris. But, of course," he laughed, "you didn't know who the hunchback really was. It was Finch Grey."

"Finch Grey!" gasped Garrett, amazed, for he was the most renowned and expert thief in the whole of Europe.

"Yes," he said, "we went to San Remo to meet him. It was like this. The Reverend Thomas was in Milan and got wind of a little *coup* at the Banca d'Italia which Finch Grey had arranged. The plot was one night to attack the strong-room of the bank, a tunnel to which had already been driven from a neighbouring house. The proceeds of this robbery—notes and gold—were to be brought down to San Remo by Finch Grey in his 'sixty,' the idea being to then meet the Princess and her niece, who were really only members of his gang. Our idea was to get friendly with the two ladies, so that when the car full of gold and notes arrived we should have an opportunity of getting hold of it. Our plans, however, were upset in two particulars, by the fact that a few days prior to my arrival the pair had quarrelled with the old hunchback, and secondly, because a friend of the Princess's, staying at the hotel, had recognised you as a 'crook.' By some means the two women suspected that, on Finch Grey's appearance, our intention was either to demand part of the proceeds of the bank robbery or expose them to the police. Therefore they put something in your coffee, the girl drove the car to the spot where you found yourself, and then they escaped to Genoa, and on to Rome. Finch Grey, who did not know who we were, was highly concerned with us regarding the non-return of the ladies. We suggested that we should go out in his 'sixty' with him to search for them, and he, fearing that you had met with an accident, consented. The rest was easy," he laughed.

"How?"

"Well, we let him get half way to Oneglia, when we just slipped a handkerchief with a little perfume upon it, over his nose and mouth, and a few minutes later we laid him quietly down behind a wall. Then I turned the car back to where we had previously stored some pots of white paint and a couple of big brushes, and in an hour had transformed the colour of the car and changed its identification-plates. Imagine our joy when we found the back locker where the tools should have been crammed with bags of gold twenty lire pieces, while under the inside seat we found a number of neat packets of fifty and one-hundred and five-hundred lire notes. Just after midnight we slipped back through San Remo, and two days ago arrived safely in Paris with our valuable freight. Like to see some of it?" he added, and rising he pushed back the bookcase, opened the panel and took out several bundles of Italian notes. I saw also within a number of small canvas bags of gold.

"By this time, Garrett," he added, laughing and pouring me out a drink, "old Finch Grey is gnashing his teeth, for he cannot invoke the aid of the police, and the women who intended to be avenged upon us for our daring are, no doubt, very sorry they ran away with our car, which, after all, was not nearly such a good one as the mysterious 'sixty.' Theirs wasn't a particularly cheery journey, was it?" and lifting his glass he added, "So let's wish them very good luck!"

IV

The Man with the Red Circle

Another story related by Garrett, the chauffeur, is worth telling, for it is not without its humorous side.

It occurred about six weeks after the return of the party from San Remo.

It was dismal and wet in London, one of those damp yellow days with which we, alas I are too well acquainted.

About two o'clock in the afternoon, attired in yellow fishermen's oil-skins instead of his showy grey livery, Garrett sat at the wheel of the new "sixty" six-cylinder car of Finch Grey's outside the Royal Automobile Club, in Piccadilly, bade adieu to the exemplary Bayswater parson, who stood upon the steps, and drew along to the corner of Park Lane, afterwards turning towards the Marble Arch, upon the first stage of a long and mysterious journey.

When it is said that the journey was a mysterious one Garrett was compelled to admit that, ever since he had been in the service of Prince Albert of Hesse-Holstein his journeys had been made for the most part with a motive that, until the moment of their accomplishment, remained to him a mystery. His employer gave him orders, but he never allowed him to know his plans. He was paid to hold his tongue and obey. What mattered if his Highness, who was such a well-known figure in the world of automobilism was not a Highness at all; or whether the Rev. Thomas Clayton held no clerical charge in Bayswater. He, Garrett, was the Prince's chauffeur, paid to close his ears and his eyes to everything around him, and to drive whatever lady who might be in the car hither and thither, just as his employer or his audacious friends required.

For two years his life had been one of constant change, as these secret records show. In scarcely a country in Europe he had not driven, while fully half a dozen times he had driven between Boulogne and the "Place" at Monte Carlo, four times from Calais due east to Berlin, as well as some highly exciting runs over certain frontiers when compelled to evade the officers of the law.

The good-looking Prince Albert, whose real name was hidden in obscurity, but who was best known as Tremlett, Burchell-Laing,

Drummond, Lord Nassington, and half a dozen other aliases, constantly amazed and puzzled the police. Leader of that small circle of bold and ingenious men, he provided the newspapers with sensational gossip from time to time, exploits in which he usually made use of one or other of his high-power cars, and in which there was invariably a lady in the car.

Prince Albert was nothing if not a ladies' man, and in two years had owned quite a dozen cars of different makes with identification plates innumerable, most of them false.

His Highness, who always found snobs to bow and dust his boots, and who took good care to prey upon their snobbishness, was a perfect marvel of cunning. His cool audacity was unequalled. The times which he passed unsuspected and unidentified beneath the very noses of the police were innumerable, while the times in which Garrett had been in imminent peril of arrest were not a few.

The present journey was, however, to say the least, a very mysterious one.

That morning at ten o'clock he had sat, as usual, in the cosy chambers in Dover Street. His Highness had given him a cigar, and treated him as an equal, as he did always when they were alone.

"You must start directly after lunch for the Highlands, Garrett," he had said suddenly, his dark, clearly defined brows slightly knit. He was still in his velvet smoking-jacket, and smoked incessantly his brown "Petroffs."

"I know," he went on, "that the weather is wretched—but it is imperative. We must have the car up there."

Garrett was disappointed, for they were only just back from Hamburg, and he had expected at least to spend a few days with his own people down at Surbiton.

"What?" he asked, "another *coup*?" His Highness smiled meaningly.

"We've got a rather ticklish piece of work before us, Garrett," he said, contemplating the end of his cigar. "There's a girl in it—a very pretty little girl. And you'll have to make a lot of love to her—you understand?" And the gay nonchalant fellow laughed as his eyes raised themselves to the chauffeur's.

"Well," remarked the man, somewhat surprised. "You make a much better lover than I do. Remember the affair of the pretty Miss Northover?"

"Yes, yes!" he exclaimed impatiently. "But in this affair it's different. I have other things to do besides love-making. She'll have to be left to you. I warn you, however, that the dainty Elfrida is a dangerous person—so don't make a fool of yourself, Garrett."

"Dangerous?" he echoed.

"I mean dangerously attractive, that's all. Neither she, nor her people, have the least suspicion. The Blair-Stewarts, of Glenblair Castle, up in Perthshire, claim to be one of the oldest families in the Highlands. The old fellow made his money at shipbuilding, over at Dumbarton, and bought back what may be, or may not be, the family estate. At any rate, he's got pots of the needful, and I, having met him with his wife and daughter this autumn at the 'Excelsior,' at Aix, am invited up there to-morrow to spend a week or so. I've consented if I may go *incognito* as Mr. Drummond."

"And I go to take the car up?"

"No. You go as Herbert Hebberdine, son of old Sir Samuel Hebberdine, the banker of Old Broad Street, a young man sowing his wild oats and a motor enthusiast, as every young man is more or less nowadays," he laughed. "You go as owner of the car. To Mrs. Blair-Stewart I explained long ago that you were one of my greatest friends, so she has asked me to invite you, and I've already accepted in your name."

"But I'm a stranger!" protested Garrett.

"Never mind, my dear fellow," laughed the audacious Prince. "Clayton will be up there too. It's he who knows the people, and is working the game pretty cleverly."

"Is it jewels?" asked the chauffeur in a low voice.

"No, it just isn't, this time! You're mistaken, as you always are when you're too inquisitive. Garrett, it's something better," he answered. "All you've got to do is to pretend to be smitten by the girl. She's a terrible little flirt, so you won't have very much difficulty. You make the running, and leave all the rest to me." His master, having shown him on the map where Glenblair was situated, half way between Stirling and Perth, added:

"I'll go up to-night, and you'll be there in three days' time. Meanwhile I'll sing your praises, and you'll receive a warm welcome from everybody when you arrive. Take your decent kit with you, and act the gentleman. There's a level thousand each for us if we bring it off properly. But," he added, with further injunctions not to fall genuinely in love with the pretty Elfrida, "the whole thing rests upon you. The girl must be devoted to you—otherwise we can't work the trick."

"What *is* the trick?" asked Garrett, his curiosity aroused.

"Never mind what it is, Garrett," he said, rising to dismiss him.

"Have your lunch and get away. You've five hundred miles of bad roads and new metal before you, so the sooner you're off the better. Call and see Clayton at his rooms. He's got a bag, or something, to put in the car, I think. When we meet in Scotland, recollect that I'm Prince Albert *incognito*. We were at Bonn together, and have been friends for many years. Good luck to you!"

And with that he left the Prince's cosy rooms, and soon found himself out in Dover Street again, much puzzled.

The real object of his visit and his flirtation at a Scotch castle filled his mind as, in the dull light of that fading afternoon, he swept along the muddy Great North Road his exhaust opened and roaring as he went ascending through Whetstone and Barnet in the direction of Hatfield. The "sixty" repainted cream with narrow gilt lines upon it certainly presented a very smart appearance, but in the back he had a couple of false number-plates, together with three big pots of dark-green enamel and a brush, so that if occasion arose, as it had arisen more than once, he could run up a by-road, and in an hour transform its appearance, so that its own maker would scarcely recognise it.

In the grey twilight as he approached Hitchin, swinging round those sharp corners at a speed as high as he dared, it poured with rain again, and he was compelled to lower the wind-screen and receive the full brunt of the storm, so blurred became everything through the sheet of plate-glass. The old "Sun" at Hitchin reached, he got a drink, lit his head-lamps, and crossing the marketplace, pushed forward, a long and monotonous run up Alconbury Hill and through Wansford to Stamford where, at the Stamford Hotel—which recalled memories of the Northovers—he ate a cold dinner and rested for an hour over a cigar.

Many were the exciting adventures he had had while acting as chauffeur to his Highness, but his instructions that morning had somehow filled him with unusual misgiving. He was on his way to pretend to make love to a girl whom he had never seen, the daughter of a millionaire shipbuilder, a man who, as the Prince had informed him, had risen from a journeyman, and like so many others who make money, had at once looked round for a ready-made pedigree, and its accompanying estate. Heraldry and family trees seem to exercise a strange and unaccountable fascination for the parvenu.

As he pushed north, on through that long dark night in the teeth of a bitter northeaster and constant rain, his mind was full of the mysterious *coup* which his Highness and his friend were about to attempt. Jewels and money were usually what they were in search of, but on this occasion it was something else. What it was, his Highness had flatly refused to tell.

Aided by the Rev. Thomas Clayton, one of the cleverest impostors who ever evaded the police, his Highness's successes had been little short of marvellous. His audacity was unparalleled. The Parson, who lived constantly in that smug circle wherein moved the newly-rich, usually marked down the victim, introduced his Highness, or the fascinating Mr. Tremlett, and left the rest to the young cosmopolitan's tact and ingenuity. Their aliases were many, while the memory of both Tremlett and Clayton for faces was extraordinary. A favourite pose of the Prince was that of military *attache* in the service of the German Government, and this self-assumed profession often gained him admission to the most exclusive circles here, and on the Continent.

Garrett's alias of Herbert Hebberdine he had assumed on one or two previous occasions—once at Biarritz, when his Highness successfully secured the splendid pearl necklace of the Duchess of Taormino, and again a few months later at Abbazia, on the beautiful shore of the Adriatic. On both occasions their *coup* had been brought off without a hitch, he recollected. Therefore, why should he, on this occasion, become so foolishly apprehensive?

He could not tell. He tried to analyse his feelings as, hour after hour, he sat at the wheel, tearing along that dark, wet, endless highway due north towards York. But all in vain. Over him seemed to have spread a shadow of impending evil, and try how he would, he could not shake off the uncomfortable feeling that he was rushing into some grave peril from which he was destined not to escape.

To describe in detail that wet, uncomfortable run from Hyde Park Corner to Edinburgh would serve no purpose in this little chronicle of an exciting chapter of an adventurous life. Suffice it to say that, late in the night of the second day after leaving London, he drew up before the North British Hotel, in Prince's Street, glad of shelter from the icy blast. A telegram from his Highness ordered him to arrive at the castle on the following evening; therefore, just as dusk was falling, he found himself before the lodge-gates of the splendid domain of the laird of Glenblair, and a moment later turned into the drive which ascended for more than a mile through an avenue of great bare beeches and oaks, on the one side a dense wood, and on the other a deep, beautiful glen, where, far below, rippled a burn with many picturesque cascades.

Once or twice he touched the button of the electric horn to give warning of his approach, when suddenly the drive took a wide curve and opened out before a splendid old mansion in the Scotch baronial style, situated amid the most romantic and picturesque scenery it had ever been his lot to witness.

At the door, brought out by the horn, stood his Highness, in a smart suit of blue serge, and the Parson, in severe clerical garb and pince-nez, while with them stood two women, one plump, elderly, and grey-haired, in a dark gown, the other a slim figure in cream with wavy chestnut hair, and a face that instantly fascinated the new-comer.

As he alighted from the car and drew off his fur glove the Prince—who was staying *incognito* as Mr. Drummond—introduced him to his hostess, before whom he bowed, while she, in turn, said:

"This is my daughter, Elfrida—Mr. Hebberdine."

Garrett bowed again. Their eyes met, and next instant the young man wished heartily that he had never come there. The Prince had not exaggerated her beauty. She was absolutely perfect. In all the years he had been a wanderer he had never seen such dainty *chic*, such tiny hands and feet, or such a sweet face with its soft pink cheeks and its red lips made for kisses. She could not have been more than eighteen or so, yet about her was none of the *gaucherie* of the school-girl. He noticed that she dropped her eyes quickly, and upon her cheeks arose just the *soupçon* of a blush.

"Had a good run, Herbert?" asked the Prince as he entered the big hall of the castle.

"Not very. The roads were infernally bad in places," replied the other, "and the new metal between York and Newcastle is most annoying."

"Good car, that of yours!" remarked the Parson, as though he had never seen it before, while his Highness declared that a six-cylinder was certainly the best of all.

After a whisky and soda, brought by the grave, antiquated butler, Garrett drove the car round to the garage some little distance from the house, where he found three fine cars belonging to his host.

Then, as he went to his room to change for dinner, he passed his Highness on the stairs.

"The game's quite easy," whispered the latter as he halted for a second. "It remains for you to make the running with Elfrida. Only be careful. Old Blair-Stewart is pretty sly—as you'll see."

At dinner in the long old-fashioned panelled room, hung with the portraits of what were supposed to be the ancestors of the Blair-Stewarts of Glenblair, Garrett first met the rather stout, coarse-featured shipbuilder who had assumed the head of that historic house, and had bought the estate at three times its market value. From the first moment of their meeting Garrett saw that he was a blatant parvenu of the worst type, for he began to talk of "my hothouses," "my motors," and "my yacht" almost in the first five minutes of their conversation.

The party numbered about fifteen at dinner, and he had the good fortune to be placed next the dainty little girl in turquoise towards whom the part allotted to him was to act as lover.

She was, he saw, of very different type to her father. She had been at school in Versailles, and afterwards had studied music in Dresden she told him, and she could, he found, speak three languages quite well. She had apparently put off her school-girl shyness when she put up her hair, and indeed she struck him as being an amusing little friend to any man. Motoring was her chief hobby. She could drive one of her father's cars, a "sixteen-twenty" herself, and often did so. Therefore they were soon upon a topic in which they were mutually enthusiastic.

A yellow-haired, thin-faced young man of elegant appearance, for he had a velvet collar to his dress-coat and amethyst buttons to his vest, was looking daggers at them. From that Garrett concluded that Archie Gould was the lover of the winning Elfrida, and that he did not approve of their mutual merriment. The Parson, who said grace, was a perfect example of decorum, and was making himself delightful to his hostess, while his Highness was joking with a pretty little married woman who, without doubt, was full of admiration of his handsome face.

What would the good people of Glenblair have thought had they been aware of the identity of the trio they were entertaining at their table? As Garrett reflected, he smiled within himself. His fellow guests were mostly wealthy people, and as he looked around the table he saw several pieces of jewellery, necklets, pendants and the like for which the old Jew in the Kerk Straat at Amsterdam would have given them very fair prices.

If jewellery was not the object of their visit, then what was?

Two days passed, and Garrett took Elfrida and the Prince for several runs on the "sixty," much to the girl's delight. He watched closely the actions of his two companions, but could detect nothing suspicious. Blair-Stewart's wife was a quaint old crow with a faint suspicion of a moustache, who fancied herself hugely as wife of the wealthy laird of Glenblair. She was busy visiting the poor of the grey straggling Highland village, and his Highness, flattering her vanity, was assisting her. Next to the Prince, the Parson was the most prominent person in the house-party, and managed to impress on every occasion his own importance upon the company.

With the dainty Elfrida, Garrett got on famously, much to the chagrin and disgust of her yellow-headed young admirer, Gould, who had recently inherited his father's estate up in Inverness-shire, and who it was currently reported, was at that moment engaged in the interesting occupation of "going through" it.

Elfrida, though extremely pretty, with a soft natural beauty all her own, was an essentially out-door girl. It being a hard frost, they had been out together on the "sixty" in the morning, and later she had been teaching him curling on the curling-pond in the park, and initiated him into the mysteries of "elbow in" and "elbow out." Indeed, every afternoon the whole party curled, a big bonfire being lit on the side of the pond, and tea being taken in the open. He had never practised the sport of casting those big round stones along the ice before, but he found it most invigorating and amusing, especially when he had as instructress such a charming and delightful little companion.

Just as the crimson light of sundown was tinting the snow with its blood-red glow one afternoon, she suddenly declared her intentions to return to the house, whereupon he offered to escort her. As soon, however, as they were away from the rest of the party she left the path by which they were approaching the avenue, saying that there was a shorter cut to the castle. It was then that they found themselves wandering over the snow in the centre of a leafless forest, where the deep crimson afterglow gleamed westward among the black trunks of the trees, while the dead silence of winter was upon everything.

Garrett was laughing with her, as was his habit, for their flirtation from the first had been a desperate one. At eighteen, a girl views nothing seriously, except her hobbies. As they walked together she presented a very neat-ankled and dainty appearance in her short blue serge skirt, little fur bolero, blue French *beret*, and thick white gloves. In the brief time he had been her father's guest, he had not failed to notice how his presence always served to heighten the colour of her cheeks, or how frequently she met him as if by accident in all sorts of odd and out-of-the-way corners. He was not sufficiently conceited to imagine that she cared for him any more than she did for young Gould, though he never once saw him with her. He would scowl at them across the table; that was all.

Of a sudden, as they went on through the leafless wood she halted, and looking into his face with her beautiful eyes, exclaimed with a girl's frankness:

"I wonder, Mr. Hebberdine, if I might trust you?—I mean if you would help me?"

"Trust me!" he echoed very surprised, as their acquaintanceship had been of such short duration. "If you repose any confidence in me, Miss Blair-Stewart, I assure you I shall respect its *secrecy*."

Her eyes met his, and he was startled to see in them a look of desperation such as he had not seen in any woman's gaze before. In that moment the mask seemed to have fallen from her, and she stood there before him craving his pity and sympathy—his sympathy above that of all other men!

Was not his position a curious one? The very girl whom he had come to trick and to deceive was asking him to accept her confidences.

"You are very kind indeed to say that," she exclaimed, her face brightening. "I hardly know whether I dare ask you to stand my friend, for we've only known each other two or three days."

"Sufficiently long, Miss Elfrida, to win me as your faithful champion," the young man declared, whereupon her cheeks were again suffused by a slight flush.

"Well, the fact is," she said with charming bluntness, "though I have lots of girl friends, I have no man friend."

"There is Archie Gould," he remarked, "I thought he was your friend!"

"He's merely a silly boy," she laughed. "I said a man friend—like yourself."

"Why are you so anxious to have one?"

She hesitated. Her eyes were fixed upon the spotless snow at their feet, and he saw that she held her breath in hesitation.

"Men friends are sometimes dangerous, you know," he laughed.

"Not if the man is a true gentleman," was her rather disconcerting answer. Then, raising her eyes again, and gazing straight into his face she asked, "Will you really be my friend?"

"As I've already said, I'd only be too delighted. What do you want me to do?"

"I—I want you to help me, and—and to preserve my secret."

"What secret?" he inquired, surprised that a girl of her age should possess a secret.

He saw the sudden change in her countenance. Her lips were trembling, the corners of her mouth hardened, and, without warning, she buried her face in her hands and burst into tears.

"Oh! come, come, Elfrida!" he exclaimed quickly, placing his hand tenderly upon her shoulder. "No, don't give way like this! I am your friend, and will help you in what ever way you desire, if you will tell me all about it. You are in distress. Why? Confide in me now that I have promised to stand your friend."

"And—and you promise," she sobbed. "You promise to be my friend—whatever happens."

"I promise," he said, perhaps foolishly. "Whatever happens you may rely upon my friendship."

Then, next instant, his instructions from his Highness flashed across his mind. He was there for some secret reason to play a treacherous part—that of the faithless lover.

She stood immovable, dabbing her eyes with a little wisp of lace. He was waiting for her to reveal the reason of her unhappiness. But she suddenly walked on mechanically, in her eyes a strange look of terror, nay of despair.

He strode beside her, much puzzled at her demeanour. She wished to tell him something of which she was ashamed. Only the desperation of her position prompted her to make the admission, and seek his advice.

They had gone, perhaps, three hundred yards still in the wood. The crimson light had faded, and the December dusk was quickly darkening, as it does in Scotland, when again she halted and faced him, saying in a faltering tone:

"Mr. Hebberdine, I—I do hope you will not think any the worse of me—I mean, I hope you won't think me fast, when I tell you that I—well, somehow, I don't know how it is—but I feel that Fate has brought you here purposely to be my friend—*and to save me!*"

"To save you!" he echoed. "What do you mean? Be more explicit."

"I know my words must sound very strange to you. But it is the truth! Ah!" she cried, "you cannot know all that I am suffering—or of the deadly peril in which I find myself. It is because of that, I ask the assistance of you—an honest man."

Honest! Save the mark! He foresaw himself falling into some horrible complication, but the romance of the situation, together with the extreme beauty of his newly found little friend held the young man fascinated.

"I cannot be of assistance, Miss Elfrida, until I know the truth."

"If we are to be friends you must call me Elfrida," she said in her girlish way, "but in private only."

"You are right. Other people might suspect, and misconstrue what is a platonic friendship," he said, and he took her hand in order to seal their compact.

For a long time he held it, his gaze fixed upon her pale, agitated countenance. Why was she in peril? Of what?

He asked her to tell him. A slight shudder ran through her, and she shook her head mournfully, no word escaping her lips. She sighed, the sigh of a young girl who had a burden of apprehension upon her sorely troubled mind. He could scarcely believe that this was the bright, happy, laughing girl who, half an hour ago, had been putting her stones along the ice, wielding her besom with all her might, and clapping her dainty little hands with delight when any of her own side knocked an opponent off "the pot lid."

At last, after long persuasion, during which time dusk had almost deepened into darkness in that silent snow-covered wood, she, in a faltering voice, and with many sentences broken by her emotion, which she vainly strived to suppress, told him a most curious and startling story to which he listened with breathless interest.

The first of the series of remarkable incidents had occurred about two years ago, while she was at school in Versailles. She, with a number of other elder girls, had gone to spend the summer at a branch of the college close to Fontainebleau, and they often succeeded, when cycling, in getting away unobserved and enjoying long runs in the forest alone. One summer's evening she was riding alone along a leafy by-way of the great forest when, by some means, her skirt got entangled in the machine and she was thrown and hurt her ankle. A rather well-dressed Frenchman who was coming along assisted her. He appeared to be very kind, gave her a card, with the name "Paul Berton" upon it, was told her name in response, and very quickly a friendship sprang up between them. He was an engineer, and staying at the Lion d'Or, in Fontainebleau, he said, and having wheeled her machine several miles to a spot quite near the college, suggested another meeting. She, with the school-girl's adventurous spirit, consented, and that proved to be the first of many clandestine rendezvous. She was not quite seventeen while he was, she thought, about twenty-six.

She kept her secret from all, even from her most intimate schoolmate, fearing to be betrayed to the head governess, so all the summer these secret meetings went on, she becoming more and more infatuated on every occasion, while he, with apparent carelessness, learned from her the history of her family, who they were, and where they resided.

"One thing about Paul puzzled me from the very first evening we met," she said reflectively as she was describing those halcyon days of forbidden love. "It was that I noticed, high upon his left wrist, about four inches from the base of the hand, a scarlet mark, encircling the whole arm. It looked as though he had worn a bracelet that had chafed him, or perhaps it had been tattooed there. Several times I referred to it, but he always evaded my question, and seemed to grow uneasy because I noticed it. Indeed, after a few meetings I noticed that he wore shirts with the cuffs buttoned over with solitaires, instead of open links. Well—" she went on slowly with a strange, far-away look in her face. "I—I hardly like to tell you further."

"Go on, little friend," he urged, "your secret is in safe keeping with me—whatever it may be. You loved the man, eh?"

"Ah! yes!" she cried. "You are right. I—I loved him—and I did not know. We met again in Paris—many times. All sorts of ruses I resorted to, in order to get out, if only for half an hour. He followed me to London—when I left school—and he came up here."

"Up here!" he gasped. "He loved you, then?"

"Yes. And when I went to Dresden he went there also."

"Why?"

She held her breath. Her eyes looked straight into his, and then were downcast.

"Because—because," she faltered hoarsely, "because he is my husband!"

"Your husband. Great heavens!"

"Yes. I married him six months ago at the registry office in the Blackfriars Road, in London," she said in a strangely blank voice. "I am Madame Berton."

He stood utterly dumbfounded. The sweet, refined face of the child-wife was ashen pale, her white lips were trembling, and tears were welling in her eyes. He could see she wished to confide further in him.

"Well?" he asked. It was the only word he could utter.

"We parted half an hour after our marriage, and I have only seen him six times since. He comes here surreptitiously," she said in a low voice of despair.

"Why?"

"Because evil fortune has pursued him. He—he confessed to me a few weeks ago that he was not so rich as he had been. He will be rich some day, but now he is horribly poor. He being my husband, it is my duty to help him—is it not?"

Garrett's heart rose against this cowardly foreigner, who had inveigled her into a secret marriage, whoever he might be, for, according to French law, he might at once repudiate her. Poor child! She was evidently devoted to him.

"Well," he said, "that depends upon circumstances. In what manner is he seeking your assistance?"

She hesitated. At last she said:

"Well—I give him a little money sometimes. But I never have enough. All the trinkets I dare spare are gone."

"You love him—eh?" asked the young man seriously.

"Yes," was her frank reply. "I am looking forward to the day when he can acknowledge me as his wife. Being an engineer he has a brilliant idea, namely, to perform a great service to my father in furthering his business aims, so that it will be impossible for him to denounce our marriage. Towards this end I am helping him. Ah! Mr. Hebberdine, you don't know what a dear, good fellow Paul is."

The young man sniffed suspiciously.

"He has invented a new submarine boat which will revolutionise the naval warfare of the future. Father, in secret, builds submarine boats, you know. But Paul is anxious to ascertain what difference there is between those now secretly building and his own invention, prior to placing it before dear old dad."

"Well?"

She hesitated.

"I wanted to ask you, Mr. Hebberdine, if you will do me a favour to-night," she said presently. "Paul is staying at the 'Star,' down in the village, in the name of Mr. James. I dare not go there, and he dare not approach me. There have been thieves about in this neighbourhood lately, and dad is having the castle watched at night by detectives."

At this Garrett pricked up his ears. Glenblair was, in those circumstances, no place for his Highness and his clerical companion.

"I wonder," she suggested, "whether you would do me a great favour and go down to the village to-night about ten and—and give him this."

From within her fur bolero she produced an envelope containing what seemed to be a little jewellery box about two inches long by an inch and a half broad. This she handed to him saying, "Give it into the hand of nobody except Paul personally. Tell him that you are my friend—and his."

So devoted was the girl-wife to her husband, and so unhappy did she seem that Garrett, filled with the romance of the affair, at once agreed to carry out his promise. Her remarkable story had amazed him. He alone knew her secret.

As they sat at dinner that night, her eyes met his once or twice, and the look they exchanged was full of meaning. He was the bearer of some secret message to her husband.

At half-past nine when the men had gone to the billiard-room, Garrett slipped upstairs to his room to put on a pair of thick boots, for he had a walk through the snow a good couple of miles to the village.

Scarcely had he closed the door when it opened again, and the Prince, his finger raised in silence, entered, and in a low excited whisper exclaimed:

"It's all up! We must get away on the car as soon as possible. Every moment's delay means increased peril. How have you got on with Elfrida?"

The chauffeur stared at him without uttering a word.

"Elfrida!" he echoed at last. "Well, she's told me a most remarkable story, and made me her confidante." Then, as briefly as possible, he told him everything. How her husband was staying in Glenblair village as Mr. James; and how he had promised to convey the little packet to him.

When he had finished the Prince fell back in his chair utterly dumbfounded. Then, taking the little packet, he turned it over in his hand.

"Great Heavens!" he cried. "You don't know what you've done, Garrett. There's something very funny about all this!" he added quickly. "Wait here, and I'll run along to Clayton," and he left the young man instantly, carrying the packet in his hand.

An hour later Garrett was driving the Prince and the Rev. Thomas Clayton in the car due south, and they were travelling for all they were worth over the hard frozen snow. Of the reason of that sudden flight, Garrett was in complete ignorance. All he knew was that he had orders to creep out to the garage, get the car, and await his companions who, in a few moments, came up out of the shadows. Their big overcoats were in the car, therefore their evening clothes did not trouble them. Then, with as little noise as possible, they ran down a back drive which his Highness, having reconnoitred, knew joined the main Perth road. An idling constable saw them, and wished them good evening. They were guests from the Castle, therefore he allowed them to pass unmolested.

The constable would scarcely have done this, however, had he known what they were carrying away with them.

They took the road by Dunblane and Stirling, and then straight south into Glasgow, where at two o'clock in the morning, Garrett's two companions alighted in a deserted snow-covered street in the suburbs of the city, and bidding him farewell, gave him orders to get back to London with all haste.

The run was a most dismal one. All through the snowstorm next day he kept on, making but poor progress.

Next night, Garrett spent alone in Carlisle, and on the following morning started direct for London, being compelled, owing to the abominable state of the roads, to take two days over the run.

A week of suspense went by, when one evening he received a note from his Highness, in consequence of which he went to Dover Street, where he found him smoking one of his "Petroffs," as was his wont.

"Well, Garrett?" he laughed. "Sit down, and have a drink. I've got eight hundred pounds for you here—your share of the boodle?"

"But I don't understand," he exclaimed. "What boodle?"

"Of course you don't understand!" he laughed. "Just carry your mind back. You told me the story of little Elfrida's unfortunate secret marriage, and that her husband had a red ring tattooed around his left wrist. That conveyed nothing to you; but it told me much. That afternoon I was walking with the ladies up Glenblair village when, to my surprise, I saw standing at a door no less a person than Jacques Fourrier, or 'Le Bravache,' as he's known in Paris, an 'international,' like ourselves."

"Le Bravache!" gasped Garrett, for his reputation was that of the most daring and successful adventurer on the Continent, besides which he knew him as his Highness's arch-enemy owing to a little love affair of a couple of years before.

"Yes. 'Le Bravache'!" the Prince went on. "He recognised me, and I

WILLIAM LE QUEUX

saw that our game was up. Then you told me Elfrida's story, and from the red circle on the man's arm I realised that Paul Berton, the engineer, and 'Le Bravache' were one and the same person! Besides, she had actually given you to take to her husband the very thing we had gone to Glenblair to obtain!"

"What was it?" he asked excitedly.

"Well, the facts are these," answered the audacious, good-looking Prince, blowing a cloud of smoke from his lips. "Old Blair-Stewart has taken, in secret, a contract from the German Government to build a number of submarine boats for naval use. The plans of these wonderful vessels are kept in a strong safe in the old chap's private office in Dumbarton, and both Fourrier and ourselves were after them—the French Intelligence Department having, in confidence, offered a big sum to any one bringing them to the Quay d'Orsay. Now you see the drift of the story of the exemplary Paul to his pretty little wife, and why he induced her to take impressions in wax of her father's safe-key, she believing that he merely wanted sight of the plans in order to ascertain whether they were any better than his own alleged invention. Fortunately for us, she induced you to be her messenger. When we sent you up there with orders to be nice to Elfrida we never anticipated such a *contretemps* as Fourrier's presence, or that the dainty little girl would actually take the impressions for us to use."

"Then you have used it?"

"Of course. On the night after leaving you, having made the false key in Glasgow, we went over to Dumbarton and got the plans quite easily. We crossed by Harwich and Antwerp to Brussels on to Paris, and here we are again. The Intelligence Department of the Admiralty are very satisfied—and so are we. The pretty Elfrida will no doubt remain in ignorance, until her father discovers his loss, but I'm half inclined to write anonymously to her and tell the poor girl the truth regarding her mysterious husband. I think I really shall, for my letter would cast a good deal of suspicion upon the Man with the Red Circle."

V

The Wicked Mr. Wilkinson

How my cosmopolitan friend, the Prince, was tricked by a woman, and how he was, entirely against his inclination, forced to run the gauntlet of the police at Bow Street at imminent risk of identification as Tremlett, form an interesting narrative which is perhaps best told in his own words, as he recounted it to me the other day in the noisy Continental city where he is at this moment in hiding.

An untoward incident, he said one afternoon as we sat together in the "sixty" on our way out into the country for a run, occurred to me while travelling from Sofia, the Bulgarian capital, to Bucharest, by way of Rustchuk. If you have ever been over that wonderfully-engineered line, which runs up the Isker defile and over the high Balkans to the Danube, you will recollect, Diprose, how grand is the scenery, and how full of interest is the journey across the battlefields of Plevna and the fertile, picturesque lands of Northern Bulgaria.

It is a corner of Europe practically unknown.

At Gornia, a small wayside station approaching the Danube, the train halts to take up water, and it was there that the mishap occurred to me. I had descended to stretch my legs, and had walked up and down the platform for ten minutes or so. Then, the signal being given to start again, I entered my compartment, only to discover that my suit-case, despatch-box, coat, and other impedimenta were missing!

The train was already moving out of the station, but, in an instant, my mind was made up, and, opening the door, I dropped out. My Bulgarian is not very fluent, as may be supposed, but I managed to make the dull station-master understand my loss.

He shrugged his shoulders, shook his head, and exhibited his palms in perfect ignorance. This rendered me furious.

Within my official-looking despatch-box were a number of valuable little objects, which I wished to keep from prying eyes my passport and a quantity of papers of highest importance. No doubt some clever railway thief had made off with the whole!

For a full ten minutes I was beside myself in frantic anger; but judge my amazement when presently I found the whole of my things piled up outside the station in the village street! They had been placed there by a half-drunken porter, who believed that I intended to descend.

Fortunately no one understood German or English, for the language I used was rather hem-stitched. My annoyance was increased on learning that there was not another train to Rustchuk—where I had to cross the Danube—for twenty-four hours, and, further, that the nearest hotel was at Tirnovo, eighteen miles distant by a branch line.

I was therefore compelled to accept the inevitable, and in the dirty, evil-smelling inn at Tirnovo—about on a par with a Russian post-house—I met, on the following day, Madame Demidoff, the queer-looking old lady with the yellow teeth, who, strangely enough, came from London.

She had with her a rather attractive young girl of about twenty, Mademoiselle Elise, her niece, and she told me that they were travelling in the Balkans for pleasure, in order to ascertain what that unbroken ground was like.

The first hour I was in Tirnovo and its rat-eaten "hotel" I longed to be away from the place; but next morning, when I explored its quaint terrace-like streets, built high upon a sleep cliff where the river below takes a sweep almost at right angles, and where dense woods rise on the opposite bank, I found it to be a town full of interest, its old white mosques and other traces of Turkish occupation still remaining.

To the stranger, Tirnovo is but a name on the map of the Balkans, but for beauty of situation and quaint interest it is surely one of the strangest towns in Europe.

The discomforts of our hotel caused me to first address the ugly old lady in black, and after luncheon she and her niece Elise strolled out upon the high bridge with me, and through the Turkish town, where the little girls, in their baggy trousers, were playing in the streets, and where grave-faced men in fezzes squatted and smoked.

Madame and her niece were a decidedly quaint pair. The first-named knew her London well, for when she spoke English it was with a distinctly Cockney accent. She said "Yers" for "Yes," and "'Emmersmith" for "Hammersmith." Mademoiselle was, however, of a type, purely Parisienne—thin, dark-haired, narrow-featured, with bright, luminous, brown eyes, a mouth slightly large, and a sense of humour that attracted me.

Both of them had travelled very extensively, and their knowledge of the Continent was practically as wide as my own. Both were, of course, much impressed by my princely position. It is marvellous what a title does, and how snobbish is the world in every quarter of the globe.

So interesting did I find the pair that I spent another day in Tirnovo, where, in the summer sunset, we were idling after dinner on the balcony overhanging the steep cliff above the river. Our *salle-a-manger* was half filled by rough, chattering peasants in their white linen clothes embroidered in red, and round pork-pie hats of fur, while our fare that night had been of the very plainest—and not over fresh at that.

But it was a distinctly curious incident to find, in that remotest corner of the Balkans, a lady whose residence was in the West End of London, and who, though a foreigner by birth, had evidently been educated "within the sound of Bow Bells."

"I love Bulgaria," the old lady had said to me as we had walked together down by the river bank that afternoon. "I bring Elise here every summer. Last June we were at Kazanlik, among the rose-fields, where they make the otto of rose. It was delightful."

I replied that I, also, knew Servia, Bulgaria, and Roumania fairly well.

"Then your Highness is travelling for pleasure?" she inquired.

I smiled vaguely, for I did not satisfy her. She struck me as being a particularly inquisitive old busybody.

When next morning Mademoiselle Elise informed me that her aunt was suffering from a headache, I invited her to go for a stroll with me out of the town, to which she at once acceded.

Her smart conversation and natural neat waisted *chic* attracted me. She used "Ideale," the very expensive Parisian perfume that to the cosmopolitan is somehow the hall-mark of up-to-date smartness. Her gown was well-cut, her gloves fresh and clean, and her hat a small toque of the very latest *mode*.

Idling beside her in the bright sunshine, with the broad river hundreds of feet below, and the high blue Balkans on every side about us, I spent a most delightful morning.

"We move down to Varna to-morrow, and then home by way of Constantinople," she replied in French in answer to my question. "Aunt Melanie has invited your Highness to our house in Toddington Terrace, she tells me. I do hope you will come. But send us a line first. In a month we shall be back again to the dreariness of the Terrace."

"Dreariness? Then you are not fond of London?"

"No." And her face fell, as though the metropolis contained for her

WILLIAM LE QUEUX

some sad memory she would fain forget. Her life with that yellow-toothed, wizen-faced old aunt could not be fraught with very much pleasure, I reflected. "I much prefer travelling. Fortunately we are often abroad, for on all my aunt's journeys I act as her companion."

"You are, however, French—eh?"

"Yes—from Paris. But I know the Balkans well. We lived in Belgrade for a year—before the Servian *coup d'etat*. I am very fond of the Servians."

"And I also," I declared, for I had been many times in Servia, and had many friends there.

They were a curious pair, and about them both was an indescribable air of mystery which I could not determine, but which caused me to decide to visit them at their London home, the address of which I had already noted.

At five o'clock that evening I took farewell of both Madams and her dainty little niece, and by midnight was in the Roumanian capital. My business—which by the way concerned the obtaining of a little matter of 20,000 francs from an unsuspecting French wine merchant—occupied me about a week and afterwards I went north to Klausenburg, in Hungary, and afterwards to Budapest, Graz, and other places.

Contrary to my expectations, my affairs occupied me much longer than I expected, and four months later I found myself still abroad, at the fine Hotel Stefanie, among the beautiful woods of evergreen laurel at Abbazia, on the Gulf of Quarnero. My friend, the Rev. Thomas Clayton from Bayswater, was staying there, and as, on the evening of my arrival, we were seated together at dinner I saw, to my great surprise, Madame Demidoff enter with the pretty Elise, accompanied by a tall, fair-haired gentlemanly young man, rather foppishly dressed.

"Hulloa?" I exclaimed to my friend, "there's somebody I know! That old woman is Madame Demidoff."

"No, my dear Prince," was my friend's reply. "You are, I think, mistaken. That is the old Countess Gemsenberg, and the girl is her daughter Elise. She's engaged to that fellow—an awful ass—young Hausner, the son of the big banker in Vienna, who died last year, leaving him thirty million kroners."

"Do you really know this?" I asked, looking the Parson straight in the face.

"Know it? Why, everybody in this Hotel knows of their engagement. I've been here five weeks, and they were here before I arrived. They're staying the season, and have the best suite of rooms in the place. The old Countess is, no doubt, very wealthy, and lives in Munich."

Neither of the women had noticed me, and I remained silent.

What my friend had told me was certainly extraordinary. Why, I wondered had Madame represented herself as a woman of the middle-class, resident in a dull West End terrace? Why had Elise not admitted to me the truth? She had seemed so charmingly frank.

With an intention to remain unseen and observant I purposely avoided the pair that evening.

Next morning I saw Elise and young Hausner strolling together on the Strandweg, that broad path which forms the principal promenade, and runs along the rocky coast from Volosca to Icici. She was smartly dressed in cream serge, girdled narrow but distinctive, and wore a large black hat which suited her admirably, while he was in an easy suit of dark blue, a panama, and white shoes. They were talking very earnestly as they walked slowly on in the bright autumn sunshine with the blue Adriatic before them. He seemed to be telling her something very seriously, and she was listening without uttering a word—or, at least, she scarcely spoke while they were within my sight.

On returning to the hotel I stumbled upon Madame Demidoff, who, seated in the hall, was chatting with a tall, bald-headed, middle-aged man in dark brown tweed, who had every appearance of an Englishman. She had just given him a letter to read, and he was laughing heartily over it. Fortunately, however, she sat with her back to the door and, therefore, did not observe me. So I was enabled to make my exit without detection.

Half an hour later I pointed out the Englishman to the Parson, asking who he was.

"I don't know," was his reply. "I've never seen him before; a fresh arrival, I suppose."

That day I lunched and dined in my private sitting-room, in order to avoid the pair, and continue my observations. That night I caught sight of Elise, whose exquisite gown of pale pink chiffon was creating a sensation among the well-dressed women, for the news of her engagement to the young millionaire banker made her the most-talked-of and admired girl in the great crowded hotel.

At eleven that night, when I believed that the ladies had gone to bed, I ventured downstairs to the *fumoir*. As I went along the corridor, I noticed Madame's English friend, with his overcoat over his evening clothes, leaving the hotel for a stroll, while almost at the same moment

Madame herself emerged from one of the rooms, and, without doubt, recognised me, I saw her start quickly, hesitate for a second, and then turn away in pretence that she had not noticed me.

Her attitude was distinctly curious, and therefore I made no attempt to claim acquaintance.

The mystery of the situation was, however, considerably increased when, next morning, I was surprised to learn that the Countess Gemsenberg had received bad news from Munich, that her husband had been injured in a lift accident, and that she and her daughter had left Mattuglie—the station for Abbazia, three miles distant—by the 8:48 train, young Hausner leaving by the same train.

From the servants I discovered that Madame and her daughter had spent half the night packing, and had not announced their departure until six that morning. No telegram had been received by either of the trio, which seemed to me a curiously interesting point.

Was it possible that Madame had fled upon recognising me? If so, for what reason?

The mystery surrounding the pair attracted me, and during the further fortnight I remained at the Stefanie, I made inquiries concerning them. It appeared that a few days after their arrival the Countess herself had told two German ladies of her daughter's engagement to young Hausner, and that the latter would arrive in a few days. This news at once spread over the big hotel, and when the young man arrived he at once became the most popular person in Abbazia.

The Countess's enemies, however, declared that one night in the hotel-garden she and Hausner had a violent quarrel, but its nature was unknown, because they spoke in English. Mademoiselle was also present, and instead of supporting her lover, took her mother's side and openly abused him.

And yet next morning the pair were walking arm-in-arm beside the sea, as though no difference of opinion had occurred.

As for the Englishman in brown, I ascertained that he did not live there, but at the Quarnero, down by the sea. Those who heard him talk declared that the Countess addressed him as Mr. Wilkinson, and that he was undoubtedly English.

Many facts I ascertained were distinctly strange. The more so when, on making inquiry through a man whom the Parson knew living at the Quarnero, I found that this Mr. Wilkinson had left Abbazia at the same hour as his three friends.

I could see no reason why my presence at the Stefanie should create such sudden terror within the mind of the old lady with the yellow teeth. The more I reflected upon the whole affair, the more mysterious were the phases it assumed.

I recollected that the old lady, whoever she might be, lived at Number 10 Toddington Terrace, Regent's Park, and I resolved to call and see her in pretence that I had not recognised her in Abbazia, and was unaware of her presence there.

Autumn gave place to winter, and I was still wandering about the Continent on matters more or less lucrative. To Venice Naples and down to Constantinople I went, returning at last in the dark days of late January to the rain and mud of London; different, indeed, to the sunshine and brightness of the beautiful Bosphorus.

One afternoon, while seated here in Dover Street, lazily looking forth upon the traffic, I suddenly made up my mind to call upon the old lady, and with that purpose took a taxi-cab.

As we pulled up before Number 10, I at once recognised the truth, for the green Venetian blinds were all down.

In answer to my ring, a narrow-faced, consumptive-looking woman, evidently the caretaker, opened the door.

"No, sir. Madame Demidoff and Elise left home again for the Continent a fortnight ago, and they won't be back till the beginning of April." She spoke of Elise familiarly without the prefix "Miss." That was curious.

"Do you know where they are?"

"I send their letters to the Excelsior Hotel, at Palermo."

"Thank you. By the way," I added, "do you happen to know who is the landlord of these houses?"

"Mr. Epgrave, sir. He lives just there—that new-painted house at the corner;" and she pointed to the residence in question.

And with that information I re-entered the cab and drove back to the club.

So Madame was enjoying the war in Sicilian sunshine! Lucky old woman. I had only been back in London a week, and was already longing for warmth and brightness again.

That night, seated alone, trying to form some plan for the immediate future, I found myself suggesting a flying visit to Palermo. The Villa Igiea was a favourite hotel of mine, and I could there enjoy the winter warmth, and at the same time keep an eye upon the modest old lady of Toddington Terrace, who appeared to blossom forth into a wealthy countess whenever occasion required.

The idea grew upon me. Indeed, a fortnight later, constant traveller that I am, I ran from Paris to Naples in the "sixty," with Garrett, and shipped the car over to Palermo, where I soon found myself idling in the big white and pale green lounge of the Igiea, wondering how best to get sight of Madame, who I had already ascertained, was at the Excelsior at the other end of the town, still passing as Countess Gemsenberg. The pretty Elise was with her, and my informant—an Italian—told me in confidence that the young Marquis Torquato Torrini, head of the well-known firm of Genoese shipowners who was staying in the hotel, was head over heels in love with her, and that engagement was imminent.

I heard this in silence. What, I wondered had become of the young Austrian millionaire, Hausner?

I, however, kept my own counsel, waited and watched. The Parson also turned up a couple of days later and started gossip and tea-drinking in the hotel. But, of course, we posed as strangers to each other.

The Igiea being the best hotel in Palermo and situated on the sea, the blue Mediterranean lapping the grey rocks at the end of the beautiful garden, it is the mode for people at other hotels to go there to tea, just as they go to the "Reserve," at Beaulieu, or the Star and Garter at Richmond.

I therefore waited from day to day, expecting her to come there. Each day I pottered about in the car, but in vain.

One morning, however, while passing in front of the cathedral, I saw her walking alone, and quickly seized the opportunity and overtook her.

"Ah! Mademoiselle!" I exclaimed in French as I raised my cap in feigned surprise and descended from the car. "Fancy, you! In Palermo! And Madame, your aunt?"

"She is quite well, thank you, Prince," she replied; and then, at my invitation, she got into the car and we ran round the town. I saw that she was very uneasy. The meeting was not altogether a pleasant surprise for her; that was very evident.

"This place is more civilised than Tirnovo," I laughed. "Since then I expect that you, like myself, have been travelling a good deal."

"Yes. We've been about quite a lot—to Vienna, Abbazia, Rome, and now to Palermo."

"And not yet to London?"

"Oh! yes. We were at home exactly eleven days. The weather was, however, so atrocious that Madame—my aunt, I mean—decided to come here. We are at the Excelsior. You are, of course, at the Igiea?"

And so we ran along through the big, rather ugly, town, laughing and chatting affably. Dressed in a neat gown of dove-grey cloth, with hat to match and long white gloves, she looked extremely *chic*, full of that daintiness which was so essentially that of the true Parisienne.

I told her nothing of my visit to Toddington Terrace, but presently I said:

"I'll come to the Excelsior, and call on your aunt—if I may?"

I noticed that she hesitated. She did not seem at all desirous to see me at their hotel. I, of course, knew the reason. The old lady was not Madame Demidoff in Palermo.

"We will call and see you at the Igiea," she said. "We have never been there yet."

"I shall be delighted," I answered her. "Only send me a note, in order that I may be in."

Beyond the town we ran along beside the calm blue sea, with the high purple hills rising from across the bay.

Bright and merry, she seemed quite her old self again—that sweet and charming self that I had first met in that rough, uncouth Bulgarian town. After an hour, we got out and seated ourselves on the rocks to rest.

She was certainly not averse to a mild flirtation. Indeed—had she not already been engaged to Hausner, broken it off, and was now half engaged to the Marquis Torrini? She was nothing if not fickle.

"Yes," she sighed at last, "I suppose we shall have to go back to humdrum London, before long. It is so much more pleasant here than in Toddington Terrace," she added in her pretty broken English.

"Ah! Mademoiselle," I laughed. "One day you will marry and live in Paris, or Vienna, or Budapest."

"Marry!" she echoed. "Ugh! No!" and she gave her little shoulders a shrug. "I much prefer, Prince, to remain my own mistress. I have been too much indulged—what you in English call spoil-et."

"All girls say that!" I laughed. "Just as the very man who unceasingly declares his intention to remain a bachelor is the first to become enmeshed in the feminine web."

"Ah! you are a pessimist, I see," she remarked, looking straight into my eyes.

WILLIAM LE QUEUX

"No, not exactly. I suppose I shall marry some day."

"And you are engaged—eh?"

"No," I laughed, "it hasn't got so far as that yet. A single kiss and a few letters—that's the present stage."

"And the lady is Engleesh?"

"Ah! The rest must, for the present, remain a mystery, mademoiselle," I laughed, wondering what the Marquis would say if he discovered us idling away the morning like that.

And so we chatted and laughed on, the best of friends. I tried to obtain some facts regarding her visit to Abbazia, but she was not communicative. Knowing that she was well aware of my visit to the Stefanie, I mentioned it casually, adding:

"You must have already left before my arrival."

For an instant she raised her eyes to mine with a keen look of inquiry, but, finding me in earnest, lowered her gaze again.

At length I saw from my watch that we must move again, if we intended to be back to luncheon, therefore we rose and re-entering the car drove by the sea-road, back to the town. She seemed delighted with her ride.

"I'll bring my aunt to call on you very soon," she said, as we parted. "I will send you a line to say the day."

"Yes, do, mademoiselle, I shall be greatly charmed. *Au revoir*!" and I lifted my hat as she gave me her tiny, white-gloved hand and then turned away.

Next afternoon, while in the car near the theatre, I saw her driving with a dark-bearded, well-dressed young man, whom I afterwards discovered was the Marquis.

She saw me raise my hat, blushed in confusion, and gave me a slight bow of acknowledgment.

That evening I made a discovery considerably increasing the puzzle.

I met the mysterious Mr. Wilkinson face to face in the hall of the Hotel de France, whither I had gone to pay a call upon some English friends who had just arrived.

Wearing the same brown suit, he passed me by and left the hotel, for he was unacquainted with me, and therefore unaware of my presence. From the hall-porter I learnt that "Mr. James Wilkinson, of London"— as he had registered in the hotel-book—had been there for the past three days.

For four days I awaited Madame's visit, but no note came from Elise. The latter was, no doubt, too occupied with her Italian lover. I could not write to her, as she had not given me the name by which she was known at the Excelsior.

Compelled, therefore, to play a waiting game, I remained with my eyes ever open to catch sight of one or other of the mysterious quartette. But I was disappointed, for on this fifth day I made inquiry, and to my utter dismay discovered that the same tactics had been adopted in Palermo as in Abbazia.

The whole four had suddenly disappeared!

Greatly puzzled, the Parson returned to London. I nevertheless remained in Italy until May, when back again I found myself, one bright afternoon about five o'clock, descending from the car outside the house in Toddington Terrace, my intention being to pay a call upon Madame Demidoff.

My ring was answered by a neat maidservant in smart cap and apron.

Next instant we stared at each other in speechless amazement. It was Elise!

Utterly confused, her face first flushed scarlet, and then blanched.

"You—you want to see Madame," she managed to stammer in her broken English. "She isn't at home!"

Beyond her, in the hall, stood the tall figure of a man, whom I at once recognised as the mysterious Wilkinson.

"But, mademoiselle," I said, smiling, yet wondering, the motive of that masquerade. "I called also to see you."

She drew herself up in an instant, replying with some hauteur:

"I think, m'sieur, you have made some mistake. We have never met before—to my knowledge."

Her reply staggered me.

"When will Madame Demidoff return?" I inquired, amazed at this reception.

"To-morrow—at this hour," was her rather hesitating reply.

"Then I shall be glad if you will give her my card, and say I will call," I said; "that is if you still deny having met me in Tirnovo and in Palermo?"

"I really do not know what you are talking about, m'sieur," she answered, and then, without further parley, closed the door in my face. I stood still, staggered.

Surely my reception at Toddington Terrace was the reverse of cordial.

Next afternoon at the same hour I called at Number 10, but there was no response to my ring, and the blinds were all down again. The place was deserted, for the tenants had evidently fled.

That same night as I sat in my rooms, a short, thick-set man, who gave the name of Payne, was ushered in.

"I think," he said, "your Highness happens to know something of an old lady named Demidoff and her friends who live in Toddington Terrace?"

"Yes," I replied, much surprised.

"Well," he explained, "I'm a police officer, and I watched you go twice to the house, so I thought you knew something about them. Are they your friends?"

"Well, no; not exactly my friends," I replied, very suspicious of my visitor. "I had never been nearer a man from Scotland Yard in all my life! Imagine my position, my dear Diprose!"

"Ah! that's a good job. They seem to have been playing a pretty smart game on the Continent of late."

"How? What was their game?" I asked eagerly.

"One that brought them in thousands a year. From the Italian and Austrian police, who are both over here, it seems that they worked like this: Old Madame Demidoff had a young and pretty French servant named Elise. On the Continent Madame took the title of countess, and Elise posed as her daughter. The latter flirted with wealthy young bachelors, and so cleverly did she play her cards, that in several instances they proposed marriage to her. Then, after the old woman had secretly spread the report of the engagement, there would suddenly appear on the scene Elise's English husband—a well-known ex-convict named Wilkinson. This latter person would at once bluster, make charges against the unsuspecting young lover, threaten exposure, and end by accepting a thousand or two to preserve secrecy, none of the young elegants, of course, caring that it should be known how completely they had been 'had.' There are over a dozen different charges against them, the most recent being a coup in Palermo a few months ago, by which they blackmailed the young Marquis Torrini to the tune of nine thousand pounds."

"I was in Palermo at the time, but I never knew that was their game."

"Were you?" he cried in triumph. "Then you'll identify them, won't you? I arrested Madame Demidoff and Wilkinson at Parkeston Quay last night, as they were getting away to the Hook. The girl tried to get to Paris, but was followed and apprehended on landing at Calais early this morning. The Italian Government are asking for the extradition of the interesting trio, and the papers are already on their way over."

I regretted having blurted forth the fact that I had known them in Palermo, for in the interests of justice—though terribly afraid of being recognised myself—I was compelled to identify Madame and Wilkinson at Bow Street next day.

She swore a terrible vengeance upon me, but at present I have no fear of her reprisals, for the Assize Court at Palermo a month ago condemned her to ten years' imprisonment, while Wilkinson—whose past record was brought up—has been sent to Gorgona for fifteen years, and the dainty Elise, his wife, is serving seven years at Syracuse.

"But," the Prince added: "By Jove! it was a narrow squeak for me. Old Never-let-go Hartley, of Scotland Yard, was in the Extradition Court. And I know he was racking his brains to remember where he had met me before."

VI

The Vengeance of the Vipers

Certain incidents in my friend's career are a closed book to all but Clayton, the exemplary Bayswater parson, the devoted valet Charles, and his smart chauffeur Garrett.

Gay, well-dressed, debonair as he always is, a veritable master of the art of skilful deception and ingenious subterfuge, he has found it more than once to his advantage to act as spy. His knowledge of the east of Europe is perhaps unique. No man possessed a wider circle of friends than Prince Albert of Hesse-Holstein, who to-day can pose perfectly as the young German Highness, and to-morrow as the wandering Englishman, and a bit of a fool to boot.

This wide acquaintance with men and matters in the Balkans first brought him in touch with the Intelligence Department of the Foreign Office, and his services as secret agent of the British Government were promptly secured. In this connection he was always known as Mr. Reginald Martin. Downing Street is rather near New Scotland Yard, where the names of Prince Albert of Hesse-Holstein and of Tremlett are a little too well-known. Therefore, to the chief of the Secret Service, and afterwards to the British Ministers and consuls resident in the Balkan countries, Servia, Bulgaria, Montenegro, and Roumania, he was for a time known as Reggie Martin.

Only on rare occasions, however, were his services requisitioned. The game of spying did not pay him nearly so well as the game of jewel-lifting. Yet he had taken to it out of mere love of adventure, and surely some of his experiences in the Orient were sufficiently perilous and exciting. More than once he had been in possession of State secrets which, if divulged, would have set two or more of the Powers flying at one another's throats, and more than once he had carried his life in his hand.

One series of incidents through which he lived last year were, in themselves, as romantic as anything seen written in fiction. They were hard solid facts—an exciting chapter from the life of a man who was a perfect and polished adventurer, a little too impressionable perhaps, where the fair sex were concerned, but keen-witted, audacious, and utterly fearless. He seldom, if ever, speaks of the affair himself, for he is not anxious that people should know of his connection with the Secret Service.

As an old college chum, and as one whom he knows is not likely to "give him away" to the police, he one day, after great persuasion, related it in confidence to me as together we spent a wearisome day in the *rapide* between Paris and Marseilles.

"Well, my dear Diprose, it happened like this," he said, as he selected one of his "Petroffs" and lit it with great care. "I was sent to the Balkans on a very difficult mission. At Downing Street they did not conceal that fact from me. But I promised to do my best. Garrett was with the 'sixty' in Vienna, so I wired sending it on to Sofia, in Bulgaria, and then left Charing Cross for the Balkans myself.

"I first went *via* Trieste down the Adriatic to Cattaro and up to quaint little Cettinje, the town of one long street, where I had audience of Prince Nicholas of Montenegro, whom I had met twice before—in my character of Reggie Martin, of course—and thence I went north to Servia, where I was received several times in private audience by King Peter. One day I arrived in Bulgaria to have confidential interviews with the Prime Minister Dimitri Petkoff, and the newly appointed Minister of Foreign Affairs. My orders from Downing Street, I may as well at once admit, were to ascertain whether Bulgaria intended to declare war against Turkey over Macedonia. The British Government was extremely anxious to ascertain Bulgaria's intentions, as well as the views of the other Balkan Powers, in order that the British policy towards the Porte might combat that of the expansion intrigues of Germany.

"Our public at home have a perfectly erroneous idea of Bulgaria, believing it to be a semi-savage land. If, however, they went to Sofia they would find a fine modern city entirely up to date—a city that must in a few years become the Paris of the Balkans.

"I had wandered along the wide tree-lined boulevards, idled outside the big white mosque, and strolled through the market alive with peasants in their sheepskins, and the girls with sequins and fresh flowers twined in their plaited hair, until it was time for me to keep my appointment with my friend the patriot Petkoff, Prime Minister.

"Half an hour later I was conducted through the long corridor of the fine Government offices opposite the Sobranje, or Parliament House, and ushered into the presence of the real ruler of Bulgaria.

"'Ah! *mon cher* Martin,' he cried in French. 'Welcome back to Sofia!

They were talking of you in the Club last night. De Corvin was saying you were delayed in Belgrade. He met you there—at our Legation, so he told us. And you have your motor-car here—eh? Good. I'll go for a run with you,' and his Excellency put out his left hand in greeting. His right sleeve hung limp and empty, for he lost his arm in the Turco-Russian Campaign, at the historic battle of the Shipka.

"Dark-eyed, dark-haired, with a pleasant face and a small pointed imperial on his chin, he was a wonderful orator and a magnificent statesman who had the full confidence of his sovereign. A dozen times had political plots, inspired by Russia, been formed to assassinate him. Indeed, he had actually been driving beside the great Stambouloff when the latter had been killed in the street. But he had always escaped. Under his direction, Bulgaria had risen to be the strong power of the Balkans, and as my personal friend I hoped that he would tell me, in strictest confidence, what was his future policy towards the Turk.

"With that object I took the seat he offered me, and lighting cigarettes, we began to chat.

"Through the open window came up the strains of martial music, as an infantry regiment in their grey uniforms on the Russian model were marching past, and as I glanced around the quiet, comfortable, red-carpeted room, I saw that the only picture was a fine full-length portrait of the Prince.

"For fully an hour we gossiped. Perfectly frankly I at last told his Excellency the object of my mission.

"He shrugged his shoulders somewhat dubiously, and smiled, declaring that each of the Powers was endeavouring to ascertain the very same thing. I pressed my point, assuring him of Britain's good-will, and explaining certain facts which, after a while, decided him.

"'But you see, *mon cher ami*,' he said, 'supposing the truth got out to Constantinople! All my efforts of the past fifteen years would be negatived. And further—it would mean dire disaster for Bulgaria!'

"'I have been entrusted with many State secrets before, your Excellency,' I replied. 'It would, for instance, not be the first time you spoke with me in confidence.'

"He admitted it, and assuring me of his good-will towards England, he declared that before he could speak, he must consult his royal master.

"Therefore, the French Minister awaiting an audience, I rose and left, having arranged to dine with him at the Union Club that evening.

"For nearly a week I idled in Sofia visiting many diplomatists and their wives, motoring about the neighbourhood, and driving out every night at one Legation or the other, no one, of course, being aware of my secret mission in the Bulgarian capital. Garrett kept eyes and ears open, of course. Useful man Garrett—very useful indeed.

"One night with the Italian minister and his wife, I went to the official ball given by the Minister-President, and among others I had as partner a rather tall, fair-haired girl with clear blue eyes and a pretty childlike face. About twenty-two, she was dressed exquisitely in white chiffon, the corsage of which was trimmed with tiny pink roses, and on her white-gloved wrist gleamed a splendid diamond bracelet. Olga Steinkoff was her name, and as we waltzed together amid the smartly dressed women and uniformed and decorated men I thought her one of the most charming of cosmopolitan girls I had ever encountered south of the Danube.

"Her chaperone was an old and rather ugly woman in dark purple silk, a stiff and starchy person who talked nearly the whole evening to one of the *attaches* of the Turkish Legation, a sallow, middle-aged, bearded man in black frock-coat and red fez.

"The girl in white chiffon was perfect in figure, in daintiness and *chic*, and a splendid dancer. We sat out two dances, and waltzed twice together, I afterwards taking her down to supper. She spoke French excellently, a little English, and a little Bulgarian, while Russian was her own language. Her father lived in Moscow, she told me, and she had spent four years in Constantinople with her aunt—the ugly old woman in purple.

"The sallow-faced, beady-eyed Turk who did not dance, and who took no champagne, was evidently her particular friend. I inquired of the Italian minister and found that the thin-faced bearded *attache* was named Mehmed Zekki, and that he had been in Sofia only a couple of months.

"Towards me he was quite affable, even effusive. He mentioned that he had noticed me in the Club, dining with the Prime Minister, and he referred to a number of people in Belgrade who were my friends. He was *attache* there, he told me, for two years—after the *coup d'etat*.

"Twice during next day I encountered the charming Olga, driving with her aunt, in a smart victoria, and during the next week met them at several diplomatic functions.

"One afternoon, Olga and her chaperone accepted my invitation for a run on the 'sixty,' and I took them for a little tour of about thirty miles around the foot of the high Balkans, returning along the winding banks of the Isker. They were delighted, for the afternoon was perfect. I drove, and she sat up beside me, her hand on the horn.

"One night, ten days later, we were sitting out together in the bright moonlight in the garden of the Austrian Legation, and I found her not averse to a mild flirtation. I knew that the frock-coated Turk was jealous, and had become amused by it. On four or five occasions she had been out for runs with me—twice quite alone.

"I mentioned the Turk, but she only laughed, and shrugging her shoulders, answered:

"'All Turks are as ridiculous as they are bigoted. Mehmed is no exception.'

"I was leaving Bulgaria next morning, and told her so.

"'Perhaps, mademoiselle, we shall meet again some day, who knows?' I added, 'You have many friends in the diplomatic circle, so have I.'

"'But you are not really going to-morrow!' she exclaimed with undisguised dismay, opening her blue eyes widely, 'surely you will stay for the ball at the palace on Wednesday.'

"'I regret that is impossible,' I replied, laughing. 'I only wish I could remain and ask you to be my partner, but I have urgent business in Bucharest.'

"'Oh! you go to Roumania!' she cried in surprise. 'But,'—she added wistfully, 'I—I really wish you could remain longer.'

"During our brief friendship I had, I admit, grown to admire her immensely, and were it not for the fact that a very urgent appointment called me to Roumania, I would have gladly remained. She had taken possession of my senses.

"But I took her soft hand, and wished her adieu. Then we returned into the ballroom, where I found several of my friends, and wished them farewell, for my train left at nine next morning.

"In a corner of the room stood the veteran Prime Minister, with a star in brilliants upon his dress-coat, the empty sleeve of which hung limply at his side.

"'*Au revoir, mon cher ami*,' he said grasping my hand warmly. 'Recollect what I told you this morning—and return soon to Bulgaria again. *Bon voyage*!'

"Then I passed the police-guard at the door, and drove back to the Hotel de Bulgarie.

"That night I slept but little. Before me constantly arose the childlike beautiful face of Olga Steinkoff that had so strangely bewitched me.

"I knew that I was a fool to allow myself to be attracted by a pair of big eyes, confirmed bachelor and constant traveller that I am. Yet the whole night through I seemed to see before my vision the beautiful face, pale and tearful with grief and sorry. Was it at my departure?

"Next day I set out in the car across the Shipka, and three nights later took up my quarters at that most expensive hotel, the 'Boulevard,' at Bucharest, the Paris of the Near East. Next day I paid several visits to diplomats I knew. Bucharest is always full of life and movement— smart uniforms and pretty women—perhaps the gayest city in all the Continent of Europe.

"On the third evening of my arrival I returned to the hotel to dress for dinner, when, on entering my sitting-room, a neat female figure in a dark travelling-dress rose from an armchair, and stood before me gazing at me in silence.

"It was Olga!

"'Why, mademoiselle!' I cried, noticing that she was without her hat, 'fancy you—in Bucharest! When did you arrive?'

"'An hour ago,' she answered, breathlessly. 'I—I want your assistance, M'sieur Martin. I am in danger—grave danger!'

"'Danger! Of what?'

"'I hardly know—except that the police may follow me and demand my arrest. This place—like Sofia—swarms with spies.'

"'I know,' I said, much interested, but surprised that she should have thus followed me. 'But why do you fear?'

"'I surely need not explain to you facts—facts that are painful!' she said, looking straight at me half-reproachfully with those wonderful blue eyes that held me so fascinated. 'I merely tell you that I am in danger, and ask you to render me assistance.'

"'How? In what manner can I assist you?'

"'In one way alone,' was her quick, breathless answer. 'Ah! if you would only do it—if you would only save my life!' And with her white ungloved hands clenched in desperation, she stood motionless as a statue.

"'Save your life!' I echoed. 'I—I really don't understand you, mademoiselle.'

"'Before they arrest me I will commit suicide. I have the means here!' and she touched the bodice of her dress. 'Ah, m'sieur, you do not know in what a position I find myself. I prefer death to save my honour, and I appeal to you, an English gentleman to help me!'

"Tears were rolling down her pale cheeks as she snatched up my hand convulsively, imploring me to assist her. I looked into her countenance and saw that it was the same that I had seen in those dark night hours in Sofia.

"'But, mademoiselle, how can I help you?' I inquired. 'What can I do?'

"'Ah! I—I hardly like to ask you,' she said, her cheeks flushing slightly. 'You know so very little of me.'

"'I know sufficient to be permitted to call myself your friend,' I said earnestly, still holding her tiny hand.

"'Then I will be frank,' she exclaimed, raising her clear eyes again to mine. 'The only way in which you can save me is to take me at once to England—to—to let me pass as your wife!'

"'As my *wife*!' I gasped, staring at her. 'But—'

"'There are no buts!' she cried, clinging to me imploringly. 'To me it is a matter of life—or death! The Orient Express passes here at three to-morrow morning for Constantza, whence we can get to Constantinople. Thence we can go by steamer on to Naples, and across to Calais by rail. For me it is unsafe to go direct by Budapest and Vienna. Already the police are watching at the frontier.'

"For a moment I was silent. In the course of years of travel I had met with many adventures, but none anything like this! Here was a charming girl in dire distress—a girl who had already enchanted me by her beauty and grace—appealing to my honour to help her out of a difficulty. Nay to save her life!

"She was Russian—no doubt a political suspect.

"'Where is Madame?' I inquired.

"'Gone to Belgrade. We parted this morning, and I came here to you.'

"'And your friend, Mehmed?'

"'Bah! the yellow-faced fool!' she cried impatiently with a quick snap of her white fingers. 'He expects to meet me at the Court ball to-night!'

"'And he will be disappointed!' I added with a smile, at the same time reflecting that upon my passport already *vised* for Constantinople—covered as it was, indeed, with *vises* for all the East—I could easily insert after my own name the words, 'accompanied by his wife Louisa.'

"Besides, though I had several times been in the Sultan's capital, I knew very few people there. So detection would not be probable.

"Olga saw my hesitation, and repeated her entreaty. She was, I saw, desperate. Yet though I pressed her to tell me the truth, she only answered:

"'The police of Warsaw are in search of me because of the events of May last. Some day, when we know each other better, I will tell you my strange story. I escaped from the "Museum of Riga"'!'

"Pale to the lips, her chest rising and falling quickly, her blue eyes full of the terror of arrest and deportment to Poland she stood before me, placing her life in my hands.

"She had escaped from the 'Museum of Riga,' that prison the awful tortures of which had only recently been exposed in the Duma itself. She, frail looking, and beautiful had been a prisoner there.

"It wanted, I reflected, still eight days to the opening of the shooting which I was due to spend with friends in Scotland. Even if I returned by the roundabout route she suggested I should be able to get up north in time.

"And yet my duty was to remain there, for at noon on the morrow, by the Orient Express from Constantza to Ostend, a friend would pass whom I particularly wanted to meet on business for a single moment at the station. If I left with my pretty companion I should pass my friend on the Black Sea a few hours out of port. It meant either keeping the appointment I had made with my friend, or securing the girl's safety. To perform my duty meant to consign her into the hands of the police.

"Acquaintance with political refugees of any sort in the Balkan countries is always extremely risky, for spies abound everywhere, and everybody is a suspect.

"I fear I am not very impressionable where the fair sex are concerned, but the romance and mystery of the situation whetted my appetite for the truth. Her sweet tragic face appealed to me. I had fallen in love with her.

"She interpreted my hesitation as an intention to refuse.

"'Ah! M'sieur Martin. Do, I beg, have pity upon me! Once in your England I shall no longer fear those tortures of Riga. See!' and drawing up her sleeve she showed me two great ugly red scars upon the white flesh scarcely yet healed. 'Once in your England!' she cried clasping her hands and falling at my feet, 'I shall be free—*free!*'

"'But how do you know that the police have followed you?'

"'Mariniski, our military *attache* in Sofia, is my cousin. He warned me that two agents of Secret Police arrived there yesterday morning.

When I got here I received a wire from him to say they are now on their way here to Bucharest. Therefore not a moment must be lost. We can leave at three, and at ten to-morrow morning will have sailed from Constantza. They are due here at eleven-thirty.'

"'To-night?'

"'No, to-morrow.'

"She held my hands in hers, still upon her knees, her gaze fixed imploringly into mine. What could I do, save to render her assistance? Ah! yes, she was delightfully charming, her face perfect in its beauty, her hands soft and caressing, her voice musical and silvery.

"I gave her my reply, and in an instant she sprang to her feet, kissing my hands again and again.

"I sent the car back to Vienna, and early that morning we entered the train of dusty *wagons-lits* which had been three days on its journey from Ostend to the Orient, and next morning in the bright sunshine, found ourselves on the clean deck of the mail steamer for Constantinople.

"There were not more than twenty passengers, and together with my dainty little companion, I spent a happy day in the bright sunshine, as we steamed down the Black Sea, a twelve-hour run. Dinner was at half-past five, and afterwards, in the evening twilight, as we passed the Turkish forts at the beautiful entrance to the Bosphorus, we sat together in a cosy corner on deck, and I held her small, soft hand.

"She had, I admit, completely enchanted me.

"She seemed to have suddenly become greatly interested in me, for she inquired my profession, and the reason I visited the East, to which I gave evasive, if not rather misleading replies, for I led her to believe that I was the representative of a firm of London railway contractors, and was in Sofia taking orders for steel rails.

"It is not always judicious to tell people one's real profession.

"When we reached the quay at Constantinople, and I had handed over my baggage to the dragoman of the Pera Palace Hotel, my pretty companion said in French:

"'I lived here for quite a long time, you know, so I shall go and stay with friends out at Sarmaschik. I will call at your hotel at, say, eleven to-morrow morning. By that time you will have ascertained what is the next steamer to Naples.'

"And so, in the dirty ill-lit custom-house at Galata, with its mud, its be-fezzed officials and slinking dogs, we parted, she entering a cab and driving away.

"Next morning she kept her appointment and was, I saw, exceedingly well-dressed.

"I told her when we met in the big vestibule of the hotel, that there was a steamer leaving for Marseilles at four that afternoon, and suggested that route as preferable to Naples.

"'I think we will delay our departure until to-morrow,' she said. 'My friends have a little family gathering to-night, and ask me to say that they would be delighted to meet you. They are not at all bigoted, and you will find them very hospitable.'

"I bowed and accepted the invitation.

"'You will not find the house alone, as Constantinople is so puzzling,' she said. 'I will send their *kavass* for you at eight o'clock.'

"And a few moments later she drove away in the smart carriage that had brought her.

"That day I idled about the Sultan's capital, looked in at St. Sophia, paused and watched the phantasmagoria of life on the Galata Bridge, and strolled in the Grand Rue at Pera, merely killing time. Case-hardened bachelor that I am, my mind was now filled with that sweet-faced, beautiful woman of my dreams who had been so cruelly tortured in that abominable prison at Riga, and whom I was aiding to the safe refuge of England's shores.

"Once, while turning a corner at the end of the Grand Rue, the busy shopping centre of the Turkish capital, a mysterious incident occurred. Among the many figures in frock-coats and fezes my eye caught one which caused me to start. It struck me curiously as that of my sallow-faced friend, Mehmed Zekki, of Sofia. Yet in a crowd of Turks all dressed alike, one is rather difficult to distinguish from another, so I quickly dismissed the suspicion that we had been followed.

"I had already dined at the hotel and was sitting in the Turkish smoking-room, when there arrived a big Montenegrin *kavass*, in gorgeous scarlet and gold, and wearing an arsenal of weapons in his belt, as is their mode.

"'Monsieur Martin?' he inquired. 'Mademoiselle Olga. She send me for you. I take you to ze house.'

"So I rose, slipped on my overcoat, and followed him out to the brougham, upon the box of which, beside the driver, sat a big black eunuch. The carriage had evidently been to fetch some ladies before calling for me.

"The *kavass* seated himself at my side, and we drove up and down many dark, ill-lit streets, where the scavenger dogs were howling, until we suddenly came out in view of the Bosphorus, that lay fairy-like beneath the full Eastern moon.

"Nicholas, the *kavass*, was from Cettinje, he told me, and when we began to talk, I discovered that his brother Mirko had been my servant on a journey through Albania two years before.

"'What! Gospodin!' cried the big mountaineer, grasping my hand and wringing it warmly. 'Are you really the Gospodin Martin? I was in Cettinje last summer, and my dear old father spoke of you! I have to thank you. It was you who brought the English doctor to him and saved his life. Fancy that we should meet here, and to-night!'

"'Why to-night?'

"The big fellow was silent. His manner had entirely changed.

"Suddenly he said: 'Gospodin, you are going to the house of Mehmed Zekki and—'

"'Zekki!' I gasped. 'Then I was not mistaken when I thought I saw him. He had followed us.'

"'Ah! Gospodin! Have a care of yourself! Take this, in case—in case you may require it,' he said, and pulling from his sash one of his loaded revolvers, he handed it to me.

"'But you said that mademoiselle had sent you for me?' I remarked surprised.

"'I was told to say that, Gospodin. I know nothing of mademoiselle.'

"'Mademoiselle Olga Steinkoff. Have you never heard of her?' I demanded.

"'Never.'

"'Then I will go back to the hotel.'

"'No, Gospodin. Do not show fear. It would be fatal. Enter and defy the man who is evidently your enemy. Touch neither food nor drink there. Then, if you are threatened, utter the words, *Shunam-al-zulah*—recollect them. Show no fear, Gospodin—and you will escape.'

"At that moment the carriage turned into a large garden, which surrounded a fine house—almost a palace—the house wherein my enemy was lying in wait.

"Entering a beautiful winter-garden full of flowers, a servant in long blue coat and fez, conducted me through a large apartment, decorated in white and gold, into a smaller room, Oriental in decoration and design, an apartment hung with beautiful gold embroideries, and where the soft cushions of the divans were of pale-blue silk and gold brocade.

"Two middle-aged Turks were squatting smoking, and as I was shown in, scowled at me curiously, saluted, and in French asked me to be seated.

"'Mademoiselle will be here in a few moments,' added the elder of the pair.

"A few seconds later the servant entered with a tiny cup of coffee, the Turkish welcome, but I left it untouched. Then the door again opened and I was confronted by the sallow-faced, black-bearded man against whom the *kavass* had warned me.

"'Good evening, Monsieur Martin,' he exclaimed with a sinister grin upon his thin face. 'You expected, I believe, to meet Mademoiselle Olga, eh?'

"'Well—I expected to meet you,' I laughed, 'for I saw you in Pera to-day.'

"He looked at me quickly, as his servant at that moment handed him his coffee on a tray.

"'I did not see you,' he said somewhat uneasily, raising his cup to his lips. Then, noticing that I had not touched mine, he asked, 'Don't you take coffee? Will you have a glass of rahki?'

"'I desire nothing,' I said, looking him straight in the face.

"'But surely you will take something? We often drank together in the Club at Sofia, remember!'

"'I do not drink with my enemies.'

"The trio started, glaring at me.

"'You are distinctly insulting,' exclaimed Mehmed, his yellow face growing flushed with anger. 'Recall those words, or by the Prophet, you do not pass from this house alive!'

"I laughed aloud in their faces.

"'Ah!' I cried, 'this is amusing! This is really a good joke! And pray what do you threaten?'

"'We do not threaten,' Zekki said. 'You are here to die.' And he laughed grimly, while the others grinned.

"'Why?'

"'That is our affair.'

"'And mine also,' I replied. 'And gentlemen, I would further advise you in future to be quite certain of your victim, or it may go ill with you. Let me pass!' And I drew the revolver the *kavass* had given me.

"'Put that thing away!' ordered the elder of the men, approaching me with threatening gesture.

"'I shall not. Let us end this confounded foolishness. *Shunam-al-Zulah!*'

"The effect of these words upon the trio was electrical.

"The sallow-faced *attaché* stood staring at me open-mouthed, while his companions fell back, as though I had dealt them both a blow. They seemed too dumbfounded to respond, as, revolver in hand, I next moment passed out of the room and from that house to which I had been so cleverly lured, and where my death had evidently been planned.

"At the hotel I spent a sleepless night, full of deep anxiety, wondering for what reason the curious plot had been arranged, and whether my dainty little companion had had any hand in it.

"My apprehensions were, however, entirely dispelled when early on the following been morning, Olga called to ask why I had absent when the *kavass* had called for me.

"I took her into one of the smaller rooms, and told her the whole truth, whereat she was much upset, and eager to leave the Turkish capital immediately.

"At seven that same evening we sailed for Naples, and without further incident duly arrived at the Italian port, took train for Rome, and thence by express to Paris and Charing Cross.

"On the journey she refused to discuss the plot of the jealous, evil-eyed Turk. Her one idea was to get to London—and to freedom.

"At eleven o'clock at night we stepped out upon Charing Cross platform, and I ordered the cabman to drive me to the Cecil, for when acting the part of Reggie Martin, I always avoided Dover Street. It was too late to catch the Scotch mail, therefore I would be compelled to spend the first day of the pheasants in London, and start north to my friends on the following day.

"Suddenly as we entered the station she had decided also to spend the night at the Cecil and leave next day for Ipswich, where a brother of hers was a tutor.

"I wished her good-night in the big hall of the hotel, and went up in the lift.

"Rising about half-past six next morning and entering my sitting-room, I was amazed to encounter Olga, fully dressed in hat and caracul jacket, standing in the grey dawn, reading a paper which she had taken from my despatch-box!

"Instantly she dropped her hand, and stood staring at me without uttering a word, knowing full well that I had discovered the astounding truth.

"I recognised the document by the colour of the paper.

"'Well, mademoiselle?' I demanded in a hard tone, 'And for what reason, pray, do you pry into my private papers like this?'

"'I—I was waiting to bid you adieu,' she answered tamely.

"'And you were at the same time making yourself acquainted with the contents of that document which I have carried in my belt ever since I left Sofia—that document of which you and your interesting friend, Zekki, have ever since desired sight—eh?' I exclaimed, bitterly. 'My duty is to call in the police, and hand you over as a political Spy to be expelled from the country.'

"'If m'sieur wishes to do that he is at perfect liberty to do so,' she answered, in quick defiance. 'The result is the same. I have read Petkoff's declaration, so the paper is of no further use,' and she handed it to me with a smile of triumph upon those childlike lips. 'Arrest or liberty—I am entirely in monsieur's hands,' she added, shrugging her shoulders.

"I broke forth into a torrent of reproach for I saw that Bulgaria had been betrayed to her arch-enemy, Turkey, by that sweet-faced woman who had so completely deceived me, and who, after the first plot had failed, had so cleverly carried the second to a successful issue.

"Defiant to the last, she stood smiling in triumph. Even when I openly accused her of being a spy she only laughed.

"Therefore I opened the door and sternly ordered her to leave, knowing, alas! that, now she had ascertained the true facts, the Bulgarian secret policy towards Turkey would be entirely negatived, that the terrible atrocities in Macedonia must continue, and that the Russian influence in Bulgaria would still remain paramount.

"I held my silence, and spent a dull and thoughtful Sunday in the great London hotel. Had I remained in Bucharest, as was my duty, and handed the document in Petkoff's handwriting to the King's Messenger, who was due to pass in the Orient express, the dainty Olga could never have obtained sight of it. This she knew, and for that reason had told me the story of her torture in the prison at Riga and urged me to save her. Zekki, knowing that I constantly carried the secret declaration of Bulgaria in the belt beneath my clothes, saw that only by my unconsciousness, or death, could they obtain sight of it. Hence the dastardly plot to kill me, frustrated by the utterance of the password of the Turkish spies themselves.

"It is useless for a man to cross swords with a pretty woman where it is a matter of ingenuity and double-dealing. With the chiefs of the Foreign Office absent, I could only exist in anxiety and dread, and when I acted it was, alas! too late.

"Inquiries subsequently made in Constantinople showed that the house in which Zekki had received me, situated near the konak of Ali Saib Pasha, was the headquarters of the Turkish Secret Service, of which the sallow-faced scoundrel was a well-known member, and that on the evening of the day of my return to London the body of Nicholas, the Montenegrin *kavass* who saved my life, had been found floating in the Bosphorus. Death had been his reward for warning me!

"Readers of the newspapers are well aware how, two months later, as a result of Turkish intrigue in Sofia, my poor friend Dimitri Petkoff, Prime Minister of Bulgaria, was shot through the heart while walking with me in the Boris Garden.

"Both Bulgarian and Turkish Governments have, however, been very careful to suppress intelligence of a dramatic incident which occurred in Constantinople only a few weeks ago. Olga Steinkoff, the secret agent employed by the Sublime Porte, was, at her house in the Sarmaschik quarter, handed by her maid a beautiful basket of fruit that had been sent by an admirer. The dainty woman with the childlike face cut the string, when, lo! there darted forth four hissing, venomous vipers. Two of the reptiles struck, biting her white wrist ere she could withdraw, and an hour later, her face swollen out of all recognition, she died in terrible agony.

"The betrayal of Bulgaria and the assassination of Petkoff, the patriot, have, indeed, been swiftly avenged."

VII

The Sign of the Cat's-Paw

Another part which the Prince played in the present-day drama now being enacted in Eastern Europe brought him in touch with "The Sign of the Cat's-Paw," a sign hitherto unknown to our Foreign Office, or to readers of the daily newspapers.

At the same time, however, it very nearly cost him his own life.

The affair occurred about a couple of months after the death of the fascinating Olga Steinkoff. He had been sent back to the Balkans upon another mission. Cosmopolitan of cosmopolitans, he had been moving rapidly up and down Europe gathering information for Downing Street, but ever on the look-out for an opening for the Parson and himself to operate in a very different sphere.

Garrett, blindly obedient to the telegrams he received, had taken the car on some long flying journeys, Vienna, Berlin and back to Belgrade, in Servia. For two months or so I had lost sight of both the mild-mannered, spectacled Clayton and the Prince, when one morning, while walking down St. James's Street, I saw Garrett in his grey and scarlet livery driving the car from Piccadilly down to Pall Mall.

By this I guessed that his Highness had returned to London, so I called at Dover Street, and twenty minutes later found myself seated in the big saddle-bag chair with a "Petroff" between my lips.

He was in his old brown velvet lounge coat and slippers, and had been at his writing-table when I entered. But on my appearance he threw down his pen, stretched himself, and sat round for a gossip.

Suddenly, while speaking, he made a quick, half-foreign gesture of ignorance in response to a question of mine, and in that brief instant I saw upon his right palm a curious red mark.

"Hullo!" I asked. "What's that?"

"Oh—nothing," he replied, rather confused I thought, and shut his hand so that I could not see it.

"But it is!" I declared. "Let me see."

"How inquisitive you are, Diprose, old chap," he protested.

So persistent was I, and so aroused my curiosity by finding a mark exactly like the imprint of a cat's-paw, that, not without considerable reluctance, he explained its meaning. The story he narrated was, indeed, a most remarkable and dramatic one. And yet he related it as though it were nothing. Perhaps, indeed, the puzzling incidents were of but little moment to one who led a life so chock-full of adventure as he.

YES, IT REALLY WAS CURIOUS, he remarked at last. It was in March. I had been in London's mud and rain for a fortnight, and grown tired of it. Suddenly a confidential mission had been placed in my hands—a mission which had for its object British support to the Bulgarian Government against the machinations of Austria to extend her sphere of influence southward across the Danube and Servia.

My destination was Sofia, the Bulgarian capital, and once more the journey by the Orient Express across Europe was a long and tedious one. I had wired to Garrett, who was awaiting me with the car at the Hungaria, in Budapest, to bring it on to Sofia.

But I was much occupied with the piece of scheming which I had undertaken to carry out. My patriotism had led me to attempt a very difficult task—one which would require delicate tact and a good deal of courage and resource, but which would, if successful, mean that a loan of three millions would be raised in London, and that British influence would become paramount in that go-ahead country, which, ere long, must be the power of the Balkans.

I knew, however, that there were others in Sofia upon the same errand as myself, emissaries of other governments and other financial houses. Therefore, in the three long never-ending days the journey occupied, my mind was constantly filled with thoughts of the best and most judicious course to pursue in order to attain my object.

The run was uneventful, save for one fact. At the Staatsbahnhof, at Vienna, just before our train left for Budapest, a queer, fussy little old man in brown entered, and was given the compartment next mine.

His nationality I could not determine. He spoke deep guttural German with the fair-bearded conductor of the train, but by his clothes—which were rather dandified for so old a man—I did not believe him to be a native of the Fatherland.

I heard him rumbling about with his bags next door, apparently settling himself, when of a sudden my quick ear caught an imprecation which he uttered to himself in English.

A few hours later, at dinner, I found him placed at the little table opposite me, and naturally we began to chat. He spoke in French—

perfect French it was—but refused to speak English, though, of course, he could had he wished.

"Ah! non," he laughed, "I cannot. Excuse me. My pronunciation is so faulty. Your English is so ve-ry deefecult."

And so we chatted in French, and I found the queer old fellow was on his way to Sofia. He seemed slightly deformed, his face was distinctly ugly, broad, clean-shaven, with a pair of black piercing eyes that gave him a most striking appearance. His grey hair was long, his nose aquiline, his teeth protruding and yellow, and he was a grumbler of the most pronounced type. He growled at the food, at the service, at the draughts, at the light in the restaurant, at the staleness of the bread we had brought with us from Paris, and at the butter, which he declared to be only Danish margarine.

His complaints were amusing. He was possessed of much grim humour. At first the *maitre d'hotel* bustled about to do the bidding of the new-comer, but very quickly summed him up, and only grinned knowingly when called to listen to his biting criticism of the Compagnie Internationale des Wagons-lits and all its works.

Next day, at Semlin, where our passports were examined, the passport-officer took off his hat to him, bowed low and *vised* his passport without question, saying, as he handed back the document to its owner:

"*Bon voyage*, Altesse."

I stared at the pair. My fussy friend with the big head must therefore be either a prince or a grand duke! Just then I was not a prince—only plain M'sieur Martin. In Roumania princes are as plentiful as blackberries, so I put him down as a Roumanian.

As I sat opposite him at dinner that night he was discussing with me the harmful writings of some newly discovered German who was posing as a cheap philosopher, and denouncing them as dangerous to the community. He leaned his elbow upon the narrow table and supported his clean-shaven chin upon his finger, displaying to me most, certainly by accident, the palm of his thin right hand.

What I discovered there caused me a good deal of surprise. In its centre was a dark livid mark, as though it had been branded there by a hot iron, the plain and distinct imprint of a cat's-paw!

It fascinated me. There was some hidden meaning in that mark, I felt convinced. It was just as though a cat had stepped upon blood with one of its fore-paws and trodden upon his hand.

Whether he noticed that I had detected it or not, I cannot say, but he moved his hand quickly, and ever after kept it closed.

His name, he told me at last, was Konstantinos Vassos, and he lived in Athens. But I took that information *cum grano*, for I knew him to be a prince travelling *incognito*. The passport-officer at Semlin makes no mistakes.

But if actually a prince, why did he carry a passport?

There is, unfortunately, no good hotel at Sofia. The best is the Bulgarie, kept by a pleasant old lady to whom I was well-known as M'sieur Martin, and in this we found ourselves next night installed. He gave his name as Vassos, and to all intents and purposes was more of a stranger in Prince Ferdinand's capital than I myself was, for I had been there at least half a dozen times before. Most of the Ministers knew me, and I was always elected a member of the smart diplomats' club, the Union, during my stay.

The days passed. From the first morning of my arrival I found myself as before in a vortex of gaiety; invitations to the Legations poured in upon me, cards for dances here and there, receptions by members of the Cabinet, and official dinners by the British and French Ministers, while daily I spent each afternoon with my friend, Colonel Mayhew, the British military *attache*, in his comfortable quarters not far from our Agency.

All the while, I must here confess, I was working my cards very carefully. I had sounded my friend, Petkoff, the grave, grey-haired Prime Minister—the splendid Bulgarian patriot—and he was inclined to admit the British proposals. The Minister of War, too, was on my side. German agents had approached him, but he would have none of them. In Bulgaria just then they had no love of Germany. They were far too Russophile.

Indeed, in this strenuous life of a fortnight or so I had practically lost sight of the ugly old gentleman who had been addressed by the passport-officer as his Highness. Once or twice I had seen him wandering alone and dejected along the streets, for he apparently knew nobody, and was having a very quiet time, Greeks were disliked in Sofia almost as much as Turks, on account of the Greek bands who massacre the Bulgars in Macedonia.

One night at the weekly dance at the Military Club—a function at which the smart set at Sofia always attend, and at which the Ministers of State themselves put in an appearance—I had been waltzing with the daughter of the Minister of the Interior, a pretty dark-haired girl in blue, whom I had met during my last visit to Bulgaria, and the Spanish *attache*, a pale-faced young man wearing a cross at his throat, had introduced to me a tall, very handsome, sweet-faced girl in a black evening-gown trimmed with silver.

A thin wreath of the same roses was in her hair, and around her neck was a fine gold chain from which was suspended a big and lustrous diamond.

Mademoiselle Balesco was her name, and I found her inexpressibly charming. She spoke French perfectly, and English quite well. She had been at school in England, she said—at Scarborough. Her home was at Galatz, in Roumania, where her father was Prefect.

We had several dances, and afterwards I took her down to supper. Then we had a couple of waltzes, and I conducted her out to the carriage awaiting her, and, bowing, watched her drive off alone.

But while doing so, there came along the pavement, out of the shadow, the short ugly figure of the old Greek Vassos, with his coat collar turned up, evidently passing without noticing me.

A few days later, when in the evening I called on Mayhew at his rooms, he said:

"What have you been up to, Martin? Look here! This letter was left upon me, with a note asking me to give it to you in secret. Looks like a woman's hand! Mind what you're about in this place, old chap! There are some nasty pitfalls, you know!"

I took the letter, opened it, read it through, and placed it in my pocket without a word.

With a bachelor's curiosity, he was eager to know who was my fair correspondent. But I refused to satisfy him.

Suffice it to say that on that same night I went alone to a house on the outskirts of Sofia, and there met at her urgent request the pretty girl Marie Balesco, who had so enchanted me. Ours seemed to be a case of mutual attraction, for as we sat together, she seemed, after apologising for thus approaching me and throwing all the convenances to the winds, to be highly interested in my welfare, and very inquisitive concerning the reasons which had brought me to Bulgaria.

Like most women of the Balkans, she smoked, and offered me her cigarette-case. I took one—a delicious one it was, but rather strong—so strong, indeed, that a strange drowsiness suddenly overcame me. Before I could fight against it the small, well-furnished room seemed to whirl

WILLIAM LE QUEUX

about me, and I must have fallen unconscious. Indeed I knew no more until on awakening I found myself back in my bed at the hotel.

I gazed at the morning sunshine upon the wall, and tried to recollect what held occurred.

My hand seemed strangely painful. Raising it from the sheets, I looked at it.

Upon my right palm, branded as by a hot iron, was the Sign of the Cat's-paw!

Horrified I stared at it. It was the same mark that I had seen upon the hand of Vassos! What could be its significance?

In a few days the burn healed, leaving a dark red scar, the distinct imprint of the feline foot. From Mayhew I tried, by cautious questions, to obtain some information concerning the fair-faced girl who had played such a prank on me. But he only knew her slightly. She had been staying with a certain Madame Sovoff, who was something of a mystery, but had left Sofia.

A month passed. Mademoiselle and Madame returned from Belgrade and were both delighted when I suggested they should go for a run in the "sixty." I took them over the same road as I had taken Olga Steinkoff. In a week Mademoiselle became an enthusiastic motorist, and was full of inquiry into the various parts of the engine, the ignition, lubrication, and other details. One day I carefully approached the matter of this remarkable mark upon my palm. But she affected entire ignorance. I confess that I had grown rather fond of her, and I hesitated to attribute to her, or to Madame, any sinister design; the strange mark on my hand was both weird and puzzling. We drove out in the car often, and many a time I recollected pretty Olga, and her horrible fate.

Vassos, who was still at the hotel, annoyed me on account of his extreme politeness, and the manner in which he appeared to spy upon all my movements. I came across him everywhere. Inquiries concerning the reason of the ugly Greek's presence in Bulgaria met with negative result. One thing seemed certain; he was not a prince *incognito*.

How I longed to go to him, show him the mark upon my hand, and demand an explanation. But my curiosity was aroused; therefore I patiently awaited developments, my revolver always ready in my hip pocket, in case of foul play.

The mysterious action of the pretty girl from Galatz also puzzled me.

At last the Cabinet of Prince Ferdinand were in complete accord with the Prime Minister Petkoff, regarding the British proposals. All had been done in secret from the party in opposition, and one day I had lunched with his Excellency the Prime Minister, at his house in the suburbs of the city.

"You may send a cipher despatch to London, if you like, Mr. Martin," he said, as we sat over our cigars. "The documents will all be signed at the Cabinet meeting at noon to-morrow. In exchange for this loan of three millions raised in London, all the contracts for quick-firing guns and ammunition go to your group of financiers." Such was the welcome news his Excellency imparted to me, and you may imagine that I lost no time in writing out a cipher message, and sending it by the man-servant to the nearest telegraph office.

For a long time I sat with him, and then he rose, inviting me to walk with him in the Boris Gardens, as was his habit every afternoon, before going down to the sitting of the Sobranje, or Parliament.

On our way we passed Vassos, who raised his hat politely to me.

"Who's that man?" inquired the Minister quickly, and I told him all I knew concerning the ugly hunchback.

In the pretty public garden we were strolling together in the sundown, chatting upon the situation in Macedonia and other matters, when of a sudden, a black-moustached man in a dark grey overcoat and round astrachan cap, sprang from the bushes at a lonely spot, and raising a big service revolver, fired point-blank at his Excellency.

I felt for my own weapon. Alas! It was not there! I had forgotten it!

The assassin, seeing the Minister reel and fall, turned his weapon upon me. Thereupon, in an instant I threw up my hands, crying that I was unarmed, and was an Englishman.

As I did so, he started back as though terrified. His weapon fell from his grasp, and with a spring, he disappeared again into the bushes.

All had happened in a few brief instants; for ere I could realise that a tragedy had actually occurred, I found the unfortunate Prime Minister lying lifeless at my feet. My friend had been shot through the heart!

READERS OF THE NEWSPAPERS WILL recollect the tragic affair, which is no doubt still fresh in their minds.

I told the Chief of Police of Sofia of my strange experience, and showed him the mark upon my palm. Though detectives searched high and low for the hunchback Greek, for Madame Sovoff, and for the fascinating Mademoiselle, none of them were ever found.

The assassin was, nevertheless, arrested a week later, while trying to cross the frontier into Servia. I, of course, lost by an ace the great financial coup, but before execution the prisoner made a confession which revealed the existence of a terrible and widespread conspiracy, fostered by Bulgaria's arch-enemy Turkey, to remove certain members of the Cabinet who were in favour of British influence becoming paramount.

Yes. It was a rather narrow squeak.

Quite unconsciously, I had, it seemed, become an especial favourite of the silent, watchful old Konstantinos Vassos. He had no idea that I was a "crook" or that I was a secret agent. Fearing lest I, in my innocence, should fall a victim with his Excellency—being so often his companion—he had, with the assistance of the pretty Marie Balesco, contrived to impress upon my palm the secret sign of the conspirators.

To this fact I certainly owe my life, for the assassin—a stranger to Sofia, who had been drawn by lot—would, no doubt, have shot me dead, had he not seen upon my raised hand "The Sign of the Cat's-paw."

VIII

Concerning a Woman's Honour

F ew people are aware of the Prince's serious love affair.

Beyond his most intimate friend, the Parson, I believe nobody knows of it except myself.

The truth I have managed to glean only bit by bit, for he has never told me himself. It is a matter which he does not care to mention, for recollections of the woman are, no doubt, ever in his heart, and as with many of us, ever painful.

No man or woman is thoroughly bad. Adventurer that he is, the Prince has ever been true and honourable, even generous, towards a good woman. The best and staunchest of friends, yet the bitterest of enemies if occasion required, he has never, to my knowledge, played an honest woman a scurvy trick.

The little romance of real life occurred in Florence about three years ago. A good many people got hold of a garbled version of it, but none know the actual truth. He loved, and because he loved he dare not pose in his usual character as a prince, for fear that she should discover the fraud. On the contrary, he was living at a small cheap hotel on the Lung Arno as Jack Cross, and posing as a man who was very hard-up and, besides, friendless.

He had entered upon the campaign with an entirely different object—an object which had for its consummation the obtaining of some very fine jewels belonging to the wife of an American who had made a corner in cotton, and who was engaged in seeing Europe. Max Mason and the Parson were both living as strangers to each other at the Savoy, in the Piazza Vittorio Emanuele, and idling daily in the Via Tornabuoni. A big coup had been planned, but instead of bringing it off, as luck would have it, his Highness had fallen hopelessly in love, and with a real royal princess, a woman whose beauty was universally proverbial.

Their love-story was full of pathos.

They were standing together in a garden one sunny afternoon, and were alone, without eavesdroppers. A moment before, he had been wondering what she would do; what she would say if she knew the ghastly truth—that he was a thief!

He had been born a gentleman—though he had no more right to the title of "prince" than I had. True, at college at Cheltenham he had been nicknamed "the prince," because of his charming manner and elegant airs. Few of us even imagined, however, that he would, in later years, pass himself off as a German princeling and gull the public into providing him with the wherewithal to live in ease and luxury.

As he stood at the handsome woman's side, thoughts of the past—bitter and regretful—flashed upon him. His conscience pricked him.

"Princess!—I—I—" he stammered.

"Well?" and her sweet red lips parted in a smile.

"I—ah! yes, it's madness. I—I know I'm a fool! I see danger in all this. I have jeopardised your good name sufficiently already. People are looking at us now—and they will surely misjudge us!"

"You are not a fool, my dear Jack," she answered in her charming broken English. "You are what you call a goose." And she laughed outright.

"But think! What will they say?"

"They may say just whatever pleases them," she answered airily, glancing at the half a dozen or so smartly dressed people taking tea in the beautiful Italian garden overlooking the red roofs and cupolas of the Lily City, Florence. "They—the world—have already said hard things about me. But what do I really care?"

"*You* care for the Prince's honour, as well as your own," he ventured in a low serious voice, looking straight into her blue eyes.

Her Imperial and Royal Highness Angelica Pia Marie Therese Crown-Princess of Bosnia, and daughter of a reigning Emperor, was acknowledged to be one of the most beautiful and accomplished women in Europe. Her photographs were everywhere, and a year before, at her brilliant marriage in Vienna, all the States of Europe were represented, and her photograph had appeared in every illustrated newspaper on the two Continents. The world, ignorant of the tragedy of life behind a throne, believed the royal marriage to be a love-match, but the bitter truth remained that it was merely the union of two imperial houses, without the desire of either the man, or the woman. Princess Angelica had, at the bidding of the Emperor, sacrificed her love and her young life to a man for whom she had only contempt and loathing.

As she stood there, a tall, frail figure, in plain white embroidered muslin, her fair hair soft beneath her big black hat, her sweet delicately moulded face and her eyes of that deep childlike blue that one so seldom sees in girls after fourteen, there was upon her countenance an undisguised love-look. She was indeed the perfect incarnation of all that was graceful and feminine; little more indeed, than a girl, and yet the wife of a prince that would ere long become a king.

For a few moments the man and the woman regarded each other in silence.

He was spell-bound by her wondrous beauty like many another man had been. But she knew, within herself, that he was the only man she had ever met that she could love.

And surely they were a curiously ill-assorted pair, as far as social equality went, she the daughter of an Emperor, while he a hard-up young Englishman, tall, dark-haired, with a handsome, serious face, lived, he had explained to her, in Florence, first, because it was cheap, and secondly, because his old aunt, who had a small house out on the Fiesole Road, practically kept him. His story to her was that he had once been on the Stock Exchange, but a run of ill-luck had broken him, so he had left England, and now managed to scrape along upon a couple of hundred or so a year paid him by a firm of Italian shipping and forwarding agents, for whom he now acted as English manager. The position was an excellent "blind." Nobody recognised him as Tremlett, alias "his Highness."

Half aristocratic Florence—those stiff-backed Italian duchesses and countesses with their popinjay, over-dressed male appendages—envied Jack Cross his intimate acquaintance with the Crown-Princess of Bosnia, who, in winter, lived at the magnificent villa on the Viale dei Colli, overlooking the town. Towards Italian society her royal Highness turned the cold shoulder. The Emperor had no love for Italy, or the Italians, and it was at his orders that she kept herself absolutely to herself.

On rare occasions, she would give a small garden-party or dinner to a dozen or so of the most prominent men and women in the city. But it was not often that they were asked, and beyond three or four people in Florence her Highness had no friends there. But part of her school-days had been spent in the big convent up at Fiesole, therefore it had been her whim after her marriage, to purchase that beautiful villa with its gorgeous rooms, marble terraces, and lovely gardens as a winter home.

And to that splendid house the Prince, alias Jack Cross, was always a welcome guest. He went there daily, and when not there, her Highness would amuse herself by chattering to him over the telephone to his office.

Envied by the society who would not know him because he was not an aristocrat, and with the sharp eye of the Florentine middle-classes upon him, little wonder was it that whispers were soon going about regarding the Princess's too frequent confidences with the unknown Englishman.

He was watched whenever he rang at the great iron gate before which stood an Italian sentry day and night, and he was watched when he emerged. In the clubs, in the salons, in the shops, in the *cafes*, the gossip soon became common, and often with a good deal of imaginary embroidery.

It was true that he often dined at the Villa Renata with her Highness, the young Countess von Wilberg, the lady-in-waiting, and the old Countess Lahovary, a Roumanian, who had been lady-in-waiting to her mother the Empress, and in whose charge she always was when outside Bosnia. The evenings they often spent in the drawing-room, Her Highness being a good pianist. And on many a night she would rise, take her shawl, and pass out into the bright Italian moonlight with the young Englishman as her escort.

It was the way they passed nearly every evening—in each other's company. Yet neither of her companions dare suggest a cessation of the young man's visits, fearing to arouse the Princess's anger, and receive their dismissal.

At risk of gossip her Imperial Highness often invited him to go for runs with her in her fine forty "Fiat" to Siena, to Bologna, or to Pisa, accompanied always, of course, by the Countess Lahovary. In those days he pretended not to possess a car, though he could drive one, and on many occasions he drove the Princess along those white dusty Italian highways. She loved motoring, and so did he. Indeed, he knew quite as much regarding the engine as any mechanic.

The Crown Prince hardly, if ever, came to Florence. His father, the King, was not on the best of terms with the Italian Court, therefore he made that an excuse for his absence in Paris, where, according to report his life was not nearly as creditable as it might have been.

Such were the circumstances in which, by slow degrees, her Highness found herself admiring and loving the quiet unassuming but good-looking young Englishman at whom everybody sneered because, to save himself from penury, he had accepted the managership of a trading concern.

Prince Albert himself saw it all, and recognised the extreme peril of the situation.

Born in the purple as the woman who had entranced him had been, she held public opinion in supreme contempt, and time after time had assured Jack that even if people talked and misconstrued their platonic friendship she was entirely heedless of their wicked untruths and exaggerations.

That afternoon was another example of her recklessness in face of her enemies.

She had invited up a few people to take tea and eat strawberries in the grounds, while a military band performed under the trees near by. But quickly tiring of the obsequiousness of her guests, she had motioned Cross aside, and in a low voice said in English: "For heaven's sake, Jack, take me away from these awful people. The women are hags, and the men tailors' dummies. Let us walk down to the rosary."

And he, bowing as she spoke, turned and walked at her side, well knowing that by taking her from her guests he was increasing the hatred already felt against him.

In her heart she loved this unknown hardworking young Englishman, while he was held captive beneath her beauty, spell-bound by the music of her voice, thrilled by the touch of the soft hand which he kissed each day at greeting her, and each evening when they parted.

Yes, people talked. Cross knew they did. Men had told him so. Max and the Parson had heard all sorts of wild gossip, and had sent him a letter telling him that he was an idiot. They wanted to handle the American woman's diamonds. They were not in Florence for sentimental reasons. The report had even reached his old aunt's ears, and she had administered to him a very severe reprimand, to which he had listened without a single word of protest, except that he denied, and denied most emphatically, that he was the Princess's lover. He was her friend, that was all.

True, she was lonely and alone there in gay Florence, the City of Flowers. Sarajevo, her own capital she hated, she had often said. "It is pleasant, my dear Jack, to be in dear old Firenze," she had declared only the previous evening as they had walked and talked together in the white moonlight. "But doubly pleasant to be near such a good, true friend as you are to me."

"I do but what is my duty, Princess," he replied in a low voice. "You have few friends here. But I am, I hope, one who is loyal and true."

Those words of his crossed her mind as they strolled away from the music and the guests that warm May afternoon, strolled on beneath the blossoms, and amid the great profusion of flowers. She glanced again at his serious thoughtful face, and sighed within herself. What were titles, imperial birth, power, and the servility of the people, to love? Why was she not born a commoner, and allowed to taste the sweets of life, that even the most obscure little waiting-maid or seamstress were allowed. Every woman of the people could seek Love and obtain it. But to her, she reflected bitterly, it was denied—because she was not of common clay, but an Emperor's daughter, and destined to become a reigning queen!

Together they walked along the cool cypress avenue; he tall, clean-limbed in his suit of white linen and panama. But they strolled on in silence, beyond the gaze of their enemies.

"You seem to fear what these wretched gossips may say concerning us, Jack," she said at last, raising her eyes to his. "Why should you?"

"I fear for your sake, Princess," he answered. "You have all to lose—honour, name, husband—everything. For me—what does it matter? I have no reputation. I ceased to have that two years ago when I left England—bankrupt."

"Poor Jack!" she sighed, in her quaint, childlike way. "I do wish you were wealthy, for you'd be so much happier, I suppose. It must be hard to be poor," she added—she who knew nothing of the value of money, and scarcely ever spent any herself, her debts and alms being paid by palace secretaries.

"Yes," he laughed. "And has it never struck you as strange that you, an Imperial Princess, should be a friend of a man who's a bankrupt—an outsider like myself?" and an ugly thought flashed through his mind causing him to wince.

"And have you not always shown yourself my friend, Jack? Should I not be ungrateful if I were not your friend in return?" she asked.

They halted almost unconsciously half way along the cypress avenue, and stood facing each other.

Prince Albert of Hesse-Holstein was struggling within himself. He loved this beautiful woman with all his heart, and all his soul. Yet he knew himself to be treading dangerous ground.

Their first acquaintance had been a purely accidental one three years ago. Her Highness was driving in the Ringstrasse, in Vienna, when her horses suddenly took fright at a passing motor-car and bolted. Jack, who was passing, managed to dash out and stop them, but in doing so was thrown down and kicked on the head. He was taken to the hospital, and not until a fortnight afterwards was he aware of the identity of the pretty woman in the carriage. Then, on his recovery, he was commanded to the palace and thanked personally by the Princess and by her father, the grey-bearded Emperor.

From that day the Princess Angelica had never lost sight of him. When she had married he had endeavoured to end their acquaintance, but she would not hear of it. And so he had drifted along, held completely beneath her spell.

He was her confidant, and on many occasions performed in secret little services for her. Their friendship, purely platonic, was firm and fast, and surely no man was ever more loyal to a woman than was the young Englishman, who was, after all, only an audacious adventurer.

In the glorious sunset of the brilliant Tuscan day they stood there in silence. At last he spoke.

"Princess," he exclaimed, looking straight into her eyes. "Forgive me for what I am about to say. I have long wished to say it, but had not the courage. I—well, you cannot tell the bitterness it causes me to speak, but I have decided to imperil you no longer. I am leaving Florence."

She looked at him in blank surprise.

"Leaving Florence!" she gasped. "What do you mean, Jack?"

"I mean that I must do so—for your sake," was his answer. "The world does not believe that a woman can have a man friend. I—I yesterday heard something."

"What?"

"That the Prince has set close watch upon us."

"Well, and what of that? Do we fear?"

"We do not fear the truth, Princess. It is the untruth of which we are in peril."

"Then Ferdinand is jealous!" she remarked as though speaking to herself. "Ah! that is distinctly amusing!"

"My friendship with you has already caused a scandal in this gossip-loving city," he pointed out. "It is best for you that we should part. Remember the difference in our stations. You are of blood-royal—while I—" and he hesitated. How could he tell her the ghastly truth?

She was silent for a few moments, her beautiful face very grave and thoughtful. Well, alas! she knew that if this man left her side the sun of her young life would have set for ever.

"But—but Jack—you are my friend, are you not?"

"How can you ask that?"

"Ah! yes. Forgive me. I—I know—you risked your life to save mine. You—"

"No, no," he cried, impatiently. "Don't let's talk of the past. Let us look at the future, and let us speak plainly. We are old friends enough for that, Princess."

"Angelica," she said, correcting him.

"Then—Angelica," he said, pronouncing her Christian name for the first time. Then he hesitated and their eyes met. He saw in hers the light of unshed tears, and bit his lip. His own heart was too full for mere words.

"Jack," she faltered, raising her hand and placing it upon his arm, "I don't quite understand you. You are not yourself this evening." The bar of golden sunlight caught her wrist and caused the diamonds in her bracelet to flash with a thousand fires.

"No, Princess—I—I mean Angelica. I am not. I wish to speak quite plainly. It is this. If I remain here, in Florence, I shall commit the supreme folly of—of loving you." She cast her eyes to the ground, flushed slightly and held her breath.

"This," he went on, "must never happen for two reasons, first you are already married, and secondly, you are of Imperial birth, while I am a mere nobody, and a pauper at that."

"I am married, it is true!" she cried, bitterly. "But God knows, what a hollow mockery my marriage has been! God knows how I have suffered, compelled as I am to act a living lie! You despise me for marrying Ferdinand, a man I could never love. Yes, you are right, you are quite—"

"I do not despise, you, Angelica. I have always pitied you," he interrupted. "I knew well that you did not love the Prince, but were compelled to sacrifice yourself."

"You knew!" she cried, clutching his arm wildly, and looking into his face. "Ah! yes, Jack. You—you knew the truth. You must have known. I could not conceal it from you."

"What?" he asked, his hand upon her slim shoulder.

"That—that I loved you," she burst forth. But next second, as if ashamed of her confession, she covered her face with her hands and sobbed bitterly.

Tenderly he placed his strong arm about her neck as her head fell upon her shoulder. For a moment he held her closely to him. Then, in a faltering voice, he said:

"Angelica, I know that our love is mutual, that is why we must part."

"No! no!" she cried through her tears. "No. Do not leave me here alone, Jack! If you go from Florence I must return to the hateful semi-imprisonment of the Palace at Sarajevo among those dull boors with whom I have not the least in common."

"But, Angelica, I am in honour bound not to compromise you further. Your enemies are all talking, and inventing disgraceful scandals that have already reached the Prince's ears. Hence his spies are here, watching all our movements."

"Spies! Yes, Bosnia is full of them!" she cried angrily. "And Ferdinand sends them here to spy upon me!" and she clenched her tiny white hands resentfully.

"They are here, hence we must part. We must face our misfortune bravely; but for your sake I must leave your side, though heaven knows what this decision has cost me—my very life and soul."

She raised her head, and with her clear blue eyes looked into his face.

At that same instant they heard a footstep on the gravel, and sprang quickly apart. But just as they did so a tall, well-dressed, brown-bearded man came into view. Both held their breath, for no doubt he had seen her in Jack's arms.

The man was the Marquis Giulio di San Rossore, a Roman nobleman, who was a friend of her husband the Prince. But that he was her secret enemy she well knew. Only a month ago he had fallen upon his knees before her, and declared his love to her. But she had spurned and scorned him in indignation. He heard her biting words in silence, and had turned away with an expression upon his face which plainly told her of the fierce Italian spirit of revenge within his heart.

But he came forward smiling and bowing with those airs and graces which the cultured son of the south generally assumes.

"They have sent me to try and find you, your Highness," he said. "The Duchess of Spezia has suggested a ball in aid of the sufferers from the earthquake down in Calabria, and we want to beg of you to give it your patronage."

And he glanced at the Princess's companion with fierce jealousy. He had, as they feared, witnessed the beautiful woman standing with her head upon his shoulder.

"Let us go back, Mr. Cross," her Highness said, "I would like to hear details of what is proposed."

And all three strolled along the fine old avenue, and skirted the marble terrace to where the guests, having now finished their tea, were still assembled gossiping with the Countess Von Wilberg and Countess Lahovary.

As they walked together, the Marquess Giulio chuckled to himself at the discovery he had made, and what a fine tale he would be able to tell that night at the Florence Club.

The truth was proved. The penniless Englishman was the Princess's lover! Florence had suspected it, but now it should know it.

That same night, after dinner, Jack was standing alone with the Princess in the gorgeous *salon* with its gilt furniture and shaded electric lights. He looked smart and well-groomed, notwithstanding that his evening clothes showed just a trifle the worse for wear, while she was brilliant and beautiful in an evening-gown of palest eau-de-nil embroidered chiffon, a creation of one of the great houses of the Rue de la Paix. Upon her white neck she wore her historic pearls, royal heirlooms that were once the property of Catherine the Great, and in her corsage a splendid true-lover's knot in diamonds, the ornament from which there usually depended the black ribbon and diamond star-cross decoration, which marked her as an Imperial Archduchess. The cross was absent that night, for her only visitor was the man at her side.

Her two female companions were in the adjoining room. They knew well their royal mistress's attraction towards the young Englishman, and never sought to intrude upon them. Both were well aware of the shameful sham of the Princess's marriage and of his neglect and cruelty towards her, and both women pitied her in her loveless loneliness.

"But, Jack!" her Highness was saying, her pale face raised to his. "You really don't mean to go? You can't mean that!"

"Yes, Angelica," was his firm reply, as he held her waist tenderly, drawing her towards him and looking deeply into her fine eyes. "I must go—to save your honour."

"No, no!" she cried, clinging to him convulsively. "You must not— you shall not! Think, if you go I shall be friendless and alone! I couldn't bear it."

"I know. It may seem cruel to you. But in after years you will know that I broke our bond of affection for your own dear sake," he said very slowly, tears standing in his dark eyes as he uttered those words. "You know full well the bitter truth, Angelica—just as well as I do," he went on in a low whisper. "You know how deeply, how fervently I love you, how I am entirely and devotedly yours."

"Yes, yes. I know, Jack," she cried, clinging to him. "And I love you. You are the only man for whom I have ever entertained a single spark of affection. But love is forbidden to me. Ah! yes I know! Had I been a commoner and not a princess, and we had met, I should have found happiness, like other women. But alas! I am accursed by my noble birth, and love and happiness can never be mine—never!"

"We love each other, Angelica," whispered the man who was a thief, softly stroking her fair hair as her head pillowed itself upon his shoulder. "Let us part, and carry tender remembrances of each other through our lives. No man has ever loved a woman more devoutly than I love you."

"And no woman has ever loved a man with more reverence and more passion than I love you, Jack—my own dear Jack," she said.

Their lips slowly approached each other, until they met in a fierce long passionate caress. It was the first time he had kissed her upon the lips—their kiss, alas! of long farewell.

"Good-bye, my love. Farewell," he whispered hoarsely. "Though parted from you in the future I shall be yours always—always. Remember me—sometimes."

"Remember you!" she wailed. "How can I ever forget?"

"No, dear heart," he whispered. "Do not forget, remember—remember that we love each other—that I shall love you always—always. Farewell!"

Again he bent and kissed her lips. They were cold. She stood immovable. The blow of parting had entirely paralysed her senses.

Once more he pressed his hot lips to hers.

"May Providence protect and help us both, my beloved," he whispered, and then with a last, long, yearning look upon the sad white countenance that had held him in such fascination, he slowly released her.

He caught up her soft white hand, kissing it reverently, as had been his habit ever since he had known her.

Then he turned, hard-faced and determined, struggling within himself, and next second the door had closed upon him, and she was left alone.

"Jack! My Jack!" she gasped. "Gone!" and grasping the edge of the table to steady herself, she stood staring straight before her.

Her future, she knew, was only a blank grey sea of despair.

Jack, the man whom she worshipped, the man whom she believed was honest, and for whom her pure affection was boundless, had gone out of her young life for ever.

WILLIAM LE QUEUX

Outside, a young Tuscan contadino, passing on to meet his love, was singing in a fine clear voice one of the old Florentine *stornelli*—those same love-songs sung in the streets of the Lily City ever since the Middle Ages. She listened:

> *Fiorin di mela!*
> *La mela e dolce e la sua buccia e amara,*
> *L'uomo gli e finto e la donna sincera.*
>
> *Fior di limone!*
> *Tre cose son difficili a lasciare:*
> *Il giuoco, l'amicizia, e il primo amore!*
>
> *Fior di licore!*
> *Licore e forte e non si puo incannare;*
> *Ma son piu forti le pene d'amore.*

She held her breath, then with sudden wild abandon, she flung herself upon the silken couch, and burying her face in its cushions gave herself up to a paroxysm of grief and despair.

Six weeks later.

Grey dawn was slowly spreading over the calm Mediterannean, the waters of which lazily lapped the golden shingle. Behind the distant blue the yellow sun was just peeping forth. At a spot upon the seashore about four miles from Leghorn, in the direction of the Maremma, five men had assembled, while at a little distance away, on the old sea-road to Rome, stood the hired motor-car which had brought one of them there.

The motive for their presence there at that early hour was not far to seek.

The men facing each other with their coats cast aside were the brown-bearded Marquess Giulio di San Rossore, and Prince Albert.

The latter, having left Florence, had learnt in Bologna of a vile, scandalous, and untrue story told of the Princess by the Marquess to the aristocratic idlers of the Florence Club, a story that was a foul and abominable lie, invented in order to besmirch the good name of a pure and unhappy woman.

On hearing it he had returned at once to the Lily City, gone to the Marquess's palazzo on the Lung' Arno, and struck him in the face before his friends. This was followed by a challenge, which Jack, although he knew little of firearms, was forced to accept.

Was he not champion and defender of the helpless and lonely woman he loved—the woman upon whom the Marquess had sworn within himself to be avenged?

And so the pair, accompanied by their seconds and a doctor, now faced each other, revolvers in their hands.

The Prince stood unflinching, his dark brow slightly contracted, his teeth hard set, his handsome countenance pale and serious.

As he raised his weapon he murmured to himself some words.

"For your honour, my own Angelica—my dear lost love!"

The signal was given an instant later, and two shots sounded in rapid succession.

Next moment it was seen that the Italian was hit, for he staggered, clutched at air, and fell forward upon his face, shot through the throat.

Quickly the doctor was kneeling at his side, but though medical aid was rendered so quickly, he never spoke again, and five minutes afterwards he was dead.

HALF AN HOUR LATER PRINCE Albert was driving the hired car for all he was worth across the great plain towards the marble-built city of Pisa to catch the express to Paris. From that day Jack Cross has concealed his identity, and has never been traced by the pretty Crown-Princess.

No doubt she often wonders what was the real status of the obscure good-looking young Englishman who spoke German so perfectly, who loved her devotedly, who fought bravely in vindication of her honour, and yet who afterwards so mysteriously disappeared into space.

These lines will convey to her the truth. What will she think?

IX

A Double Game

L ord Nassington drove his big red sixty horse-power six-cylinder "Napier" slowly up the Corso in Rome.

By his side was his smart chauffeur, Garrett, in dark-green livery with the hand holding a garland proper, the crest of the Nassingtons, upon his bright buttons.

It was four o'clock, the hour of the *passeggiata*, the hour when those wintering in the Eternal City go forth in carriages and cars to drive up and down the long, narrow Corso in order to see, and be seen, to exchange bows with each other, and to conclude the processional drive at slow pace owing to the crowded state of the street by a tour of the Pincian hill whence one obtains a magnificent view of Rome and the Tiber in the sunset.

Roman society is the most exclusive in the world. Your Roman princess will usually take her airing in her brougham with the windows carefully closed, even on a warm spring afternoon. She holds herself aloof from the crowd of wealthy foreigners, even though her great gaunt palazzo has been denuded of every picture and work of art years ago, and she lives with a *donna di casa* in four or five meagre rooms on the first floor, the remainder of the great place being unfurnished and untenanted.

There is more pitiful make-believe among the aristocracy of Rome than in any other city in the world. The old principessa, the marchesa, and the contessa keep themselves within their own little circle, and sneer at the wealthy foreigner and his blatant display of riches. One hears girls of the school-room discussing the social scale of passers-by, and disregarding them as not being "of the aristocracy" like themselves.

Truly the Eternal City is a complex one in winter, and the Corso at four o'clock, is the centre of it all. You know that slowly-passing almost funereal line of carriages, some of them very old and almost hearse-like, moving up and down, half of them emblazoned with coronets and shields—for the Italian is ever proud of his heraldry—while the other half hired conveyances, many of them ordinary cabs in which sit some of the wealthiest men and women in Europe who have come south to see the antiquities and to enjoy the sunshine.

Behind the lumbering old-fashioned brougham of a weedy marchesa, Lord Nassington drove his big powerful car at snail's pace, and almost silently. In such traffic the flexibility of the six-cylinder is at once appreciated.

Both Garrett and his master had their eyes about them, as though in search of some one.

A dozen times pretty women in furs bowed to Lord Nassington, who raised his motor-cap in acknowledgment. The smart, good-looking young peer had spent a couple of months there during the previous winter and had become immensely popular with the cosmopolitan world who gather annually in the Italian capital. Therefore, when he had arrived at the Excelsior, a week before, word had quickly gone round the hotels, clubs, pastrycooks, and *cafes* that the young English motoring milord had returned.

Upon the table of his luxurious little sitting-room at the hotel were lying a dozen or so invitations to dinners, receptions, the opera, and a luncheon-party out at Tivoli, while Charles, his man, had been busy spreading some picturesque gossip concerning his master.

For the nonce his Highness Prince Albert of Hesse-Holstein was *incognito*, and as was the case sometimes, he was passing as an English peer, about whose whereabouts, position, and estates Debrett was somewhat vague. According to that volume of volumes, Lord Nassington had let his ancestral seat in Northamptonshire, and lived in New Orleans. Therefore, his Highness had but little to fear from unwelcome inquiry. He spoke English as perfectly as he could speak German when occasion required, for to his command of languages his success had been in great measure due.

Such a fine car as his had seldom, if ever, been seen in Rome. It was part of his creed to make people gossip about him, for as soon as they talked they began to tumble over each other in their endeavour to make his acquaintance. Both Garrett and Charles always had some interesting fiction to impart to other servants, and so filter through to their masters and mistresses.

The story running round Rome, and being passed from mouth to mouth along the Corso, in Aregno's, in the Excelsior, and up among the idlers on the Pincio, was that that reckless devil-may-care young fellow in motor-coat and cap, smoking a cigar as he drove, had only a fortnight before played with maximums at Monte Carlo, and in one day alone had won over forty thousand pounds at roulette.

The rather foppishly dressed Italians idling along the Corso—every man a born gambler—were all interested in him as he passed. He was a favourite of fortune, and they envied him his good luck. And though they wore yellow gloves and patent-leather boots they yearned for a *terno* on the Lotto—the aspiration of every man, be he *conte* or *contadino*.

As his lordship approached the end of the long, narrow street close to the Porta del Popolo, Garrett gave him a nudge, and glancing at an oncoming carriage he saw in it two pretty dark-haired girls. One, the better looking of the pair, was about twenty-two, and wore rich sables, with a neat toque of the same fur. The other about three years her senior, wore a black hat, a velvet coat, and a boa of white Arctic fox. Both were delicate, refined-looking girls, and evidently ladies.

Nassington raised his cap and laughed, receiving nods and merry laughs of recognition in return.

"I wonder where they're going, Garrett?" he remarked after they had passed.

"Better follow them, hadn't we?" remarked the man.

A moment later, however, a humble cab passed, one of those little open victorias which the visitor to Rome knows so well, and in it was seated alone a middle-aged, rather red-faced English clergyman.

His lordship and he exchanged glances, but neither recognised each other.

"Good!" whispered the man at the wheel to his servant beside him. "So the Parson's arrived. He hasn't been long on the way from Berlin. I suppose he's keeping his eye upon the girls."

"Trust him," laughed the chauffeur. "You sent him the snap-shot, I suppose?"

"Of course. And it seems he's lost no time. He couldn't have arrived before five o'clock this morning."

"When Clayton's on a good thing he moves about as quickly as you do," the smart young English chauffeur remarked.

"Yes," his master admitted. "He's the most resourceful man I've ever known—and I've known a few. We'll take a run up the Pincio and back," and, without changing speed, he began to ascend the winding road which leads to the top of the hill.

Up there, they found quite a crowd of people whom Nassington had known the previous season.

Rome was full of life, merriment and gaiety. Carnival had passed, and the Pasqua was fast approaching; the time when the Roman season is at its gayest and when the hotels are full. The court receptions and balls at the Quirinale had brought the Italian aristocracy from the various cities, and the ambassadors were mostly at their posts because of the weekly diplomatic receptions.

Surely it is a strange world—that vain, silly, out-dressing world of Rome, where religion is only the cant of the popular confessor and the scandal of a promenade through St. Peter's or San Giovanni.

At the summit of the Pincio Lord Nassington pulled up the car close to the long stone balustrade, and as he did so a young Italian elegant, the Marquis Carlo di Rimini, stepped up and seizing his hand, was profuse in his welcome back to Rome.

The Englishman descended from the car, lit one of his eternal "Petroffs," and leaned upon the balustrade to chat and learn the latest scandal. The Marquis Carlo and he were fellow members of the Circolo Unione, one of the smartest clubs in Rome, and had played bridge together through many a night.

A whisper had once gone forth that the source of the over-dressed young noble's income was cards, but Nassington had always given him his due. He had never caught him cheating, and surely if he had cheated the Englishman would have known it.

As they stood there, gazing across the city below, the sky was aflame in all the crimson glory of the Roman sunset, and even as they spoke the Angelus had, of a sudden, clashed forth from every church tower, the bells clanging discordantly far and near.

It was the hour of the *venti-tre*, but in the city nobody cared. The patient toilers in the Campagna, however, the *contadini* in the fields and in the vineyards who had been working on the brown earth since the dawn, crossed themselves with a murmured prayer to the Madonna and prodded their ox-teams onward. In Rome itself nowadays, alas! the bells of the *venti-tre* of spring and winter only remind the gay, giddy cosmopolitan crowd that it is the hour for tea in the halls of the hotels, or the English tea-rooms in the Corso.

An hour later, when his lordship entered his room at the Excelsior, he found the Reverend Thomas Clayton seated in his armchair patiently smoking and awaiting him.

"By Jove! old chap. You got through quick," cried his lordship throwing off his coat and cap. "Well?"

"It's a soft thing—that's my opinion, the girl Velia is devilish pretty, and the cousin isn't half bad-looking. I haven't been idle. Got in at six—an hour late, of course, had a bath and breakfast and out. Saw a dozen people I know before noon, lunched at that little *trattoria* behind the post office where so many of the Deputies go, and learnt a lot. I'm no stranger here you know—lived here a year once—did a splendid bit of business, but had to slip. That was the year before we joined our forces."

"Well, what do you know?"

"Boncini, her father is, of course, Minister of the Interior, and a pretty slick customer. Made pots of money, they say, and only keeps in office by bribery. Half the money subscribed by charitable people on behalf of the sufferers from the recent earthquake down in Calabria went into his pocket. He bought a big villa, and fine estate, close to Vallombrosa a month or so afterwards."

His lordship grunted.

"Picks up what he can?" he remarked. "One of us—it seems!"

"Exactly. And to do any business, we'll have to be pretty cute. He's already seen and heard a lot of you, and he knows that you've met his pretty daughter. Perhaps he fancies you'll marry her."

"The only use of marriage to a man, my dear Clayton," exclaimed the devil-may-care adventurer blowing a cloud of cigarette smoke from his lips, "is to enable him to make a settlement upon his wife, and so wriggle from the clutches of his creditors." The Parson laughed. Regarding the marriage tie his Highness, or "his lordship" rather as he was at that moment called, was always sarcastic.

"Really, old chap, you spread your fame wherever you go. Why, all Rome is talking about this wonderful coup of yours at Monte."

"It was Garrett's idea. He told them down in the garage, and Charles told a lady's maid or two, I think. Such things are quite easy when one starts out upon a big bluff. But if what you've discovered about his Excellency the Minister Boncini is really true, then I shall alter my tactics somewhat. I mean that I must make the dark-haired daughter a stepping-stone to her father."

"With care—my dear fellow," exclaimed the Parson in that calm, clerical drawl habitual to him. "The girl's cousin, Miss Ethel Thorold, is English. The sister of the Signora Boncini married a man on the London Stock Exchange, named Thorold."

"That's awkward," exclaimed his lordship thoughtfully, "upsets my plans."

"But he's dead," the Parson declared. His companion nodded satisfaction.

"Now Miss Ethel is, I've found, a rather religiously inclined young person—all praise to her. So I shall succeed very soon in getting to know her. Indeed, as you've already made her acquaintance you might introduce me as the vicar of some living within your gift."

"Excellent—I will."

"And what's your plans?"

"They're my own secrets at present, Tommy," was the other's quick answer. "You're at the Grand, aren't you? Well, for the present, we must be strangers—till I approach you. Understand?"

"Of course. Give me five hundred francs will you. I'm short?"

His lordship unlocked his heavy steel despatch-box and gave his friend five one-hundred franc notes without a word.

Then they reseated themselves, and with Charles, the faithful valet, leaning against the edge of the table smoking a cigarette with them, their conversation was both interesting and confidential.

A fortnight went by, and Rome was in the middle of her Pasqua *fetes*. The night was perfect, bright and star-lit.

The great gilded ballroom of the huge old Peruzzi Palace, in the Via Nazionale, the residence of his Excellency the Minister Boncini, was thronged by a brilliant crowd, among whom Lord Nassington made his way, ever and anon bowing over some woman's hand.

The bright uniforms, the glittering stars and coloured ribbons worn by the men, and the magnificent toilettes of the women combined to form a perfect phantasmagoria of colour beneath the huge crystal electroliers.

The political and social world of Rome had gathered there at the monthly reception of his Excellency, the rather stout grey-bearded man with the broad cerise-and-white ribbon of the Order of the Crown of Italy across his shirt-front, and the diamond star upon his coat. His Lordship strode through the huge painted *salons* with their heavy gilt mirrors and giant palms, and approached the man of power in that complex nation, modern Italy.

At that moment his Excellency was chatting with the French Ambassador, but on the Englishman's approach he turned to him exclaiming in French:

"Ah! Lord Nassington! I am so pleased you could come. Velia told me of the slight accident to your car yesterday. I hope you were not hurt at all?"

"Oh! no," laughed the debonair young man. "I had perhaps a close shave. My car is a rather fast one, and I was driving recklessly on the Maremma Road—a sharp turn—and I ran down a bank, that's all. The car will be all right by to-morrow."

"Ah, milord. The automobile is an invention of the future, without a doubt."

"Most certainly. Indeed, as a matter of fact, I thought of making a suggestion to your Excellency—one which I believe would be most acceptable to the Italian nation. But, of course, here it's quite impossible to talk."

"Then come to-morrow morning to my private cabinet at the Ministry—or better still, here to luncheon, and we can chat."

His Lordship expressed his thanks, and then moved off in search of the pretty Velia.

For the greater part of the evening he dangled at the side of the good-looking girl in turquoise chiffon, having several waltzes with her and afterwards strolling out upon the balcony and sitting there beneath the starlight.

"What a charming man your friend Mr. Clayton is!" exclaimed the girl in English, as they were sitting together apart from the others. "Papa is delighted with him."

"Oh, yes—a most excellent fellow for a parson," his Lordship laughed, and then their conversation turned upon motors and motoring.

"How is your shoulder this evening?" she inquired.

"Not at all painful," he declared. "It's nearly all right again. The car will be ready for the road to-morrow afternoon. I'm lunching with you here, and I wonder if you and your cousin will come with me for a run out to Tivoli afterwards?"

"I should be delighted," she said. "Our car is only a sixteen 'Fiat' you know, and we never travel faster than a cab. It would be such fun to have a run in your beautiful 'sixty'! I don't suppose papa would object."

"I'll ask him to come, too," laughed the man by whom she had become so attracted, and then they returned for another dance. Her ears were open, and so were those of the shrewd old man who controlled the internal affairs of the kingdom. There were whisperings everywhere, regarding the young man's wealth, his good fortune, and his aristocratic family.

His Excellency had not failed to notice the attraction which the young English peer held for his daughter, and also that he paid her marked attention. Therefore the old man was extremely self-satisfied.

Next day after the little family luncheon at the Peruzzi Palace at which only the Signora Boncini, Velia, and her cousin Ethel were present, his Excellency took his guest aside in his small private room for their coffee and cigarettes.

Nassington offered the Minister one of his "Petroffs" which was pronounced excellent.

Then, after a brief chat, his Lordship came to the point.

"The fact is, your Excellency," he said, "a suggestion has occurred to me by which the Italian Government could, while benefiting the country to an enormous extent, at the same time secure a very handsome sum annually towards the exchequer."

"How?" inquired the shrewd old statesman.

"By granting to a group of substantial English financiers a monopoly for the whole of the motor-transport of Italy," his Lordship replied, blowing a cloud of smoke from his lips. "You have, in every part of the kingdom, great tracts of productive country without railways or communications. At the same time you have excellent roads everywhere. The concession, if granted, would be taken up by a great firm who handle motor-traction, and certain districts, approved by your government, would be opened up as an experiment. Would not that be of national benefit?"

"I see," replied the statesman stroking his beard thoughtfully. "And you propose that the earnings of the syndicate should be taxed by our Department of Finance?"

"Exactly."

A keen, eager look was in the old man's eyes, and did not pass unrecognised by the man lounging in the armchair in picturesque indolence.

"And suppose we were to go into the matter," the Minister said. "What attitude would your Lordship adopt?"

"Well—my attitude would be this," Nassington replied. "You give me the proper concession, signed by the Ministers, and I guarantee to find the capital among my personal friends in financial circles in London. But on one condition," he added. "That the whole matter is kept secret. Afterwards, I venture to think the whole country, and especially the rural population will be grateful to your Excellency."

Boncini instantly saw that such a move would increase his popularity immensely in the country. The idea appealed to him. If Lord Nassington's friends were ready with capital, they would also be ready, he foresaw, with a very substantial sum for bribery. Personally he cared not a rap for the progress of Italy. While in office, he intended to amass as much as he could. He was the all-powerful man in Italy at the moment. But next year he might be—well where more than one Minister as powerful as he, had found himself—in prison!

"There are difficulties," his Excellency said with some hesitation. "My colleagues in the Cabinet may raise objections. They may not see matters in the light that I do. And the Senate, too—they—"

"I know. I quite understand your Excellency," exclaimed his Lordship, lowering his voice into a confidential whisper. "Let us speak quite frankly. In a gigantic matter of this sort—a matter of millions—certain palm-oil has to be applied—eh?"

The old man smiled, placed his hands together and nodded.

"Then let us go further," Lord Nassington went on. "I submit in all deference—and, of course, this conversation is strictly in private between us, that should you think favourably of the scheme—my friends should secretly place a certain sum, say one hundred thousand pounds sterling at your Excellency's command, to apply in whatever way you may think best to secure the success of the proposition. Are you willing?"

The old man rose from his chair, and standing before the younger man stretched forth his hand.

"Perfectly," he said as the other grasped it. "We agree."

"And if I frame the form of the concession you will agree to it and, in return for an undertaking of the payment of one hundred thousand pounds into—where shall we say—into the head office of the Credit Lyonnais in Paris in the name of your nominee, you will hand me the legal concession confirmed by the Italian Government?"

"I agree to hand you the necessary documents within a fortnight," responded his Excellency. "The adoption of motor-traction in the remote districts for bringing wine and produce to the nearest railways will be of the greatest boon to our country."

"Of course, my friends will leave the whole of the details, as far as finance on your side is concerned, to you," his Lordship said. "You can administer the official backsheesh so much better than any one else."

"Within a fortnight you shall be able, my lord, to hand your friends the actual concession for motor-transport throughout the kingdom of Italy."

For another half-hour they discussed certain details, Lord Nassington talking big about his wealthy friends in London. Then, with his daughter and his niece, his Excellency accepted his guest's invitation for a run out to Tivoli to take tea.

The "sixty" ran splendidly, and the Minister of the Interior was delighted. Before the girls, however, no business was discussed. Velia's father, who, by the way had once been a clever advocate in Milan, knew better than to mention affairs of State before women.

During the run, however, he found himself counting upon the possibilities of Velia's marriage with the amiable young English aristocrat who, upon his own initiative, had offered to place one hundred thousand sterling unreservedly in his hands. At most the present Cabinet could last another year, and then—well, oblivion if before then he did not line his nest snugly enough. The thought of the poor widows and orphans and starving populace down in Calabria sometimes caused him a twinge of conscience. But he only laughed and placed it aside. He had even been unscrupulous, and this young English peer was his friend, he would use to best advantage.

Though Lord Nassington was an eligible husband for his daughter, yet, after all, he was not a business man, but a wealthy "mug." As such he intended to treat him.

At the little *cafe*, near the falls, where they took tea the conversation ran on motors and motoring, but his Excellency could not disguise from himself that the young peer was entirely fascinated by his good-looking daughter.

They lingered there until the mists began to rise and the red afterglow was fast disappearing; then they ran past the sulphur springs and on the broad highway back to the Eternal City at such a pace that his Excellency's breath was taken away. But Lord Nassington drove, and notwithstanding the accident of two days previously, the Minister felt himself perfectly safe in his hands.

Three weeks went by. His Lordship took a flying visit to London, and quickly returned. Both he and the highly respectable clergyman of the English church, the Reverend Thomas Clayton, became daily visitors at the Peruzzi Palace. In the Corso the pretty Signorina Boncini and her cousin were often seen in his Lordship's car, and already the gossip-loving world of Rome began to whisper that an engagement was about to take place.

The valet, Charles, also made a quick journey to London and back, and many telegrams were exchanged with a registered cable address in London.

WILLIAM LE QUEUX

One afternoon, in the private cabinet of that colossal building, the Ministry of the Interior, his Excellency handed his English friend a formidable document bearing many signatures with the official seal of the Government embossed, a document which gave Lord Nassington the exclusive right to establish motor-transport for both merchandise and passengers upon every highway in the kingdom. In exchange, his Excellency received an undertaking signed by a responsible firm in the City of London to place to the account of Madame Boncini at the Credit Lyonnais in Paris the respectable sum of one hundred thousand pounds within seven days.

"I shall return at once to London," his Lordship said replacing the formidable document in its envelope, "and in exchange for this, the financial group will at once pay in the sum to Madame's account in Paris, while the actual sum for the concession will be paid here, in Rome, to the Department of Finance, on the date stipulated."

"Benissimo," replied the grey-bearded statesman, holding one of his long Toscano cigars in the candle which he had lit for that purpose. "It is all settled. You will dine with us at home to-night."

His Lordship accepted, and after further discussion regarding several minor details of the concession he rose and left.

That night he dined at the Peruzzi Palace, seated next his Excellency's charming daughter, and next morning left the Excelsior in his big red car, to run as far as Bologna and thence return to London by rail.

With her father's consent Velia her cousin and Signora Ciullini, her aunt, accompanied him and they set out across the Maremma for marble-built Pisa, where the girls were to return home by rail.

The more direct road was by Orvieto, but it is not so good as that wide, open road across the fever-marshes of the Maremma, therefore his Lordship resolved on taking the latter.

The day was glorious, and travelling for all they were worth with only two stops to refill with petrol, they ran into Pisa late that same night. The sleeping-car express from Paris to Rome was due in half an hour, therefore after a scrambling meal at the Victoria the aristocratic motorist saw the girls and their aunt safely into the train—kissing Velia in secret by the way—and waving them "addio," watched the train glide out of the big echoing station again.

Then, with Garrett at his side, he turned the big car with its glaring head-lights out of the big gates through the town along the Lung' Arno and into the high road for Florence.

In the early morning he passed through the dimly-lit deserted streets of the City of the Medici, and away beyond, through Prato, to the foot-hills of the Appenines where he began to ascend that wonderfully engineered military road which runs, with many dangerous turns for motorists, high up across the mountain range, and ends in the long colonnaded street of old Bologna.

It was noon ere he drew into the Piazza before the station, and giving Garrett instructions to continue on to Milan and north to Berlin where the car was to be garaged, he took the afternoon express for the frontier at Chiasso, travelling thence *via* Bale to Ostend and London.

On entering his snug chambers at five o'clock one afternoon, he found Charles and the Parson smoking and awaiting him. That evening the trio held a long and earnest consultation. The official document was carefully examined, and the names of many city firms mentioned. The Parson seemed to possess a remarkable intimate knowledge of city life.

"Old Boncini is a clever old thief," remarked the reverend gentleman. "He's feathering his nest finely—all the money in his wife's name."

"My dear fellow, half the Cabinet Ministers of Europe only use their political influence in order to gain fortune. Except the British Government there isn't a single one which isn't corrupt."

"Well, Albert, my dear boy, you certainly seem to have got hold of a good thing," the Parson remarked. "His Corrupt Excellency seems to place every faith in you. Your four-flush was admirable all the time."

"It took a bit of working, I can tell you. He's as slick as a rat."

"But he doesn't suspect anything wrong?"

"Hasn't the slightest idea of it, my dear Tommy. He fancies I'm going to marry his daughter. The fat old mother is already imagining herself mother-in-law of a British peer."

"Yes. All Rome knows that you've fallen in love with the pretty Velia, and that you've told her the tale. What a fellow you are with the ladies."

"Why?" he laughed taking a cigarette. "They are all very charming and delightful. But in my career I generally manage to make them useful. It's really remarkable what a woman will do in the interests of the man whom she fancies is in love with her. Fortunately, perhaps, for me, I've only been in love once."

"And it resulted in a tragedy," remarked the Parson quietly, knowing that he referred to the Princess.

His Lordship sighed, flinging himself down in his armchair, worn out by long travel.

WILLIAM LE QUEUX

"My dear boy," he said with a weary sigh, "if I ever got married I'd soon go mothy—everybody does. Married people, whatever their position in life, settle down into the monotonous groove that is the death of all romance. Before a man marries a girl they have little dinners together at restaurants, and little suppers, and all seems so bright and gay under the red candle-shades. We see it on every hand. But why should it all be dropped for heavy meals and dulness, just because two people who like one another have the marriage service read over them?"

The Parson laughed. His friend was always amusing when he discussed the question of matrimony.

During the next four days his Lordship, in the character of Mr. Tremlett—as he was known in certain circles in the City—was busy with financiers to whom he offered the concession. His story was that it had been granted by the Italian Government to his cousin, Lord Nassington, and that the latter had given it into his hands to negotiate.

In the various quarters where he offered it the concession caused a flutter of excitement. The shrewdest men in the City saw that it was a good thing, and one after the other craved a day to think it over. It really was one of the best things that had been offered for a long time. The terms required by the Italian Government were not at all heavy, and huge profits were certain to be made out of such a monopoly.

The great tracts of fertile land in central and southern Italy would, by means of motor-transport, be opened up to trade, while Tremlett's picturesque story of how the concession had been snatched away from a strong group of German financiers was, to more than one capitalist, most fascinating.

Indeed he saw half a dozen of the most influential men in the City, and before a week was out he had got together a syndicate which could command a couple of millions sterling.

They were all of them shrewd men, however, and he saw that it behoved him to be on the alert. There is such a thing in the City as to be "frozen out" of a good thing, even when one holds it in one's hand.

By dint of close watching and clever observation, he discovered something, and this caused him to ponder deeply. The syndicate expressed themselves ready to treat, but for the present he was rather unwilling.

Some hitches occurred on technicalities, and there were a number of meetings to consider this point and that. By all this Mr. Tremlett saw that he was losing time, and at the same moment he was not keeping faith with the old statesman concerning the amount to be paid into Madame's account in Paris. At last one morning, after the Parson had left for an unknown destination, he took a taxi-cab down to the City with a bold resolve.

The five prominent financiers were seated together in an office in Old Broad Street when Mr. Tremlett, leaning back in his chair, said:

"Well, gentlemen, it seems that we are as far away as ever from coming to terms, and I think it useless to discuss the matter further. I must take the business elsewhere."

"We admit," exclaimed an old bald man, a director of one of London's largest banks, "that it is a good thing, but the price you ask is prohibitive."

"I can get it in Paris. So I shall go there," was Tremlett's prompt reply.

"Well," exclaimed the bald man, "let's get straight to facts. Your cousin, Lord Nassington, wants sixty thousand pounds in cash for the concession and a percentage of shares, and that, we have decided, is far too much."

"Those are his figures," remarked Tremlett.

"Well, then all we can offer is one-half—thirty thousand in cash and ten per cent, of shares in the company," said the other, "and," he added, "I venture to say that ours is a very handsome offer." Tremlett rose from the table with a sarcastic smile.

"Let us talk of something else," he said. "I haven't come down here to the City to play at marbles."

"Well," asked the old man who was head of the syndicate. "What are your lowest terms?"

"I've stated them."

"But you don't give us time to inquire into the business," he complained.

"I have shown you the actual concession. Surely you are satisfied with it!"

"We are."

"And I've told you the conditions of the contract. Yet you postpone your decision from day to day!"

The five men glanced at each other, rather uneasily Tremlett thought.

"Well," he went on. "This is the last time I shall attend any meeting. We come to a decision this morning, or the matter is off. You, gentlemen, don't even show *bona fides*!"

WILLIAM LE QUEUX

"Well, I think you know something of the standing of all of us," the banker said.

"That is so. But my cousin complains that he, having offered the concession, you on your part do not attempt to show your intention to take it up."

"But we do. We wish to fix a price to-day," remarked another of the men.

"A price, gentlemen, which is ridiculous," declared Tremlett.

The five men consulted together in undertones, and in the end advanced their offer five thousand pounds. At this Tremlett only shook his shoulders. A further five thousand was the result, and a long discussion followed.

"Have you your cousin's authority to accept terms?" asked one of the capitalists.

"I have."

"Then forty thousand is all we can offer."

Tremlett hesitated.

"I have a number of payments to make for bribery," he declared. "It will take half that sum."

"That does not concern us, my dear sir," said the bald-headed banker. "We know that a concession such as this can only be obtained by the judicious application of palm-oil."

"But I must pay out nearly twenty thousand almost immediately," Tremlett said.

At this there was another long discussion, whereupon at last the bald-headed man said:

"If the payment of the bribes is imperative at once, we will, on consideration of the business being to-day concluded on a forty thousand pound basis, hand you over half the sum at once. That is our final decision."

Tremlett was not at all anxious. Indeed he took up his hat and cane, and was about to leave, when two of the men present exercising all their powers of persuasion, got him at last to reseat himself and to accept the sum of twenty thousand pounds down, and twenty thousand thirty days from that date, in addition to a percentage of shares in the company to be formed.

Memoranda were drawn up and signed by all parties, whereupon Tremlett took from his pocket the official concession and handed it to the head of the syndicate.

That same afternoon, before four o'clock, he had received a draft for twenty thousand pounds, with which he had opened an account in Charles's name at a branch bank in Tottenham Court Road.

At nine o'clock that same evening he left for Paris, putting up at a small obscure hotel near the Gare du Nord where he waited in patience for nearly a week.

Once or twice he telegraphed, and received replies.

Late one night the Parson arrived unexpectedly and entered the shabby bedroom where his Lordship was lounging in an armchair reading a French novel.

He sprung up at the entrance of the round-faced cleric, saying:

"Well, Tommy? How has it gone? Tell me quick."

"You were quite right," exclaimed the clergyman. "The crowd in London were going behind your back. They sent two clever men to Rome, and those fellows tried to deal with Boncini direct. They arrived the day after I did, and they offered him an extra twenty thousand if he would rescind your concession, and grant them a new one. Boncini was too avaricious and refused, so they then treated with you."

"I got twenty thousand," remarked his Lordship, "got it in cash safe in the bank."

"Yes. I got your wire."

"And what did you do?" asked his friend.

"I acted just as you ordered. As soon as I was convinced that the people in London were working behind our backs, I laid my plans. Then when your wire came that you'd netted the twenty thousand, I acted."

"How?"

"I took all the signed proof you gave me of old Boncini's acceptance of the bribe, and of Madame's banking account at the Credit Lyonnais, to that scoundrel Ricci, the red-hot Socialist deputy in the Chamber."

"And what did he say?" asked his Lordship breathlessly.

"Say!" echoed the other. "He was delighted. I spent the whole evening with him. Next day, he and his colleagues held a meeting, and that afternoon he asked in the Chamber whether his Excellency, the Minister of the Interior, had not been bribed by an English syndicate and put a number of similarly awkward questions. The Government had a difficulty in evading the truth, but imagine the sensation when he waved proofs of the corruptness of the Cabinet in the face of the House. A terrible scene of disorder ensued, and the greatest sensation has been caused. Look here,"—and he handed his friend a copy of *Le Soir*.

WILLIAM LE QUEUX

At the head of a column on the front page were the words in French, "Cabinet Crisis in Italy," and beneath, a telegram from Rome announcing that in consequence of the exposure of grave scandals by the Socialists, the Italian Cabinet had placed their resignations in the hands of his Majesty.

"Serve that old thief Boncini right," declared his Lordship. "He was ready to sell me for an extra few thousands, but I fortunately got in before him. I wonder if the pretty Velia has still any aspirations to enter the British peerage?"

And both men laughed merrily at thought of the nice little nest-egg they had managed to filch so cleverly from the hands of five of the smartest financiers in the City of London.

X

Love and the Outlaw

B y Jove!" I exclaimed, "Who's the girl, Prince?"

"That's Zorka. Pretty, isn't she, Diprose?"

"Pretty!" I echoed. "Why, she's the most beautiful woman I've seen in the whole of Servia!"

We were driving slowly together in the big "sixty" up the main street of the city of Belgrade, and were at that moment passing the iron railings of the palace of his Majesty King Peter. It was a bright dry afternoon, and the boulevard was thronged by a smart crowd, ladies in Paris-made gowns, and officers in brilliant uniforms and white crosses with red and white ribbons on their breasts.

Belgrade, though constantly in a ferment of political storm and stress, and where rumours of plots against the throne are whispered nightly in the corners of drawing-rooms, is, nevertheless, a quiet and pleasant place. Its picturesque situation, high up upon its rocks at the confluence of the Save with the Danube, its pretty Kalemegdan gardens, its wide boulevard and its pleasant suburbs, combine to offer considerable attraction to the foreigner. It is the gateway to eastern Europe. At quiet old Semlin—or Zimony—on the opposite bank of the Danube is Hungary, the fringe of western Europe: in Belgrade the Orient commences.

I happened to be at the Grand at Belgrade, and had there found the Prince, or Reggie Martin, as he always called himself in the Balkans. He was idling, with no apparent object. Only the faithful Garrett was with him. Both Charles and the Parson he had left behind in London. Therefore, I concluded that the reason of his presence in Servia was to learn some diplomatic secret or other, for he only went to the Balkans with that one object.

Of his business, the Prince seldom, if ever, spoke. Even from his most intimate associate, the Rev. Thomas Clayton, he usually concealed his ulterior object until it was attained. The Parson, Garrett, and Charles acted in blind obedience. They were paid to obey, not to reason, he often told them.

And so it was that although we had been together a week in King

Peter's capital, I was in entire ignorance of the reason of his presence there.

As we had brought the big car slowly along the boulevard, a dark-eyed peasant-girl, with a face full of wondrous beauty, had nodded saucily to him, and this had caused me to notice and admire her. Belgrade is full of pretty women, but not one was half so handsome. She was about twenty, I judged, and the manner in which her hair was dressed with the gay-coloured handkerchief upon it was in the style of unmarried women.

"I want to speak to her, to ask her a question," the Prince said suddenly, after we had gone some distance. And driving the car down into the square we turned back in order to overtake her.

"An old friend of yours?" I inquired.

"Yes, my dear Diprose," he laughed as he touched the button of the electric horn. "And a girl with a very remarkable past. Her story would make a good novel—by Jove it would."

Five minutes later we had overtaken her, and pulled up at the kerb. The girl blushed and appeared confused as my companion, stopping the car, got down and stood at her side with his motor-cap raised. He spoke to her in his best Servian, for he knew a smattering of that difficult language, and appeared to be inviting her to enter the car and come for a run.

At first she was disinclined to accept the invitation, because of the crowd of smart promenaders. She was probably shy at being seen in the company of two foreigners. At last her curiosity as to what conveyance by automobile might be got the better of her, and she reluctantly entered the door held open for her.

Then Reggie introduced us, and got back to his seat at the wheel, I mounting again to my place beside him.

In a few minutes we were out on the broad Semendria road, a fine well-kept military highway, and on getting clear of the town, put on a "move" until the speedometer before me registered fifty miles an hour.

Zorka, now alone with us, clapped her hands with childish delight. She was an Eastern beauty of rare type, with full red lips, magnificent luminous eyes, and a pink and white complexion that any woman of Mayfair would envy.

Ten miles from Belgrade, we stopped at a small wine-shop and had some refreshment. She sat at the little table before us laughing at me because we could not understand each other. In lieu of paying the rustic beauty compliments, I raised my glass and bowed. She accepted my homage with queenly grace. Indeed, in her peasant costume of scarlet and black, with golden sequins on the bodice, she reminded me of a heroine of opera.

We sat in the little garden above the broad blue Danube until the sun grew golden with departing day, the Prince chatting with her and laughing merrily. He seemed to be asking many questions, while I, in my curiosity, kept pestering him to tell the story of our beautiful companion—the story which he had declared to be so remarkable and romantic.

He had offered her one of his "Petroffs" from his gold cigarette-case, and she was smoking with the air of one accustomed to the use of tobacco. Our eyes met suddenly, and blowing a cloud of smoke from her pretty lips she suddenly burst out laughing. Apparently she was enjoying that unconventional meeting to its full bent. She had never before ridden in a motor-car—indeed, there are but few in Servia—and the rush through the air had exhilarated her. I noted her well-formed hands, her splendid bust, and her slim, graceful figure, and I longed to hear her story. The Prince possessed, indeed, a wide circle of friends ranging from princes of the blood down to peasants.

At last he made some remarks, whereupon our delightful little companion grew suddenly silent, her great dark eyes fixed upon me.

"Zorka is not Servian, Diprose," the Prince began. "She's Turkish. And this meeting to-day has recalled to me memories, of a strange and very remarkable incident which occurred to me not so very long ago." And then he went on to relate the following chapter of his amazing life-story. I will here record it in his own words:

That silent night was glorious. I shall preserve its memory for ever.

High up to that mountain fastness I was the first stranger to ascend, for I was the guest of a wild tribe of Albanian brigands, those men of the Skreli who from time to time hold up travellers to ransom, and against whom the Turkish Government are powerless.

It was a weird, never-to-be-forgotten experience, living with those tall, handsome fellows in white skin-tight woollen trousers with big snake-like bands running up the legs, black furry boleros, and white fezes. Every man was armed to the teeth with great silver-hilted pistols and long knives in their belts, and nobody went a dozen yards without his rifle ready loaded.

Ever since the days before we were together at Cheltenham, Diprose,

I had read stories of brigands, but here was the real thing—the free-booters of the mountains, who would never let me go about without a dozen men as guard, lest I should be mistaken for a stranger and "picked off" by one of the tribe lurking behind a rock. Life is, indeed, cheap in the Skreli country, that great range of inaccessible mountains east of gallant little Montenegro.

On that night in the early autumn I was seated upon a rock with a tall, thin, wiry, but handsome, young man, named Luk, known in his tribe as "The Open Eye," whom the great chieftain, Vatt Marashi, had given me as head of my body-guard, while beside was the dark-faced Albanian who, speaking Italian, acted as my guide and interpreter. Zorka was spinning her flax close by.

In the domain of his Imperial Majesty the Sultan, the moon seems to shine with far greater brilliancy than it does anywhere else in the world, and surely the panorama of high mountain and deep dark valley there spread before us was a veritable stage-picture, while the men at my side were as romantic looking a pair as could be found anywhere in real life.

Many times, as at night I lay down upon my humble bed of leaves, had I reflected how insecure was my position, and how easily my hosts could break their word, hold me to ransom, and worry the Foreign Office. Yet, let me here assert that all, from the chieftain, down to the humblest tribesman, treated me with a kindness, courtesy, and forethought, that, from the first, caused me to admire them. They might be brigands, and the blood-curdling stories of their cruelty might possibly be true, but they were, without doubt, a most gentlemanly gang of ruffians.

We had eaten our evening meal, and were sitting in the calm night smoking cigarettes, prior to turning in. The two men beside me had placed their rifles upon the ground, where the moonbeams glinted along the bright barrels, and our conversation had become exhausted.

Below, in that dark valley, ran the mule-track to Ipek, therefore day and night it was watched for passing travellers, as indeed were all the paths at the confines of the territory over which my friend Vatt Marashi, defiant of the Turks, ruled so firmly and yet so justly.

Luk, rolling a fresh cigarette, was making some remark to Palok, my guide, in his peculiar soft-sounding but unwritten language, when it suddenly occurred to me to ask him to give me some little reminiscence of his own adventurous life.

He was silent for a few moments, his keen gaze upon the shining rifle-barrel before him, then, with Palok translating into Italian, he told me the story of how he earned his nickname of "The Open Eye."

About two years before, when his tribe were at feud with their neighbours, the powerful Kastrati, who live in the opposite range of mountains, he was one dark night with a party of his fellow tribesmen in ambush, expecting a raid from their enemies. The false alarms were several when, of a sudden, Luk discerned a dark figure moving slowly in the gloom. Raising his rifle he was on the point of firing when some impulse seized him to stay his hand and shout a challenge.

The reply was a frightened one—and in Turkish.

Luk came forth from his hiding-place, and a few seconds later, to his great surprise, encountered the stranger, who proved to be a woman wearing her veil, and enshrouded by an ugly black shawl wrapped about her. He knew sufficient Turkish to demand her name, and whence she had come, but she refused to satisfy him. She had already recognised by his dress, that he was of the tribe of the Skreli, therefore she knew that she had fallen into the hands of enemies.

"Speak!" he cried, believing her to be a spy from the Kastrati. "Tell me who sent you here to us? Whither are you going?"

"I know not," was her reply in a sweet voice which told him at once that she was quite young, and he, being unmarried, became instantly interested.

"Where are you from?" he asked, expecting that she had come from Skodra, the nearest Turkish town.

"From Constantinople," was her reply.

"Constantinople!" gasped Luk, to whom the capital was so far off as to be only a mere city of legend. It was, indeed, many hundred leagues away. In the darkness he could not see her eyes. He could only distinguish that the lower part of her face was veiled like that of all Mahommedan women.

"And you have come here alone?" he asked.

"Yes, alone. I—I could not remain in Constantinople longer. Am I still in Turkey?"

"Nominally, yes. But the Sultan does not rule us here. We, of the Skreli, are Christians, and our country is a free one—to ourselves, but not to our captives."

"Ah!" she said with failing heart. "I see! I am your captive—eh? I have heard in Constantinople how you treat the Turks whom you capture."

"You may have heard many stories, but I assure you that the Skreli never maltreat a woman," was the brigand's proud answer. "This path is unsafe for you, and besides it is my duty to take you to our chief Vatt Marashi that he may decide whether we give you safe conduct."

"No, no!" she implored. "I have heard of him. Take pity upon me—a defenceless woman! I—I thought to escape from Turkey. I have no passport, so I left the train and hoped to get across the mountains into Montenegro, where I should be free."

"Then you have escaped from your harem—eh?" asked Luk, his curiosity now thoroughly aroused.

"Yes. But I have money here with me—and my jewels. I will pay you—pay you well, if you will help me. Ah! you do not know!"

Luk was silent for a moment.

"When a woman is in distress the Skreli give their assistance without payment," was his reply, and then, as day was breaking, he led her up the steep and secret paths to that little settlement where we now were—the headquarters of the all-powerful Vatt Marashi.

At the latter's orders she unwound the veil from her face, disclosing the beautiful countenance of a Turkish girl of eighteen, and when she took off her cloak it was seen that beneath she wore a beautiful harem dress, big, baggy trousers of rich mauve and gold brocade, and a little bolero of amaranth velvet richly embroidered with gold. Upon her neck were splendid emeralds, pearls, and turquoises, and upon her wrists fine bracelets encrusted with diamonds.

She stood in the lowly hut before the chief and her captor Luk, a vision of perfect beauty—looking "a veritable houri as promised by Mahommed," as Luk put it.

Vatt Marashi listened to her story. She had, she told him, escaped from her father's harem because she was betrothed, as is usual in Turkey, to a man whom she had never seen. She had taken money from the place where one of the black eunuchs hoarded it, and with the assistance of a young officer, a cousin of hers, had succeeded in leaving the capital in the baggage-waggon of the Orient Express. Unable to procure a passport, however, she dare not attempt to cross the frontier into Bulgaria, for she would at once be detected, refused permission to travel, and sent back. For a Turkish woman to attempt to leave Turkey in that manner the punishment is death. So at some small station near the frontier, the name of which she did not know, she had, under cover of night, left the train, and taken to the mountains. For four days she had wandered alone, until Luk had discovered her.

"And what was done with her?" I inquired, much interested.

"Well," replied my companion. "She elected to remain with us, our chief giving her assurance that she would be well and honourably treated. He pointed out that had she been a man he would have demanded of the Sultan a heavy ransom for her release, but as she was a defenceless woman, and alone, she was not to remain a prisoner. If she cared to accept the offer of the protection of the Skreli, then every man of his tribe would defend her, and her honour to the last drop of blood remaining in their veins. The word of Skreli, once given, is, as you know, never broken."

And his was no idle boast. The code of honour among the tribes of Northern Albania would put even ours of England to the blush. The Skreli are very bad enemies, but they are, as I know from personal experience, most firm and devoted friends.

"And so it came about," Luk went on, "that Zorka—that was her name—was placed in my mother's charge, and discarded her veil, as do our own women. Well—I suppose I may confess it—I loved her. It was only to be expected, I suppose, for she was very lovely, and every unmarried man in the tribe was her devoted admirer. Though she lived with us, no word of affection passed between us. Why should it? Would it not have been folly?—she the daughter of a great Pasha who was seeking for her all over Turkey, and I a poor humble tribesman, and a Christian into the bargain? And so a year went over. We often walked together, and the others envied me my friendship with the delicate and beautiful girl who preferred our free untrammelled life of the mountains to the constant confinement of her father's harem on the Bosphorus. Unlike that of our women, her skin was lily white, and her little hands as soft as satin. Ah! yes, I loved her with all my soul, though I never dared to tell her so. She became as a sister to me, as a daughter to my mother. It was she who said the last word to me when I went forth upon a raid; she who waited to welcome me on my return."

"And you said nothing," I remarked, with some surprise.

"Nothing. Our chief had ordered that no man should declare his love to her. She was our guest, like yourself, and she was therefore sacred. Well," he went on, gazing thoughtfully across the dark valley, the white moonbeams shining full upon his thin, sun-tanned countenance. "One day our men down yonder, on the northern border, discovered three

WILLIAM LE QUEUX

strangers who were examining the rocks and chipping pieces off—
French mining engineers we afterwards found them to be. They were
captured, brought up here, and held to ransom. Two were elderly men,
but the third was about twenty-eight, well-dressed with a quantity of
French banknotes upon him. At first the price we asked of the Sultan
was too high. The Vali of Skodra refused to pay, but suggested a smaller
sum. We were in no hurry to compromise, so the three remained
prisoners, and—"

"And what?"

"Well, during that time the younger of the three saw Zorka, and fell
in love with her. I caught the pair one night walking together. They sat
here, at this very spot. The Frenchman had been in Constantinople,
and, speaking a little Turkish, could converse with her. I crept up and
overheard some of their conversation. Next day I told the chief, and
when he heard it he was angry, and ordered that the prisoners were to
be released and sent away—without ransom—that very day. Zorka was
one of ourselves. So that afternoon the three strangers were escorted
down to the Skodra road, and there told to begone."

Here Luk broke off, slowly rolling a fresh cigarette in silence. By the
light of the brilliant moon I saw the sudden change in his countenance.

"Well?" I asked.

"There is not much more to tell," he said hoarsely, hard lines showing
at the corners of his mouth. "A few weeks later we one night missed
Zorka. The whole tribe went forth to search for her. Some men of
the Hoti, down on the way to Skodra, had seen a woman pass. Vatt
Marashi took me with some others down to the lake-side, where we
heard that she had escaped on the little steamer that runs up the lake
to Ryeka, in Montenegro. And further that she had a male companion
who, from his description, we knew to be the Frenchman whose life
we had spared. With the man was an elderly woman. He had evidently
returned to Skodra, and sent Zorka a message in secret. At risk of arrest
by the Turks we went down into Skodra itself, and saw the captain of
the steamer, from whom we learnt that the Frenchman's name was Paul
Darbour, and that he was a mining engineer, living in Paris. While
on the boat he had chatted to the captain in French, and mentioned
that he was going first to Ragusa, down on the Dalmatian coast. The
Skreli punish an insult to their women with death, therefore that same
night, upon the lake shore, we twelve men and our good chief raised
the blood-feud, and I was ordered to go forth in search of the man

who had enticed away our Zorka. None of them, however knew how deeply I loved her myself. Well, I left, wearing the Montenegrin dress, the blue baggy trousers, scarlet jacket, and pork-pie hat. Through Montenegro, down to Cattaro, I followed them, and took the steamer along the Adriatic to Ragusa. But they had already left. For a month I followed the trio from place to place, until late one night, in Trieste, I met Zorka in European dress, walking with her lover along the quays. He was speaking sharply to her, evidently trying to induce her to act against her will, for she was weeping bitterly. I crept after them unseen in the shadows. From words she let drop in Turkish I knew that he was treating her with cruelty, now that he had got her in his power—that she bitterly regretted listening to his love-speeches. I clenched my teeth, took a few sharp steps, and next instant my keen knife was buried up to the hilt behind our enemy's shoulder. He fell forward almost without a cry."

"And Zorka?" I asked.

"I brought her safely back again to us," was his simple answer. "See. She is my wife!"

Luk is here, outside Belgrade, the Prince added. But in secret, for a price is set upon his head. He is a Turkish brigand, and he and his band terrorise the Montenegrin border. The Servian Government offered, only a month ago, twenty thousand dinars for his capture. They little dream he is in hiding in a cave over in yonder mountain, and that he is supplied with food by his faithful little wife here!

And true sportsman that he was, he raised his glass again to her—and to her husband.

XI

Touching the Widow's Mite

One

THE PRINCE, KEEN MOTORIST THAT he was, had—attended by the faithful Garrett, of course—been executing some remarkably quick performances on the Brooklands track.

About a month before he had purchased a hundred horse-power racing-car, and now devoted a good deal of his time to the gentle art of record-breaking. Some of his times for "the mile" had been very creditable, and as Mr. Richard Drummond, son of a Manchester cotton magnate, his name was constantly appearing in the motor journals. Having for the time being discarded the purple, and with it his cosy chambers off Piccadilly, he had now taken up his quarters at that small hotel so greatly patronised by motorists, the "Hut," on the Ripley Road.

Among the many road-scouts, with their red discs, in that vicinity he had become extremely popular on account of his generosity in tips, while to the police with his ugly grey low-built car with its two seats behind the long bonnet he was a perpetual source of annoyance.

Though he never exceeded the speed limit—in sight of the police—yet his open exhaust roared and throbbed, while his siren was the most ear-piercing of any on the road. A little bit of business up in Staffordshire which he had recently brought to a successful issue by the aid of the faithful Charles, the Parson, and Mr. Max Mason, had placed them all in funds, and while the worthy Bayswater vicar was taking his ease at the "Majestic" up at Harrogate—where, by the way, he had become extremely popular among his fellow guests—Mason was at the Bath at Bournemouth for a change of air.

To the guests at Harrogate the Rev. Thomas Clayton had told the usual tale which seems to be on the lips of every cleric, no matter how snug his living—that of the poor parish, universal suffering, hard work, small stipend, ailing wife and several small children. Indeed, he admitted to one or two of the religious old ladies whose acquaintance he had made, that some of his wealthier parishioners, owing to his nervous breakdown, had subscribed in order to send him there for a month's holiday.

Thus he had become indispensable to the tea-and-tattle circle, and the ladies soon began to refer to him as "that dear Mr. Clayton." With one of them, a certain wealthy widow named Edmondson, he had become a particular favourite, a fact which he had communicated in a letter to the good-looking motorist now living at the pretty wayside inn in front of the lake on the Ripley Road.

While the Parson was enjoying a most decorous time with the philanthropic widow, Dick Drummond, as he soon became known, had cultivated popularity in the motor-world. To men in some walks of life, and especially to those on the crooked by-paths, popularity is a very dangerous thing. Indeed, as the Prince had on many occasions pointed out in confidence to me, his popularity greatly troubled him, making it daily more difficult for him to conceal his identity.

At that moment, because he had lowered a record at Brooklands, he was living in daily terror of being photographed, and having his picture published in one or other of the illustrated papers. If this did occur, then was it not more than likely that somebody would identify Dick Drummond the motorist, with the handsome Prince Albert of Hesse-Holstein?

He led a life of ease and comfort in all else, save this constant dread of recognition, and was seriously contemplating a sudden trip across the Channel with a run through France and Germany when he one morning received a registered letter bearing the Harrogate postmark.

He read it through half a dozen times. Then he burned it.

Afterwards he lit a "Petroff" and went out for a stroll in the sunshine along the road towards Ripley village.

"It's really wonderful how clerical clothes and a drawling voice attract a woman. They become fascinated, just as they do when they meet a Prince. By Jove!" he laughed merrily to himself. "What fools some women—and men, too, for the matter of that—make of themselves! They never trouble to institute inquiry, but accept you just at your own value. Take myself as an instance! In all these four years nobody has ever discovered that I'm not Prince Albert. Nobody has taken the trouble to trace the real prince to his safe abode, the Sanatorium of Wismar. Yet the great difficulty is that I cannot always remain a prince."

Then he strode along for some time in thoughtful silence. In his well-cut blue serge suit and peaked motor-cap he presented the smart devil-may-care figure of a man who would attract most women. Indeed, he was essentially a ladies' man, but he always managed to turn his amorous adventures to monetary advantage.

Only once in his life had he been honestly in love. The tragic story of his romance in Florence I have already explained in a previous chapter. His thoughts were always of his real princess—ever of her. She had been his ideal, and would always remain so. He had defended her good name, but dared not return to her and expose himself as a fraud and a criminal. Better by far for her to remain in ignorance of the truth; better that he should possess only sweet sad memories of her soft lips and tender hands.

As he walked, a young man passed in a dirty white racing-car, on his way to Brooklands, and waved to him. It was George Hartwell, the holder of the one-mile record, and an intimate friend of his.

The Prince was debating within himself whether he should adopt the Parson's suggestion, abandon motor-racing for the nonce, and join him up in Yorkshire.

"I wonder whether the game's worth the candle?" he went on, speaking to himself after the cloud of dust has passed. "If what Clayton says is true, then it's a good thing. The old woman is evidently gone on him. I suppose he's told her the tale, and she believes he's a most sanctified person."

He halted at a gate near the entrance to Ripley village, and lighting another cigarette puffed vigorously at it.

"My hat!" he exclaimed at last. "A real parson must have an exceedingly soft time of it—snug library, pretty girls in the choir, tea-fights, confidences, and all that kind of thing. In the country no home is complete without its tame curate." Then, after a long silence, he at length tossed away the end of his cigarette, and declared:

"Yes, I'll go. There'll be a bit of fun—if nothing else."

And he walked to the village telegraph office and wired one word to his bosom friend and ingenious accomplice. It was a word of their secret code—Formice—which Clayton would interpret as "All right. Shall be with you as soon as possible, and will carry out the suggestions made in your letter."

Then he walked back to the "Hut," where he found Garrett sitting out in that little front garden against the road, which is usually so crowded by motorists on warm Sunday afternoons.

"Better go and pack," he said sinking into a chair as his supposed servant rose and stood at attention. "We're going back to town in an hour."

Garrett, without asking questions, returned into the hotel. He saw by the Prince's sharp decided manner that something new was in the wind.

An hour later Dick Drummond motor-maniac, drew the car along the road towards Esher, and as he disappeared around the bend among the trees, he ceased to exist. Prince Albert became himself again.

Direct to Dover Street they went—and there found the discreet Charles awaiting them. Fresh kit was packed while Garrett, in a garage over in Westminster where he was unknown, was busily engaged in repainting the ugly racer with its big bonnet a bright yellow.

That evening the Prince spent alone in his pretty sitting-room consuming dozens of his pet Russian cigarettes, and thinking hard. For an hour he was busy upon some accounts written in German—accounts from a Jew dealer in precious stones in Amsterdam. The gentleman in question was a good customer of the Prince's, gave fair prices, and asked no questions. His Highness seemed troubled about one item, for as he rested his brow upon his hand, still seated at his desk, he murmured in a low voice to himself:

"I'm sure the old Hebrew has done me out of four hundred and fifty! Eighteen hundred was the price agreed for that carroty-headed woman's pendant. That's what comes of leaving business matters to Max." And sighing, he added: "I shall really have to attend to the sales myself, for no doubt we're swindled every time. The old Jew doesn't believe in honour among thieves, it seems!"

Some letters which had arrived during his absence were put before him by the valet, Charles. Among them were several invitations to the houses of people struggling to get into society—by the back door, and who wanted to include the name of Prince Albert of Hesse-Holstein in the list of their guests.

"Are we likely to be away for long?" asked the valet, at the same time helping himself to a cigarette from his master's silver box.

"I haven't the slightest idea," laughed the good-looking young adventurer. "You'll go down to the 'Majestic' at Harrogate by the first train in the morning and take the best suite for me. Garrett and I will arrive in the car. Of course you'll tell the usual story to the servants of my wealth, and all that."

"The Parson's down there, isn't he?"

"Yes, but you'll take no notice of him. Understand?"

So the smart young crook who posed as valet, having received his master's instructions, retired to pack his own clothes.

At ten next morning Garrett brought round the hundred "racer," now covered in yellow enamel and bearing a different identification-plate from that it had borne the previous day, and with the Prince up beside him wearing a light dust-coat and his peaked cap turned the wrong way, so as not to catch the wind, drew out into Piccadilly, and turned up Shaftesbury Avenue due northward.

Throughout that warm summer's day they tore along the Great North Road as far as Doncaster, wary always of the police-traps which abound there. Then, after a light meal, they pushed on to Ferrybridge, taking the right-hand road through Micklefield to the cross-roads beyond Aberford, and then on the well-kept old Roman way which runs through Wetherby to Plampton Corner, and ascends the hill into Harrogate.

The last forty miles they did at tearing speed, the great powerful engine running like a clock, leaving a perfect wall of white dust behind. The car was a "flyer" in every sense of the word. The Prince had won the Heath Stakes at Brooklands, therefore, on an open road, without traffic or police-traps, they covered the last forty miles within the hour.

The sun had already sunk, and the crimson afterglow had spread before they reached the Stray, but as the car drew up before the great hotel, Charles, bareheaded and urbane, came forth to receive his master, while behind him stood the assistant manager and a couple of attendants also in bareheaded servitude.

Charles, who always acted as advance-agent had already created great excitement in the hotel by the announcement that his Highness was on his way. Quite a small crowd of visitors had concluded their dinner early, and assembled in the hall to catch first sight of the German princeling who preferred residence in England to that in his native principality.

As he passed across the great hall and entered the lift, dusty after his journey, his quick eyes caught sight of the sedate modest-looking parson seated away from the others, chatting with a rather buxom, florid-looking, red-necked woman of about fifty.

The Parson had his face purposely averted. At present he did not wish to claim acquaintance with the new-comer, whom he allowed to ascend to the fine suite of rooms reserved for him.

Next morning, as the Prince crossed the hall to go out for a stroll about the town he created quite a flutter in the hotel, especially among the female guests. The place was filled by summer holiday-makers from London, each of whom was eager to rub elbows with a real live Prince. Indeed many were the flattering words whispered by pretty lips regarding his Highness's good looks and general bearing.

The worthy Bayswater vicar was chatting with Mrs. Edmondson in his usual clerical drawl, when the Prince's sudden appearance caused him to look up. Then turning to her again, he exclaimed:

"Oh, here's Prince Albert! I knew him quite well when I was British chaplain in Hanover," and crossing to his Highness he shook hands heartily, adding in the next breath: "I wonder if your Highness would allow me to present to you my friend here, Mrs. Edmondson?"

"Delighted, I'm sure," replied the younger man bowing before the rather stout, dark-haired lady, whose blatant pomposity crumpled up instantly, and who became red and white in turns.

The introduction had been effected so suddenly that the relict of Thomas Edmondson, Esquire, J.P., D.L., of Milnthorpe Hall, near Whitby, had been taken completely off her feet—or "off her perch," as the merry cleric afterwards jocosely put it. She knew Mr. Clayton to be a most superior person, but had no idea of his intimate acquaintance with princes of the blood-royal.

She succeeded in stammering some conventional expressions of pleasure at being presented, and then lapsed into ignominious silence.

"Mrs. Edmondson has kindly expressed herself very interested in my poor parish," explained the Parson, "just as your Highness has been interested. I wrote to you a month ago to Aix-les-Bains, thanking you for your generous donation towards our Children's Holiday Fund. It was really extremely kind of you."

"Oh, don't mention it, Mr. Clayton," replied his Highness. "I've been in your parish twice, remember, and I know well how very hard you work, and what a number of the deserving poor you have. I'm just going down in the town for a stroll. Perhaps I'll see you after lunch? Come to my room for a smoke."

And then, bowing to the obese widow, he replaced his grey felt hat and strode out.

"What a very charming man!" declared the widow when she recovered herself sufficiently to speak. "So he has been to your parish!"

"Oh, yes. He gives me most liberal donations," answered Clayton in a low tone of confidence. "But he always prefers to remain anonymous, of course. He has been my best friend for years. I had no idea he was in England. He wrote me last from Aix."

But the widow's brain was already active. Though possessing a deep religious feeling, and subscribing liberally to all sorts of charities just as her late husband had done, she was nevertheless a snob, and was already wondering whether, with the assistance of the pleasant-faced cleric, she could not induce the Prince to be her guest at Milnthorpe. She knew that his presence there would give to her house a *cachet* which had always been lacking, and would raise her social position in the select county of Yorks a hundred per cent.

"Most delightful man!" she repeated as they went forth into the grounds. "I hope I shall have the pleasure of a long chat with him."

"Oh, that won't be very difficult, my dear Mrs. Edmondson," her companion replied. "Any one introduced by me will, I feel assured, be received most cordially by him. He does me the honour of reposing the most implicit trust in myself."

"A trust which certainly is not misplaced," declared the stout widow in her self-satisfied way, as she strutted along in a new grey cotton gown of latest *mode*, a large hat to match, a big golden chatelaine at her side, and a blue silk sunshade.

"You are very flattering," replied Clayton. "I—I fear I do not deserve such kind words, I only do my duty to my bishop and my parish, and prosecute the line of life which Providence has laid out for me."

"There are clergymen—and clergymen," the woman said with affected wisdom. "I have known more than one who has been utterly worthless. It is, therefore, very gratifying to meet a man with such a high mind, and such a keen sense of responsibility towards his poor backsliding fellow creatures as yourself."

He was silent, for he was biting his nether lip. What would this estimable widow think if she knew the truth that he had no parish, no wife, no little children, and that he had no right to the sombre garb of religion in which he stood before her?

A moment later he succeeded in changing the subject.

The Prince lunched alone in his private room, as he always did in hotels in order to impress both management and guests. It was another habit of his, in order to cause servants to talk, to have a big bottle of eau de Cologne placed in his bath each morning. The chatter of servants as to his generosity, and his careless extravagance, was often most useful to him. While the Parson was always parsimonious—which, by the way, was rather belied by his rubicund complexion—the Prince was ever open-handed.

The good-looking, well-dressed young man's slight foreign accent entirely disappeared whenever he became Tremlett or Lord Nassington, or Drummond, or any other imaginary person whose identity he from time to time assumed. At present, however, he spoke with just sufficient error of grammar and speech to betray his foreign birth, and as he rose, and stood looking out of the window he presented, in his cool, grey flannels, the ideal young foreign prince of English tastes and English education.

Already in the reading-room below, the "Almanach de Gotha" had been handled a dozen times by inquisitive half-pay colonels, and mothers with marriageable daughters. And what had been found printed there had caused a flutter in many hearts.

The Prince's audacity was superb. The suspicion of any little *coup* he made as prince he always managed to wriggle out of. Even though some evil-disposed persons had made ugly allegations against him at times, yet they were not believed. He was a prince and wealthy, therefore what motive had he to descend to the level of a thief? The Parson, too, always managed to evade suspicion. His voice, his manner, and his general get-up were perfect.

Those who had visited his house in Bayswater, not far from Queen's Road station, had found it to be the ideal and complete clergyman's home, with study and half-written sermons on the writing-table.

Their victims, indeed, were as puzzled as were the police. The Prince's magnificent impertinence and amazing boldness carried him through it all. He was a fatalist. If he and his friends Clayton, Garrett, and Mason were ever caught—well it would be just Fate. Till they actually fell into the hands of the police they would have a good time, and act fearlessly.

As he stood at the window, with the eternal Russian cigarette between his lips, gazing thoughtfully out upon the garden below, the door opened and the Parson entered.

"Well, Tommy, old chap!" exclaimed his Highness, when in a few moments the two men were lounging in easy-chairs opposite each other. "Now, tell me all about the old girl," he said laughing. "She walks like a pea-hen."

"There's not much more to tell than what you already know," responded the Parson, "except that she's all in a flutter at meeting you, and wants to chat with you again."

"Have you made any inquiries concerning her?"

"Of course. A week ago I ran over in secret to Milnthorpe Hall. Fine place, big park, large staff of servants, butler an Italian. Husband was partner in a firm of shipbuilders at Barrow, and left nearly a million to his wife. One son recently passed into the Army, and just now stationed in Cawnpore. Rather rackety, his mother says. The old woman dotes on parsons."

"And quite gone on you—eh?" Clayton laughed.

"She gave me a cheque for fifty pounds for my Children's Holiday Fund last week," he said. "She's promised to come down and go round my parish one day, soon." His Highness smiled knowingly.

"Is her place far from Whitby?" he inquired, between whiffs of his cigarette.

"About four miles, on the high road just past a place called Swarthoe Cross. Grosmount station, on the Pickering line is nearest."

"The old girl, as far as I've been able to observe, is a purse-proud old crow," his Highness remarked.

"Rather. Likes her name to figure in subscription lists. The old man built and endowed some almshouses in Whitby, and offered twenty thousand to his Party for a knighthood, but was refused. It's a sore point, for she badly wanted to be Lady Edmondson."

"How long since the dear one departed?"

"Two years."

"And she's looking for a second, I suppose?"

"That's my belief."

"I wonder if she'd be attracted by the title of princess?" he laughed.

"Why, the very suggestion would take the silly old woman's breath away," declared the Reverend Thomas.

"Well, if she's so confoundedly generous, what is to prevent us from benefiting a bit? We sadly need it, Tommy," the Prince declared. "I had a letter from Max the day before yesterday. He wants fifty wired without fail to the Poste Restante at Copenhagen. He's lying low there, just now."

"And one of the best places in Europe," the Parson exclaimed. "It's most snug at the 'Angleterre,' or at the 'Bristol.' I put in six months there once. Stockholm is another good spot. I was all one summer at that little hotel out at Salsjobaden, and had quite a good time. I passed as an American and nobody recognised me, though my description had been circulated all over Europe. The Swedish and Danish police are a muddle-headed lot—fortunately for fellows like ourselves who want to lie undisturbed. Have you sent Max the money?"

"I wired twenty-five this morning, and promised the balance in seven days," responded his Highness, lighting a fresh cigarette with his half-consumed one. He always smoked in the Russian style, flinging away the end when only half finished.

Of the proceeds of the various *coups* made, his Highness took one-third, with one-third to Clayton, who was a schemer almost as ingenious as the Prince himself, and the remaining third was divided between Max Mason, Charles, and Garrett, the chauffeur.

The pair of conspirators spent the greater part of the afternoon together in exchanging confidences and arranging plans. Then his Highness rang for Garrett, and ordered him to bring round the car at five o'clock.

The Parson descended to the hall below, being followed ten minutes later by his Highness. The latter found his friend lounging picturesquely with the fascinated widow, and joined them at tea, greatly to the gratification of the "pompous old crow," as Prince Albert had designated her half an hour before.

As they finished the tea and muffins, the big yellow racing-car drew slowly up to the door, and on seeing it the widow began to discuss motors and motoring.

"I have a car at home—a sixty-Mercedes—and I'm awfully fond of a run in it," she told the Prince. "One gets about so quickly, and sees so much of the country. My poor husband hated them, so I never rode in one until after his death."

"The car I have with me is a racer, as you see," remarked his Highness. "It's a hundred horse-power, and made a record on the Brooklands track just before I bought her. If you were not of the feminine sex, Mrs. Edmondson, I'd invite you to go for a run with me," he laughed. "It's rather unsociable, for it's only a two-seater, with Garrett on the step."

"I'd love to go for a run," she declared. "It—well it really wouldn't be too great a breach of the convenances for a woman to go out on a racing-car, would it?"

"I don't think so, Mrs. Edmondson," remarked the Reverend Thomas, in his most cultivated clerical drawl. "But I would wrap up well, for the Prince travels very fast on a clear road."

So "the old crow" decided to accept his Highness's invitation, and ascended to put on her brown motor-cap and veil and a thick coat against the chill, evening winds.

Two

A QUARTER OF AN HOUR later, with Garrett—in his grey and red livery—seated on the step, and the widow up beside him, the Prince drew the great ugly yellow car out of the hotel entrance, while the Parson, standing amid the crowd of jealous onlookers, waved his hand in merry farewell.

In a few moments the siren screamed, and the open exhaust roared and spluttered as they crossed the Stray, taking the road through Starbeck to Knaresborough, thence south by Little Ribston to Wetherby.

Having turned off to the left through the town, they came upon a straight open road where, for the first time his Highness, accustomed as he was to all the vagaries of his powerful car, put on a "move" over the ten miles into York, a run at such a pace that the widow clung to her seat with both hands, almost breathless.

She had never travelled half so fast before in all her life.

In York they ran round by the station past the old grey minster, then out again through Clifton, as far as Shipton Moor, turning up to Beningborough station, and thence into the by-roads to Newton-upon-Ouse, in the direction of Knaresborough.

Once or twice while they tore along regardless of speed-limits or of police-traps, the powerful engine throbbing before them, she turned to his Highness and tried to make some remarks. But it was only a sorry attempt. Travelling at fifty miles an hour over those white roads, without a glass screen, or even body to the car, was very exhilarating, and after the first few minutes of fright, at the tearing pace, she seemed to delight in it. Curious though it is, yet it is nevertheless a fact that women delight in a faster pace in a car than men, when once the first sensation of danger has passed.

When they were safely back again in the hall of the hotel she turned to him to express her great delight at the run.

"Your car is, indeed, a magnificent one, your Highness. I've never been on a racer before," she said, "but it was truly delightful. I never had a moment's anxiety, for you are such a sure and clever driver."

Her eye had been from time to time upon the speedometer, and she had noted the terrific rate at which they had now and then travelled, especially upon any downward incline.

The Prince, on his part, was playing the exquisite courtier. Had she been a girl of twenty he could not have paid "old crow" more attention.

As he was dressing for dinner with the aid of the faithful Charles, the Parson entered, and to him he gave an accurate description of the run, and of the rather amorous attitude the obese widow had assumed towards him.

"Good, my dear boy," exclaimed the urbane cleric, "I told you that she's the most perfect specimen of the snob we've ever met."

A week went by—a pleasant week, during which Mrs. Edmondson, her nose now an inch higher in the air than formerly, went out daily with the Prince and his chauffeur for runs around the West Riding.

One afternoon they ran over to Ripon, and thence across to the fine old ruins of Fountains Abbey. Like many women of her class and character, the buxom lady delighted in monastic ruins, and as the pair strolled about in the great, roofless transept of the Abbey she commenced an enthusiastic admiration of its architecture and dimensions. Though living at Whitby she had, curiously enough, never before visited the place.

"Crowland, in Lincolnshire is very fine," she remarked, "but this is far finer. Yet we have nothing in England to compare with Pavia, near Milan. Have you ever been there, Prince?"

"Only through the station," his Highness replied. Truth to tell he was not enthusiastic over ruins. He was a very modern up-to-date young man.

They idled through the ruins, where the sunshine slanted through the gaunt broken windows, and the cawing rooks flapped lazily in and out. One or two other visitors were there besides themselves, and among them a lonely pale-faced man in grey, wearing gold pince-nez who, with hands behind his back, was studying the architecture and the various outbuildings.

The Prince and his companion brushed close by him in the old refectory, when he glanced up suddenly at a window.

His face was familiar enough to his Highness, who, however, passed him by as a stranger.

It was Max Mason, only yesterday returned from Copenhagen.

That afternoon the widow grew confidential with her princely cavalier in motor clothes, while he, on his part, encouraged her.

"Ah!" he sighed presently as they were walking slowly together in a distant part of the great ruined fabric. "You have no idea how very lonely a man can really be, even though he may be born a prince. More often than not I'm compelled to live *incognito*, for I have ever upon me the fierce glare of publicity. Every movement, every acquaintance I make, even my most private affairs are pried into and chronicled by those confounded press fellows. And for that reason I'm often compelled to hold aloof from people with whom I could otherwise be on terms of intimate friendship. Half my time and ingenuity is spent upon the adoption of subterfuges to prevent people from discovering who I really am. And then those infernal illustrated papers, both here and on the Continent, are eternally republishing my photograph."

"It really must be most annoying, Prince," remarked the widow sympathetically.

"I often adopt the name of Burchell-Laing," he said, "and sometimes—well," and he paused, looking her straight in the face. "I wonder, Mrs. Edmondson, whether I might confide in you—I mean whether you would keep my secret?"

"I hope I may be permitted to call myself your Highness's friend," she said in a calm, impressive tone. "Whatever you may tell me will not, I assure you, pass my lips."

"I am delighted to have such a friend as yourself," he declared enthusiastically. "Somehow, though our acquaintanceship has been of such brief duration, yet I feel that your friendship is sincere, Mrs. Edmondson."

By this speech the widow was intensely flattered. Her companion saw it in her countenance.

He did not allow her time to make any remark, but added: "My secret is—well a rather curious one, perhaps—but the fact is that I have a dual personality. While being Prince Albert of Hesse-Holstein, I am also known as Dick Drummond, holder of two records on the Brooklands motor-track. In the motor-world I'm believed to be a young man of means, who devotes his time to motor-racing—a motor-maniac in fact."

The widow stared at him in blank astonishment.

"Are you really the Mr. Drummond of whose wonderful feat I read of only the other day in the papers?"

"I won the race at Brooklands the other day," he said carelessly, "I won it with the car I have here now."

"And nobody suspects that this Mr. Drummond is a prince!" she exclaimed.

"Nobody. I could never afford to go racing in my own name. The Kaiser would not allow it, you know. I have to be so very careful."

"I quite understand that," remarked the widow. "But what an excellent motor-driver you must be! What a fine performance your record was! Why, there was half a column in the *Morning Post* about it!"

"It was not any more difficult, or more dangerous, than some of the long quick runs I've made on the Continent. From Rome up to Berlin, for instance, or from Warsaw to Ostend, I'm racing again at Brooklands next week."

"And may I come and see you?" she asked. "Do let me. I will, of course, keep your secret, and not tell a soul."

He hesitated.

"You see nobody knows but yourself and Garrett, my chauffeur—not even Clayton. He's a good fellow, but parsons," he laughed, "are bad hands at keeping secrets. Too much tea and gossip spoils them, I suppose."

"But I'll swear to remain secret. Only let me know the day and hour, and I'll go south and see you. I should love to see a motor-race. I've never seen one in my life."

So at last, with seeming reluctance, his Highness, having taken the flattered widow into his confidence, promised on condition that she said nothing to anybody, she should know the day and hour when to be at Brooklands.

As the warm summer days slipped by, it became more and more apparent to the Parson that his friend, the widow, had become entirely fascinated by the lighthearted easy-going prince. She, on her part, recognised how, because of her intimate acquaintance with his Highness, and the fact that he honoured her table with his presence sometimes at dinner, every one in the hotel courted her friendship in the hope that they might be introduced to the cousin of the Kaiser.

Prince and Parson were, truth to tell, playing a very big bluff. Max had taken up his quarters at the Spa Hydro, and though meeting his two accomplices frequently in the streets, passed them by as strangers.

Now and then the Parson went up to smoke with the Prince after the wealthy widow had retired, and on such occasions the conversation was of such a character that, if she had overheard it, she would have been considerably surprised.

One evening, when they were together, the valet, Charles, entered, closing the door carefully after him.

"Well," asked his master, "what's the news?"

"I've just left Max down in the town," replied the clean-shaven servant. "He got back from Milnthorpe Hall this morning. He went there as an electrical engineer, sent by Cameron Brothers, of London, at the old woman's request, and examined the whole place with a view to a lighting installation. He reports that, beyond a few good paintings—mostly family portraits of the original owners—and a little *bric-a-brac*, there's nothing worth having. The old woman keeps her jewels in the bank at York, as well as greater part of the plate. What's in general use is all electro. Besides, there are burglar-alarms all over the place."

"Then the old woman's a four-flush!" declared the Parson tossing away his cigarette angrily. "I thought she'd got some good stuff there. That was my impression from the outside."

"Afraid of thieves, evidently," remarked the Prince. "She's a lone woman, and according to what you say, the only men in the house are the Italian butler, and a young footman."

"If there's nothing there, what's the use troubling over her further?"

His Highness puffed thoughtfully at his "Petroff." He was reflecting deeply, bitterly repenting that he had been such a fool as to tell her the truth regarding his motor-racing *nomade-guerre*. He could not afford to allow her to become his enemy. To abandon her at once would surely be a most injudicious action.

"At present let's postpone our decision, Tommy," he exclaimed at last. "There may be a way to success yet. You, Charles, see Max to-morrow, and tell him to go to London and lie low there. I'll wire him when I want him. You have some money. Give him a tenner."

And the man addressed soon afterwards withdrew.

The events of the next two days showed plainly that the original plans formulated by the Rev. Thomas Clayton had been abandoned.

The widow, with some trepidation, invited the Prince and his clerical friend to be her guests at Milnthorpe, but they made excuses, much to her chagrin. The exemplary vicar was compelled to return to his Bayswater parish, while the Prince was also recalled to London to race at Brooklands, making the journey, of course, on the car.

Thus Mrs. Edmondson found herself left alone in the "Majestic," with her fellow guests full of wonder at what had really occurred.

The widow, however, had been buoyed up by a few whispered words of the Prince at the moment of his departure.

"Preserve my secret as you promised, Mrs. Edmondson, and come to London one day next week. You always go to the Langham—you say. I'll call on you there next Friday. *Au revoir*!"

And he lifted his cap, shook her hand, and mounted at the wheel of the big mustard-coloured "racer."

On the day appointed he called at the Langham and found her installed in one of the best suites, prepared to receive him.

He told her that, on the morrow at noon, he was to race at Brooklands against Carlier, the well-known Frenchman, both cars being of the same horse-power. The distance was one hundred miles.

She was delighted, and promised to observe every secrecy, and come down to witness the struggle. He remained to tea, chatting with her pleasantly. When he rose and bade her adieu, she sat alone for a long time thinking.

Was she dreaming? Or was it really a fact that he, Prince Albert of Hesse-Holstein, had, for a few moments, held her hand tenderly? The difference of their ages was not so much, she argued—about twelve years. She was twelve years older. What did that matter, after all?

If she, plain Mrs. Edmondson, of Milnthorpe, became Princess Albert of Hesse-Holstein! Phew! The very thought of it took her breath away.

She was a clever scheming woman, and had always been, ever since her school-girl days. She flattered herself that she could read the innermost secrets of a man's heart.

Yes. She was now convinced. This man, who had reposed confidence in her and told her of his dual personality, was actually in love with her. If he did not marry her, it certainly should not be her fault.

With that decision she called Marie, her French maid, and passed into her room to dress for dinner with her sister-in-law and her husband—a barrister—with the theatre and Savoy to follow.

Next day at noon she was down at Brooklands, where a number of motor enthusiasts and men "in the trade" had assembled. She saw a tall, slim figure in grey overalls and an ugly helmet-shaped cap with dark glasses in the eye-holes, mount upon a long grey car, while a mechanic in blue cotton and a short jacket buttoned tightly, gave a

WILLIAM LE QUEUX

last look round to see that all was working properly. The man mounted the step, the signal was given by the starters, and the two cars, pitted against each other, both grey, with huge numbers painted on the front of their bonnets, came past her like a flash, while the mechanics swung themselves half out, in order to balance the cars as they went round the bend.

After the first two or three laps the pace became terrific, and as the widow sat watching, she saw the Prince *incognito*, his head bent to the wind, a slim, crouched figure at the wheel driving the long car at a pace which no express train could travel.

At first he slowly forged ahead, but presently, after twenty minutes, the Frenchman gradually crept up, inch by inch. It was the test of the two cars—a comparatively new English make against a French firm.

Dick Drummond had many friends on the course. He was popular everywhere, and at regular intervals as he passed the stand where the widow was seated, a crowd of young, smart, clean-shaven men shouted to his encouragement.

Each time, with slight dust flying behind, he went round the bend, Garrett, in his dirty blue clothes, swung himself out to balance the car, while to the Prince himself all has become a blur. Travelling at that terrific pace, the slightest swerve would mean a terrible accident, therefore, he had no eyes save for the track before him. Garrett was busy every moment with the lubrication, and at the same time both feared tyre-troubles, the bugbear of the racing motorist. Such speed sets up tremendous friction and consequent heat, therefore tyre-bursts are likely, and if a tyre does "go off" while a car is travelling at that pace, the consequences may be very serious.

Many a bad accident had occurred on that track, and more than one good man had lost his life. Yet the Prince, sportsman that he was, knowing that the widow's eyes were upon him, set his teeth hard and drove until once again he gradually drew away from his opponent, the renowned Carlier.

There were present representatives of the daily and the motor press. The race would be chronicled everywhere on the morrow. If the Frenchman won, it would be an advertisement worth many thousands of pounds to the firm for whom he was driving.

To-day every maker of motor-cars vies with his competitors, and strives strenuously to obtain the greatest advertisement. Like so many other things about us, alas! it is not the quality of the car, or of the materials used, but a car's excellence seems to be judged by its popularity. And that popularity is a mere matter of advertisement.

The best car ever turned out by the hand of man would never be looked at if not advertised and "boomed."

The French driver, a man who had won a dozen races, including the Circuit of the Ardennes, and the Florio Cup, was trying to get an advertisement for the particular company for whom he was the professional racer, while Dick Drummond was merely trying his English car against the Paris-built variety.

The whirr-r was constant, now approaching and now receding, as the two cars went round and round the track with monotonous regularity. Experts, men interested in various makes, stood leaning over the rails making comment.

It was agreed on every hand that Drummond was a marvel of cool level-headedness. His driving was magnificent, and yet he had apparently nothing to gain, even if he won the race. He was not financially interested, as far as was known, in the make of car he drove. He was merely a man of means, who had taken up motor-car racing as a hobby.

The Frenchman drove well, and the race, after the first three-quarters of an hour, was a keenly contested one. First Drummond would lead, and then Carlier. Once Drummond spurted and got half a lap ahead, then with the Frenchman putting on speed, he fell behind again till they were once more neck and neck.

Time after time they shot past the widow, who had eyes only for her champion. Her blue sunshade was up, and as she stood there alone she hoped against hope that the Prince—the man who had told her his secret—would prove the victor.

When he was in front, loud shouts rent the air from the men interested in the make of car he was driving, while, on the other hand, if the Frenchman gained the vantage the applause from his partisans was vociferous.

Over all was a cloud of light dust, while the wind created by the cars as they rushed past fanned the cheeks of the woman watching her champion with such deep interest.

A group of men near her were discussing him.

"Drummond is a magnificent driver," one remarked in admiration. "Look at him coming up now. Cagno never drove like that, even in his very best race."

"I wonder what interest he has in the Company? He surely wouldn't race for the mere excitement," remarked another.

"Interest!" cried a third man—and, truth to tell, he was Max Mason—"Why he has the option to buy up the whole of the concern, lock, stock, and barrel. I heard so yesterday. The company gave it to him a fortnight ago. Lawrence, the secretary, told me so. Why, by Jove! if he wins, the fortune of that make of car is secured. I suppose he has capital behind him, and will buy up the whole concern. I only wish I were in it. A tenth share would be a fortune."

"You're right," remarked the first man. "Dick Drummond is a shrewd chap. If he wins he'll make a pot of money on the deal—you see. It'll be the biggest advertisement that a car has ever had in all the whole annals of motoring."

Mrs. Edmondson listened to all this in silence. She quite understood. The Prince, in his character of Dick Drummond, had entered into the affair with a view to a big financial deal—the purchase of the important company who were responsible for the car he was driving.

The car in question, be it said, was the actual mustard-coloured one in which she had careered about the West Riding, although she did not recognise it in its garb of dirty slate-grey.

She found it quite fascinating, standing there watching those two cars with their powerful roaring engines striving for the mastery, as mile after mile was covered at that frightful break-neck speed. Her heart was with the man bent over his wheel, whom every one believed to be a commoner, and whom she alone knew to be a prince.

And he, the cousin of the Kaiser, had actually squeezed her hand!

As the end of the race approached the excitement increased. The onlookers grouped themselves in little knots, watching critically for any sign of weakness in one or the other. But there was none. Carlier was as dogged as his opponent, and kept steadily on until at the eightieth mile he gradually overhauled the Englishman.

There were still twenty miles to cover. But Dick Drummond was behind, quite an eighth of a lap. Carlier had apparently been husbanding all his strength and power. The car he was driving was certainly a splendid one, and was behaving magnificently. Would it beat the English make?

As the last few laps were negotiated at a frightful speed the knots of onlookers became more and more enthusiastic. Some cheered Dick until they were hoarse, while others, with an interest in the car Carlier was driving, cried "Bravo! Bravo!"

The blood ran quickly in the widow's veins. Ninety-five miles had been covered, and still Drummond was behind more than half a lap. She watched his crouching figure, with head set forward, his position never altering, his chin upon his breast, his eyes fixed upon the track before him. Garrett seemed ever at work, touching this and that at the order of his master, whose face was wholly protected from the cutting wind by the ugly mask, save mouth and chin.

As the board showed ninety-seven miles he came at a fearful pace past the spot where Mrs. Edmondson had again risen from her seat in her excitement. He was spurting, and so valiantly did he struggle, getting every ounce out of the hundred horse-power of his car, that he slowly, very slowly, crept towards the flying Frenchman.

"Keep on, Drummond!" shrieked the men, taking off their caps and waving them. "Don't be beaten, old man!"

But he could not hear them above the terrible roar of his exhaust. No express train ever designed had run so quickly as he was now travelling. Official timekeepers were standing, chronometers in hand, calmly watching, and judges were making ready to declare the winner.

Every spectator stood breathless. It was really marvellous that one hundred miles could have been covered in that brief space of time while they had been watching.

Again, and yet again, the two cars flashed by, yet still Dick lagged behind.

Suddenly, however, they came round for the last lap, and as they passed the watchful widow, the Englishman like a shot from a gun, passed his opponent and won by twenty yards.

When he pulled up, after having run again round the course to slacken speed, he almost fell into the arms of the crowd of men who came up to congratulate him.

Mrs. Edmondson had left her post of vantage and stood near by. She overheard one of them—it was Mason—say:

"By Jove, Dick! This is a wonderful run. You've broken the five, ten, and hundred mile records! The fortune of your car is made?"

Then the victor turned to his opponent and shook his hand, saying in French:

"Thank you, my dear Carlier, for a very excellent race."

The widow, after a brief chat, returned to town by rail, while Garrett drove his master back to Dover Street.

WILLIAM LE QUEUX

That night his Highness dined with the widow at the Langham, and she bestowed upon him fulsome praise regarding his prowess.

"What make of car is yours?" she asked while they were lingering over their dessert in the widow's private sitting-room.

"It's the St. Christopher," he answered.

"St. Christopher!" she echoed. "What a funny name to give a car!"

"It may appear so at first sight, but St. Christopher has been taken by motorists on the Continent as their patron saint—the saint who for ages has guarded the believer against the perils of the way. So it's really appropriate, after all."

"I heard them say that you've made the fortune of the car by your success to-day," she remarked.

"Yes," he answered carelessly. "Anybody who cared to put in a few thousands now would receive a magnificent return for their money—twenty-five per cent, within a year."

"You think so?" she asked interestedly. "Think, Mrs. Edmondson?" he echoed. "I'm sure of it! Why, the St. Christopher now holds the world's record, and you know what that means. The makers will begin to receive far more orders than they can ever execute. Look at the Napier, the Itala, the Fiat, and others. The same thing has happened. The St. Christopher, however, is in the hands of two men only, and they, unfortunately, lack capital."

"You should help them, if it's such a good thing."

"I'm doing so. Now I've won the race I shall put in fifteen thousand—perhaps twenty. They are seeing me to-morrow. As a matter of fact," he added, lowering his tone, "I mean to hold controlling interest in the concern. It's far too good a thing to miss."

The fat widow, with her black bodice cut low, and the circle of diamonds sparkling upon her red neck, sipped her wine slowly, but said nothing.

His Highness did not refer to this matter again. He was a past-master of craft and cunning.

Later on, the Rev. Thomas Clayton was announced, and the trio spent quite a pleasant evening, which concluded by the lady inviting them both to Milnthorpe the following week.

At first the Prince again hesitated. The widow sat in breathless expectancy. At all hazards she must get his Highness to visit her. It would be known all over the county. She would pay a guinea each to the fashionable papers to announce the fact, for it would be worth so very much to her in the county.

"I fear, Mrs. Edmondson, that I must go to Berlin next week," replied the Prince. "I'm sure it's very good of you, but the Emperor has summoned me regarding some affairs of my brother Karl."

"Oh! why can't you postpone your visit, and come and see me first?" she urged in her most persuasive style. "Mr. Clayton, do urge the Prince to come to me," she added.

"You can surely go to Germany a week later, Prince," exclaimed the cleric. "Where's the Kaiser just now?"

"At Kiel, yachting."

"Then he may not be in Berlin next week?"

"He has appointed to meet me at Potsdam. His Majesty never breaks an engagement."

"Then you will break yours, Prince, and go with me to Milnthorpe," declared the Parson.

"Yes," cried Mrs. Edmondson; "and we will have no further excuses, will we, Mr. Clayton?"

So his Highness was forced to accept, and next day the wily widow returned to Yorkshire to make preparations for the visit which was to shed such social lustre upon her house.

Three

THE PRINCE AND THE PARSON held several long interviews in the two days that followed, and it was apparent from one meeting which took place, and at which both Mason and Garrett were present, that some clever manoeuvre was intended. The quartette held solemn councils in the Prince's chambers, and there was much discussion, and considerable laughter.

The latter, it appeared, was in consequence of Max's recollection of the wonderful record of his Highness at Brooklands.

On the day appointed both Prince and parson, attended by the faithful Charles, left King's Cross by train for Whitby, Garrett having started alone on the "forty," with orders to travel by way of Doncaster and York, and arrive at Milnthorpe by noon next day.

The fine old place was, the Prince found, quite a comfortable residence. The widow did the honours gracefully, welcoming her guests warmly.

When the two friends found themselves alone in the Prince's room, his Highness whispered to the exemplary vicar:

"I don't like the look of that Italian butler, Tommy. Do you know I've a very strange fancy?"

"Of what?"

"That I've met that fellow before, somewhere or other."

"I sincerely hope not," was the clergyman's response.

"Where I've met him I can't remember. By Jove! It'll be awkward for us if he recollects me."

"Then we'll have to watch him. I wonder if—"

And the Parson crossed noiselessly to the bedroom door and opened it suddenly.

As he did so there was the distinct sound of some one scuffling round the corner in the corridor. Both men detected it.

There had been an eavesdropper! They were suspected!

At dinner that night the pair cast furtive glances at the thin, clean-shaven face of the middle-aged Italian butler, whose head was prematurely bald, but whose manners as a servant were perfect. Ferrini was the name by which his mistress addressed him, and it was apparent that he was very devoted to her. The young footman was English—a Cockney, by his twang.

In the old panelled room, with its long family portraits and its old carved buffet laden with well-kept silver—or rather electro-plate, as the pair already knew—a well-cooked dinner was served amid flowers and cunningly-concealed lights. The table was a round one, and the only other guest was a tall, fair-haired young girl, a Miss Maud Mortimer, the daughter of a neighbouring squire. She was a loosely built, slobbering miss, with a face like a wax doll, and a slight impediment in her speech.

At first she seemed shy in the presence of the Kaiser's cousin, but presently, when her awkwardness wore off, she grew quite merry.

To the two visitors the meal was a perfect success. Those dark watchful eyes of the Italian, however, marred their pleasure considerably. Even the Parson was now convinced that the man knew something.

What was it? Where had the fellow met the Prince before? Was it under suspicious circumstances—or otherwise?

Next day Garrett arrived with the car, while to the White House Hotel at Whitby came a quietly dressed and eminently respectable golfer, who gave his name as Harvey, but with whom we are already familiar under the name of Mason.

The afternoon was a hot, breathless one, but towards five o'clock the Prince invited his hostess to go for a run on the "forty"—repainted, since its recent return from the Continent, dark blue with a coronet and cipher upon its panels.

Garrett who had had a look round the widow's "sixty" Mercedes, in confidence told his master that it was all in order, and that the chauffeur was an experienced man.

With the widow and her two guests seated together behind, Garrett drove the car next day along the pretty road by Pickering down to Malton, returning by way of Castle Howard. The pace they travelled was a fast one, and the widow, turning to his Highness, said:

"Really, Prince, to motor with you is quite a new experience. My man would never dare to go at such a rate as this for fear of police-traps."

"I'm pretty lucky in escaping them," responded the good-looking adventurer, glancing meaningly at the man in black clerical overcoat and cap.

"The Prince once ran from Boulogne to Nice in twenty-eight hours on his St. Christopher," remarked the Rev. Thomas. "And in winter, too."

"Marvellous!" declared the widow, adjusting her pale-blue motor-veil, new for the occasion. "There's no doubt a great future before that car—especially after the record at Brooklands."

"Rather!" exclaimed the rubicund vicar. "I'm only a poor parson, but if I had a little capital I should certainly put it in. I have inside knowledge, as they say in the City, I believe, Mrs. Edmondson," he laughed.

"From the Prince?"

"Of course. He intends having the largest interest in the concern. They've had eight orders for racers in the last six days. A record at Brooklands means a fortune to a manufacturer."

His Highness was silent, while the self-satisfied widow discussed the future of the eight-cylinder St. Christopher.

Returning to the Hall, Ferrini came forth bowing to his mistress, and casting a distinctly suspicious glance at the two visitors. Both men noticed it, and were not a little apprehensive. They had played some clever games, but knew not from one moment to the other when some witness might not point a finger at them in open denunciation.

While the Prince was dressing for dinner Charles said:

"That butler fellow is far too inquisitive for my liking. I found him in here an hour ago, and I'm positive he had been trying to unlock your crocodile suit-case. He made an excuse that he had come to see whether you had a siphon of soda. But I actually caught him bending over your bag."

The Prince remained grave and silent.

"Where have we met that fellow before? I can't remember."

"Neither can I. His face is somehow familiar. I'm sure we've seen him somewhere!"

"That's what the Parson says. Write to Max at Whitby, and tell him to come over on some pretext or other and get a glance at the man. Post the letter yourself to-night."

"Perhaps the fellow is afraid of his plate," the valet exclaimed in an undertone, laughing.

"He needn't be. It's all 'B' electro—not worth taking away in a dungcart. The only thing I've seen is the old woman's necklet, and that she keeps in her room, I fancy. If the sparklers are real they're worth a couple of thousand to the Dutchman."

"They are certainly real. She's got them out of the bank in your honour. Her maid told me so to-day. And she means, I believe, to give a big dinner-party for some of the county people to meet you."

"Are you sure of this?" asked his master quickly.

"The cook told the footman, who told me. The housekeeper to-day ordered a lot of things from London, and to-morrow the invitations are to be sent out."

"Are people coming here to dine and sleep?"

"Yes. Eight bedrooms are to be prepared."

"Then keep an eye on that confounded Italian. Send that letter to Max, and tell him to reply to you in cipher. His letter might fall into somebody else's hands. Max might also inquire into what the police arrangements are about here—where the village constable lives, and where is the nearest policestation."

"Couldn't you send me in to Whitby, and I'd give him all instructions, and tell him the state of affairs?"

"Yes. Go in the morning. Garrett will take you in on the car. Say you're going to buy me a book I want."

And with that his Highness finished tying his cravat with care, and descended into the pretty drawing-room, where the widow, lounging picturesquely beneath the yellow-shaded lamp, awaited him.

That evening the Parson, who complained of headache on account of the sun during a walk in the morning, retired to his room early, and until past eleven the Prince sat alone with his fat and flattered hostess.

As she lolled back in the big silk-covered easy-chair, slowly fanning herself and trying to look her best, he, calm, calculating person that he was, had his eyes fixed upon her sparkling necklet, wondering how much the old Jew in Amsterdam would give for it.

"What a splendid ornament!" he remarked, as though he had noticed it for the first time.

"Do you like it?" she asked with a smile. "It belonged to my husband's family."

"Beautiful!" remarked his Highness, bending closer to examine it, for he had the eye of a connoisseur, and saw that it was probably French work of the eighteenth century.

"Many people have admired it," she went on. "My husband was very fond of jewellery, and gave me quite a quantity. I never keep it here, however, for a year ago an attempt was made to break into the place."

"So you keep them in a safe deposit?" he exclaimed; "and quite right, too. Diamonds are always a sore temptation to burglars."

"I'm asking a few people to dinner next Wednesday, and am sending to the bank in York for some of my ornaments," remarked the widow. "I hope they'll be safe here. Since the attempt by thieves, I confess I've been awfully nervous."

"Oh, they'll be safe enough," declared the audacious adventurer, taking a fresh Russian cigarette from his case.

"I hope so. I have invited a few people—the best in the county—to meet your Highness. I hope you won't object."

"Not at all," he replied affably. "Only, as you know, I much prefer to remain *incognito*."

"You're one of the most modest men I've ever met," she declared, in a soft voice, intended to be seductive.

"I find life as a commoner much more agreeable than as a prince," he responded. "In *incognito*, I always enjoy freedom of speech and freedom of action, which, as a royalty, it is impossible to obtain."

The widow's mind was ever active. She was straining her utmost to fascinate her guest. The difference in their ages was really not so very great. Her secret hope was that she could induce him to make a declaration of love. Fancy her, plain Mrs. Edmondson, ridiculed by the county and only tolerated by a certain section of it, suddenly becoming a princess!

Milnthorpe was a beautiful old place, but to her it was but a sepulchre. She hated it because, while in residence there, she was buried alive. She preferred Monte Carlo, Paris, or even Cairo.

"Then the dinner-party will be a very smart one?" he remarked for want of something better to say. "And my hostess herself will surely be the smartest of them all," he added with a bow and an intent to flatter.

"Ah! I fear not," replied the widow with a slight sigh. "I dare say the diamonds which poor Tubby gave me are as good as any worn by the other women, but as for smartness—well, Prince, a woman's mirror does not lie," and she sighed again. "Youth is but fleeting, and a woman's life is, alas! a long old age."

"Oh, come!" he laughed, lounging back in his chair. "You haven't yet arrived at the regretful age. Life is surely still full of youth for you!"

She was much gratified at that little speech of his, and showed it.

He continued to flatter her, and with that cunning innate within him he slowly drew from her the fact that she would not be averse to a second marriage. He was fooling her, yet with such cleverness that she, shrewd woman that she was, never dreamed that he was laughing at her in his sleeve.

So earnest, so sensible, so perfectly frank and straightforward was he, that when after half an hour's *tete-a-tete* she found him holding her hand and asking her to become Princess, she became utterly bewildered. What she replied she hardly knew, until suddenly, with an old-fashioned courtliness, he raised her fat, bejewelled hand gallantly to his lips and said:

"Very well. Let it be so, Mrs. Edmondson. We are kindred spirits, and our souls have affinity. You shall be my princess."

"And then the old crow started blubbering," as he forcibly described the scene afterwards to the Parson.

For a few moments he held her in his embrace, fearful every moment that the ferret-eyed Italian should enter. Indeed, his every movement seemed to be watched suspiciously by that grave, silent servant.

They mutually promised, for the present, to keep their secret. He kissed her upon the lips, which, as he declared to the Parson, were "sticky with some confounded face-cream or other." Then Ferrini suddenly appeared, and his mistress dismissed him for the night. The Prince, however, knew that he would not retire, but lurk somewhere in the corridor outside.

He stood before the old Jacobean fireplace, with its high overmantel of carved stone and emblazoned arms, a handsome man who would prove attractive to any woman. Was it therefore any wonder that the ambitious widow of the shipbuilder should have angled after him?

He had entirely eclipsed the Parson.

First their conversation was all of affection; then it turned upon something akin, money. Upon the latter point the Prince was utter careless. He had sufficient, he declared. But the widow was persistent in telling him the state of her own finances. Besides the estate of Milnthorpe, which produced quite a comfortable income, she enjoyed half the revenue from the great firm her husband had founded, and at that moment, besides other securities, she had a matter of seventy thousand pounds lying idle at her bank, over which she had complete control.

She expected this would interest him, but, on the contrary, he merely lit a fresh cigarette, and having done so, said:

"My dear Mrs. Edmondson, this marriage of ours is not for monetary interest. My own estates are more than sufficient for me. I do not desire to touch one single penny of your money. I wish you to enjoy your separate estate, and remain just as independent as you are to-day."

And so they chatted on until the chimes of the stable clock warned them it was two in the morning. Then having given him a slobbery good-night kiss, they separated.

Before his Highness turned in, he took from his steel despatch-box a small black-covered book, and with its aid he constructed two cipher telegrams, which he put aside to be despatched by Charles from the Whitby post office in the morning.

The calm, warm summer days went slowly by. Each afternoon the widow—now perfectly satisfied with herself—accompanied her two guests on runs on the Prince's "forty"—one day to Scarborough, the next over the Cleveland Hills to Guisborough, to Helmsley on to the ruins of Rievaulx, and to other places.

One afternoon the Parson made an excuse to remain at home, and the widow took the Prince in to York in her own Mercedes. Arrived there, they took tea in the coffee-room of the Station Hotel, then, calling at a solicitor's office in Coney Street, appended their joint names to a document which, at the widow's instigation, had already been prepared.

A quarter of an hour later they pulled up before the West Riding Bank in Stonegate, and though the offices were already closed, a clerk on duty handed to the widow a box about eighteen inches square, tied with string, and sealed with four imposing red seals. For this she scribbled her name to a receipt, and placing it in the car between them, drove back by way of Malton, Pickering, and Levisham.

"This is the first time I've had my tiara out, my dear Albert, since the burglars tried to get in," she remarked when they had gone some distance, and the Mercedes was tearing along that level open stretch towards Malton.

"Well, of course, be careful," answered her companion. Then after a pause he lowered his voice so the chauffeur could not overhear, and said: "I wonder, Gertrude, if you'll permit me to make a remark—without any offence?"

"Why, certainly. What is it?"

"Well, to tell the truth, I don't half like the look of that foreign servant of yours. He's not straight. I'm sure of it by the look in his eyes."

"How curious! Do you know that the same thought has occurred to me these last few days," she said. "And yet he's such a trusty servant. He's been with me nearly two years."

"Don't trust him further, Gertrude, that's my advice," said his Highness pointedly. "I'm suspicious of the fellow—distinctly suspicious. Do you know much of him?"

"Nothing, except that he's a most exemplary servant."

"Where was he before he entered your service?"

"With Lady Llangoven, in Hertford Street. She gave him a most excellent character."

"Well, take my warning," he said. "I'm sure there's something underhand about him."

"You quite alarm me," declared the widow. "Especially as I have these," and she indicated the sealed parcel at her side.

"Oh, don't be alarmed. While I'm at Milnthorpe I'll keep my eyes upon the fellow, never fear. I suppose you have a safe in which to keep your jewels?"

"Yes. But some of the plate is kept there, and he often has the key."

His Highness grunted suspiciously, thereby increasing the widow's alarm.

"Now you cause me to reflect," she said, "there were several curious features about this recent attempt of thieves. The police from York asked me if I thought that any one in the house could have been in league with them. They apparently suspected one or other of the servants."

"Oh!" exclaimed the Prince. "And the Italian was at that time in your service?"

"Yes."

"Then does not that confirm our suspicions? Is he not a dangerous person to have in a house so full of valuable objects as Milnthorpe?"

"I certainly agree. After the dinner-party on Wednesday, I'll give him notice."

"Rather pay the fellow his month's money, and send him away," her companion suggested. Then in the same breath he added: "Of course it is not for me to interfere with your household arrangements. I know this is great presumption. But my eyes are open, and I have noted that the man is not all he pretends to be. Therefore I thought it only my duty to broach the subject."

"My interests are yours," cooed the widow at his side. "Most decidedly Ferrini shall go. Or else one morning we may wake up and find that thieves have paid us a second visit."

Then, the chauffeur having put on a "move," their conversation became interrupted, and the subject was not resumed, for very soon they found themselves swinging through the lodge-gates of Milnthorpe.

Wednesday night came. Milnthorpe Hall was aglow with light, the rooms beautifully decorated by a well-known florist, the dinner cooked by a *chef* from London, the music played by a well-known orchestra stationed on the lawn outside the long, oak-panelled dining-room; and as one guest after another arrived in carriages and cars they declared that the widow had certainly eclipsed herself by this entertainment in honour of his Highness Prince Albert of Hesse-Holstein.

Not a word of their approaching marriage was allowed to leak out. For the present, it was their own secret. Any premature announcement might, he had told her, bring upon him the Kaiser's displeasure.

Four

IN THE LONG DRAWING-ROOM, RECEIVING her guests, stood the widow, handsome in black and silver, wearing her splendid tiara and necklet of diamonds, as well as a rope of fine, well-matched pearls, all of which both the Parson and his Highness duly noted. She certainly looked a brilliant figure, while, beside her, stood the Prince himself, with the miniature crosses of half a dozen of his decorations strung upon a tiny gold chain across the lappel of his dress-coat.

Several guests had arrived earlier in the day to dine and sleep, while the remainder, from the immediate neighbourhood, included several persons of title and social distinction who had accepted the invitation out of mere curiosity. Half the guests went because they were to meet a real live prince, and the other half in order to afterwards poke fun at the obese tuft-hunter.

The dinner, however, was an unqualified success, the thanks being in a great measure due to his Highness, who was full of vivacity and brilliant conversation. Everybody was charmed with him, while of course later on, in the corner of the drawing-room, the Bayswater parson sang his friend's praises in unmeasured terms.

The several unmarried women set their caps pointedly at the hero of the evening, and at last, when the guests had left and the visitors had retired, he, with the Parson and two other male visitors, Sir Henry Hutton, and a certain Lionel Meyer, went to the billiard-room.

It was two o'clock when they went upstairs. The Bayswater vicar had to pass the Prince's room, in order to get to his own, but he did not enter further than the threshold. Both men looked eagerly across at the dressing-table, upon which Charles had left two candles burning.

That was a secret sign. Both men recognised it, and the Prince instantly raised his finger with a gesture indicative of silence. Then he exclaimed aloud: "Well, good-night, Clayton. We'll go for a run in the morning," and closed his door noisily, while the Parson went along to his own room.

The Prince, always an early riser, was up at eight o'clock, and was already dressed when Charles entered his room.

"Well?" he inquired, as was his habit.

"There's a rare to-do below," exclaimed the valet. "The whole house has been ransacked in the night, and a clean sweep made of all the jewellery. The old woman is asking to see you at once."

Without ado, his Highness descended, sending Charles along to alarm the Parson.

In the morning-room he found the widow, with the two male guests and two ladies, assembled in excited conclave. As he entered, his hostess rushed towards him, saying:

"Oh, Prince! A most terrible thing has happened! Every scrap of jewellery, including my tiara and necklet, has been stolen!"

"Stolen!" he gasped, pretending not to have heard the news.

"Yes. I placed them myself in the safe in the butler's pantry, together with several cases the maids brought me from my guests. I locked them up just after one o'clock and took the key. Here it is. It has never left my possession. I—"

She was at that moment interrupted by the entrance of the Parson, who, having heard of the robbery from the servants, began:

"My de-ah Mrs. Edmondson. This is really a most untoward circumstance—most—"

"Listen," the widow went on excitedly. "Hear me, and then advise me what to do. I took this key,"—and she held it up for their inspection—"and hid it beneath the corner of the carpet in my room. This morning, to my amazement, my maid came to say that the safe-door had been found ajar, and that though the plate had been left, all the jewellery had disappeared. Only the empty cases remain!"

"How has the safe been opened?" asked the Prince, standing amazed.

Was it possible that some ingenious adventurer had got ahead of him? It certainly seemed so.

"It's been opened by another key, that's evident," replied the widow.

"And where's Ferrini?" inquired his Highness quickly.

"He's missing. Nobody has seen him this morning," answered the distressed woman. "Ah, Prince, you were right—quite right in your surmise. I believed in him, but you summed him up very quickly. I intended to discharge him to-morrow, but I never dreamed he possessed a second key."

"He has the jewels, evidently," remarked Sir Henry Hutton, himself a county magistrate. "I'll run into Whitby, and inform the police, Mrs. Edmondson. We have no idea which direction the fellow has taken."

At that moment the door opened, and Garrett, cap in hand, stood on the threshold.

"Well, what's the matter?" asked his master.

"Please, your Highness, our car's gone. It's been stolen from the garage in the night!"

The announcement caused an electrical effect upon the assembly.

"Then this man could also drive a car, as well as wait at table!" exclaimed Sir Henry. "Myself, I always distrust foreign servants."

"Ferrini had one or two lessons in driving from my chauffeur, I believe," remarked the widow, now in a state of utter collapse.

"Never mind, Mrs. Edmondson," said his Highness cheerily. "Allow Sir Henry and myself to do our best. The fellow is bound to be caught. I'll give the police the number of my car, and its description. And what's more, we have something very valuable here." And he drew out his pocket-book. "You recollect the suspicions of Ferrini which I entertained, and which I explained in confidence to you? Well, my valet has a pocket camera, and with it three days ago I took a snap-shot of your exemplary servant. Here it is!"

"By Jove. Excellent!" cried Sir Henry. "This will be of the greatest assistance to the police."

And so it was arranged that the police of Whitby should be at once informed.

At breakfast—a hurried, scrappy meal that morning—every one condoled with the Prince upon the loss of his car. Surely the whole affair had been most cleverly contrived by Ferrini, who had got clear away.

Just as the meal had concluded and the Parson had promised to accompany Sir Henry over to Whitby to see the police, he received a telegram calling him to his brother, who had just landed in Liverpool from America, and who wished to see him at the Adelphi Hotel that evening.

To his hostess he explained that he was bound to keep the appointment, for his brother had come from San Francisco on some important family affairs, and was returning to New York by the next boat.

Therefore he bade adieu to Mrs. Edmondson—"de-ah Mrs. Edmondson," he always called her—and was driven in the dog-cart to Grosmont station, while a few minutes later, the Prince and Sir Henry set out in the widow's Mercedes for Whitby.

The pair returned about one o'clock, and at luncheon explained what they had done.

In the afternoon, the widow met his Highness out in the tent upon the lawn, and they sat together for some time, he enjoying his eternal "Petroff." Indeed, he induced her to smoke one, in order to soothe her nerves.

"Don't upset yourself too much, my dear Gertrude," he urged, placing his hand upon hers. "We shall catch the fellow, never fear. Do you know, I've been wondering whether, if I went up to town and saw them at Scotland Yard, it would not be the wisest course. I know one of the superintendents. I met him when my life was threatened by anarchists, and the police put me under their protection. The Whitby police seem very slow. Besides, by this time Ferrini is far afield."

"I really think, Albert, that it would be quite a good plan," exclaimed the widow enthusiastically. "If you went to Scotland Yard they would, no doubt, move heaven and earth to find the thief."

"That's just what I think," declared his Highness. "I'll go by the six-twenty."

"But you'll return here to-morrow, won't you?" urged the widow. "The people I have here will be so disappointed if you don't—and—and as for myself," she added, her fat face flushing slightly—"well, you know that I am only happy when you are near me."

"Trust me, Gertrude. I'll return at once—as soon as ever I've set the machinery of Scotland Yard in motion. I have the negative of the photo I took, and I'll hand it to them."

And so that evening, without much explanation to his fellow guests, he ran up to town, leaving Charles and most of his baggage behind.

Next day, Mrs. Edmondson received a long and reassuring telegram from him in London.

Two days passed, but nothing further was heard. Garrett, without a car, and therefore without occupation, decided to go up to London. The theft of the car had utterly puzzled him. Whatever *coup* his master and his friends had intended had evidently been effected by the man Ferrini. All their clever scheming had been in vain.

They had been forestalled.

XII

CONCLUSION

A week later.

The soft summer afterglow flooded the pretty pale-blue upholstered sitting-room in the new Palast Hotel, overlooking the Alster at Hamburg, wherein the Prince, the Parson, and the pale-faced Englishman, Mason, were seated together at their ease.

The Prince had already been there two days, but Clayton was staying over at the Hamburgerhof, while Mason, who had arrived *via* Copenhagen only a couple of hours before, had taken up his quarters at the Kronprinzen, a smaller establishment in the Jungfernstieg.

The trio had been chatting, and wondering. Mason had just shown them a telegram, which apparently caused them some apprehension.

Suddenly, however, a waiter entered with a card for Herr Stoltenberg, as the Prince was there known.

"Show the gentleman in," he ordered in German.

A moment later a well-dressed gentlemanly-looking young Englishman in light travelling overcoat and dark-green felt hat entered. It was the valet Charles.

"By Jove!" he exclaimed, as soon as the door had closed, "I had a narrow squeak—a confoundedly narrow squeak. You got my wire from Amersfoort?" he asked of Mason.

"Yes. I've just been explaining to the Prince what happened on the night of the dinner-party," replied the pale-faced man.

"Tell me. I'm all anxiety to know," urged the valet. "I left Garrett in Rosendaal. He's utterly puzzled."

"I expect he is," Mason responded. "The fact is that he's just as much puzzled as the wily Italian himself. It's a good job I was able to locate that fellow as one of old Blair-Stewart's servants up at Glenblair Castle. You remember—when we met 'Le Bravache' on his own ground," Mason went on. "Well, I played the part of detective, and wrote to him secretly, asking him to meet me in Whitby. He did so, and to him I confided my suspicions of you all, promising him a police reward of two hundred pounds if he kept his eye on you, watched, and informed me of all that was in progress. Of course I bound him to the most complete secrecy. He tumbled into the trap at once. The Prince had, of course, previously got wax-impressions of the widow's safe-key, for she had one day inadvertently given her key to him to go and unlock a cabinet in the library. Three times the suspicious butler met me, and made secret reports on your doings. He watched you like a cat. Then, on the night of the dinner-party, I had an appointment with him at one o'clock in the morning. I stole our car, and ran it noiselessly by the back road through the park to the spot where he was to meet me. He came punctually, and got in the car at my side to be driven into Whitby, where he supposed three detectives were in waiting. My story was that we were to pick them up at the hotel, drive back to the Hall, and arrest the lot of you. He was delighted with the project, and on joining me had a nip of whisky from my flask just to keep out the night air. Ten minutes later he was *hors de combat*. I'd doctored the whisky, so, pulling up, I bound and gagged him, and deposited him in a disused cow-house on the opposite side of a field on the edge of Roxby High Moor—a place I'd previously prospected. Having thus got rid of him, I turned the car back again to a spot within a mile of Milnthorpe lodge-gates—previously arranged with the Prince—and there, close by a stile, I found a biggish packet wrapped hurriedly in brown paper. Its feel was sufficient to tell me that it was the boodle. The Prince and the Parson had secured it after Ferrini had absented himself, and having placed it there in readiness for me, had quietly returned to their beds. With it under the seat I drove south as hard as I could by Driffield into Hull. Before I got there I changed the identification plate, obliterated the coronets on the panels with the enamel I found in readiness, and leaving the car in a garage, got across to Bergen, in Norway, and thence by train down to Christiania, Copenhagen, and here."

"Well, you put me into a fine hole, Prince," protested the valet good-humouredly. "I waited, expecting to hear something each day. The old woman telegraphed frantically to London a dozen times at least, but got no reply. She was just about to go up to town herself to see what had become of you, and I was beginning to feel very uneasy, I confess, when an astounding thing happened. The Italian on the morning of the third day turned up, dirty, dazed, and in a state of terrible excitement. I saw him in the hall where he made a long rambling statement, mostly incoherent. The old woman and Sir Henry, however, would hear no explanation, and, calling the village constable, had him arrested at once. An hour later they carted him off to Whitby. Then I made an excuse,

WILLIAM LE QUEUX

cleared out, and here I am! But I tell you," he added, "I had a narrow shave. He made an allegation that I was in the swindle, but every one thought he'd either gone mad, or was trying to bluff them."

"It was unavoidable, my dear Charles. I couldn't communicate with you," the Prince explained. "Never mind, my boy. There's a good share coming to you. The sparklers are worth at least ten thousand to our old friend the Jew, and they'll be in his hands and out of their settings by this time to-morrow. Besides, the silly old crow who thought she'd got a mug, and was going to marry me, has put up twenty thousand pounds in cash to get into the St. Christopher car deal. I got the money out of my bank safely yesterday, and it's now paid into a new account in the Dresdener Bank, in the name of Karl Stoltenberg."

"Well, you absolutely misled me," Charles declared.

"Because it was imperative," replied Herr Stoltenberg, as he said he wished to be known in the immediate future. "The old crow was a fool from the very first. She was too ambitious, and never saw through our game or how the record at Brooklands was faked entirely for her benefit. The Parson's first idea was mere vulgar burglary. If we'd brought it off we should have found only a lot of worthless electro. But I saw a little farther. She had money, and with a little working would no doubt part. She did. I suppose by this time the poor vain old woman has given up all idea of becoming Princess Albert of Hesse-Holstein."

"Well, my dear Prince," exclaimed the Parson, "my own idea is that we should separate and all lie doggo for at least a year, now that we have so successfully touched the widow's mite."

And this course was at once unanimously agreed.

I happen, as an intimate friend of his audacious Highness, to know his whereabouts at the present moment, and also the snug and unsuspected hiding-places of each of his four accomplices. But to reveal them would most certainly put my personal friends at New Scotland Yard upon their track.

As a matter of fact, I am pledged to absolute secrecy. If I were not, my old college chum would never have dared to furnish me with the details of these stirring adventures of a romantic life of daring and subterfuge—adventures which I have here recounted, and in which perhaps the most prominent if sadly-deceived character has always been "The Lady in the Car."

The End

A Note About the Author

William Le Queux (1864–1927) was an Anglo-French journalist, novelist, and radio broadcaster. Born in London to a French father and English mother, Le Queux studied art in Paris and embarked on a walking tour of Europe before finding work as a reporter for various French newspapers. Towards the end of the 1880s, he returned to London where he edited *Gossip* and *Piccadilly* before being hired as a reporter for *The Globe* in 1891. After several unhappy years, he left journalism to pursue his creative interests. Le Queux made a name for himself as a leading writer of popular fiction with such espionage thrillers as *The Great War in England in 1897* (1894) and *The Invasion of 1910* (1906). In addition to his writing, Le Queux was a notable pioneer of early aviation and radio communication, interests he maintained while publishing around 150 novels over his decades long career.

A Note from the Publisher

Spanning many genres, from non-fiction essays to literature classics to children's books and lyric poetry, Mint Edition books showcase the master works of our time in a modern new package. The text is freshly typeset, is clean and easy to read, and features a new note about the author in each volume. Many books also include exclusive new introductory material. Every book boasts a striking new cover, which makes it as appropriate for collecting as it is for gift giving. Mint Edition books are only printed when a reader orders them, so natural resources are not wasted. We're proud that our books are never manufactured in excess and exist only in the exact quantity they need to be read and enjoyed.

bookfinity™

Discover more of your favorite classics with Bookfinity™.

- Track your reading with custom book lists.
- Get great book recommendations for your personalized Reader Type.
- Add reviews for your favorite books.
- AND MUCH MORE!

Visit **bookfinity.com** and take the fun Reader Type quiz to get started.

Enjoy our classic and modern companion pairings!

Classic & Modern